"How long ar asked.

"Not sure."

Sunny quickly lowered her gaze. Something was bothering her. Was it concern about her dad and how easily she could have lost him, too?

The Breckinridges had suffered more loss than any family should.

"Come down to the barn tomorrow," he said, wanting to divert her thoughts away from her sudden mood change. "One of the cats had kittens not long ago. I bet the twins would like them."

"Sounds like a good idea."

When Sunny smiled at him, that problematic jittery feeling he often had around her kicked into high gear in his middle. This time he was the one who needed to lower his gaze to his dinner.

Think about kittens. Think about kittens. Think about kittens.

It didn't matter how cute those barn kittens were. They were never going to be enough to shove thoughts of Sunny Breckinridge's smile out of his mind.

Dear Reader,

It's nice to be back bringing you another tale of love in the American West after a bit of time away. I'm happy to be writing a story set in my fictional town of Jade Valley, Wyoming, a little slice of the Cowboy State that has a lot of wide-open spaces and stunning natural beauty. And, of course, romance is in the air for local girl turned world-traveling business consultant Sunny Breckinridge and her longtime friend Dean Wheeler, who never left their little hometown or the ranch where they both grew up.

The Rancher's Unexpected Twins is a modern-day marriage of convenience story filled with the ups and downs, humor and sorrow, and love and loss that fill all of our lives. Sunny and Dean have to navigate all of it on the road from fake romance to true love.

This is my first venture into writing for Harlequin Heartwarming, and I hope you enjoy the result. I love to hear from readers, and you can contact me through my website at trishmilburn.com or via my various social media, which you can find linked on my site.

Trish Milburn

HEARTWARMING

The Rancher's Unexpected Twins

Trish Milburn

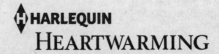

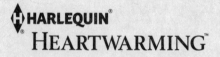

HARLEQUIN®
HEARTWARMING™

Recycling programs
for this product may
not exist in your area.

ISBN-13: 978-1-335-42638-3

The Rancher's Unexpected Twins

Copyright © 2021 by Trish Milburn

This edition published by arrangement with Harlequin Books S.A.

For questions and comments about the quality of this book,
please contact us at CustomerService@Harlequin.com.

Harlequin Enterprises ULC
22 Adelaide St. West, 40th Floor
Toronto, Ontario M5H 4E3, Canada
www.Harlequin.com

Printed in U.S.A.

Trish Milburn is the author of more than fifty novels and novellas, romances set everywhere from quaint small towns in the American West to the bustling city of Seoul, South Korea. When she's not writing or brainstorming new stories, she enjoys reading, listening to K-pop, watching K-dramas, spending probably way too much time on Twitter and, since she lives in Florida, yes, walks on the beach.

Books by Trish Milburn

Harlequin Western Romance

Blue Falls, Texas

Visit the Author Profile page at Harlequin.com for more titles.

CHAPTER ONE

THE LAST THING Sunny Breckinridge expected to do while driving toward Jade Valley, Wyoming, was laugh so hard she snorted. But she dared anyone who knew the owners of the only two restaurants in her hometown to not do the same. The two small signs advertising Trudy's Café and Alma's Diner that had once stood on opposite sides of the rural highway had graduated to full-size billboards throwing shade at each other.

Visit Alma's Diner, Best Food in Jade Valley.

Trudy's Cafe, Where the Locals Eat... For Good Reason.

It seemed the ladies' mysterious, long-standing feud was still going strong.

But that wasn't surprising, for various reasons. Things didn't change much in Jade Valley. Sure, the names on the teachers' rosters were different from year to year, but not that different. Generation after generation of the same families had called this valley home since Samuel Tillson had first settled here in 1842, deciding he'd had enough of a trip westward along the Oregon Trail. When he'd chosen a name for his new home, he'd selected it because of the color of area vegetation, having no clue that actual jade would be discovered in Wyoming decades later and become the state gemstone. Of course, that little historical tidbit didn't keep shopkeepers in Jade Valley from selling jade items to the occasional tourist who wandered through as if it was the source of the town's name all along.

She slowed down when a coyote dashed across the road ahead of her, allowing it to pass to the other side, then proceeded on into town. As she drove into the small business district, it felt as if she'd entered a time capsule. Sure, there were a couple of noticeable cosmetic changes since she'd visited at Christmas. The bank had a new sign and the corner lot where the long-out-of-business movie-rental store had been now held a small farmer's market.

Her best friend, Maya Pine, had said the abandoned store had burned down after some New Year's fireworks went awry. When the rubble that remained was cleared away early in the summer, people started setting up impromptu tents to sell their extra garden items, from-scratch pies, handmade soaps and such. And thus the pop-up Jade Valley Farmer's Market was born, with vendors and wares varying from day to day.

With no stoplights in town, she breezed through to the other side and headed farther into the valley, toward the Riverside Ranch. The happiness at being back in the valley where she'd lived until going away to college started to give way to the sadness that was inextricably a part of any visit home now.

Sunny shook her head. She couldn't focus on the losses, even though they had led to this unexpected trip home.

Ten minutes later, she made the turn onto the gravel entrance road that ran along the western edge of the ranch and bordered the river where her dad had taught her and her brother, Jason, to fish. The number of times she'd sat beside that river while doing homework or reading for pleasure were immeasurable. With the mountains rising in the distance, some of them tipped with snow year-round, this really was one of the most beautiful places in the world to her, even considering how much she'd traveled around the globe.

She passed the small log home where the ranch foreman lived. Dean Wheeler held that post now, taking over when his dad retired from the job he'd held since before Sunny and Dean were born. She didn't see either Dean or his truck, but since it was late afternoon he was probably still out working on the ranch somewhere.

Ranch work never stopped, and this time of year he could be directing the movement of cattle from one pasture to another, doing the first hay cut of the year, mending fences or any number of other tasks. Were it not for the cast on his leg, her father would no doubt be right there beside Dean working in the late spring flowing into early summer air.

Even with a foreman and ranch hands to handle the work, her dad didn't show any signs of slowing down. At least not until he had fallen off his horse and broken his tibia, and had been forced to take it easy.

She followed the curve in the road and finally spotted the larger house that she'd called home until leaving for the University of Wyoming and then on to LA after graduation.

Her heart filled with love and nostalgia…and with loss.

After parking, she took a slow, deep breath, determined not to bring any of the sadness inside with her. There had been too much sorrow within those walls, and she was determined that there would be no more. At least not the overt, heavily weighted kind that had threatened to suffocate her in the weeks following each loss of a family member.

When she stepped through the front door a couple of minutes later, two blond little heads turned her way from where they stood in their playpen watching a fishing show on the TV alongside their grandpa. Lily gave her a slobbery grin, but Liam returned his attention to the TV. Yeah, that little boy was going to be the spitting image of Jason, in appearance as well as personality. Sunny thought that might give her both comfort and heartache, in equal measures. And her dad probably saw it too, every day. Did the resemblance affect him the same way?

"I'd stand up and give you a hug, but I just managed to get comfortable," her dad said from his perch in his favorite leather recliner.

She smiled. "Then I guess I'll come to you, you klutz."

"Hey!"

Sunny laughed as she crossed the room, then bent over to give her dad a hug.

"Did you forget how to ride a horse in your old age?" Anyone could have fallen off a horse spooked by a rattlesnake, but she liked to tease her dad nonetheless. It was better than thinking about how much worse his fall could have been. If he'd hit his head…

No, don't go there. Don't borrow trouble.

"I think you got extra sassy since the last time you were here."

"That's me, sassy Sunny."

Lily started bouncing on her chubby little legs, her arms stretched above her head in the universal sign of babies who wanted to be picked up. Auntie Sunny complied and lifted the little darling into her arms, booping her on the nose with her own, eliciting a riot of giggles.

The fact that his sister had been sprung from the baby jail finally registering, Liam abandoned his TV viewing and started to whimper.

"Are you jealous?" Sunny asked as she bent over and retrieved him with her other arm. "Oh, you two are a lot heavier than I expected."

"I swear if you sit and watch them for a few minutes, you'll actually see them grow," her dad said. "Bring him here."

"He'll be all wiggly. I don't want him to hurt you."

"Who do you think holds them when you're not here?"

Sunny froze, and her dad's eyes widened. "I didn't mean anything by that."

She knew he didn't, at least she didn't think he did, but the guilt still ate at her. She'd spent as much time as she could helping out after Jason and Amanda's accident, but she'd eventually had to go back to LA or risk losing her job. But as she'd sat at her desk that first day back, it had been all she could do to keep from crying—for the loss of her brother, her sweet sister-in-law, for the twins who'd have no memory of their parents and for her dad.

He'd lost the love of his life, then raised Sunny and Jason alone after their mother's death. But Sunny had been thirteen then, Jason fifteen, old enough to take care of themselves. Twin infants were a different story altogether, and she'd left him there to fend for himself while he was also grieving the loss of his son and daughter-in-law.

Sunny remembered how she'd hidden in

the company ladies' room and called her dad, tears streaming down her face, saying she'd quit her job and come home. His response had bordered on angry as he'd told her she'd do no such thing.

"Where'd your mind drift off to?"

Her dad's question brought her back to the present. "Huh?"

He shook his head and motioned for her to give Liam to him. As she carried Liam over to his doting grandfather, Sunny wondered if her dad also had those kinds of moments where his thoughts took sudden detours into the past. Of course he did. How could he not?

She glanced toward the kitchen.

"Did Judy leave already? I thought she'd wait until I got here."

"Looks to the contrary, I do manage when she's not here. It's more difficult now, but I manage. I put them in the stroller and we all shuffle along. I told Judy to leave early. She's been cooking for two solid days, stocking the fridge and freezer for the zombie apocalypse or something."

Sunny laughed a little at the words *zombie apocalypse* coming out of her dad's mouth. He was about as likely to watch a zombie film as she was to watch one of his hunting and fishing shows. She didn't mind fishing, but she didn't understand the allure of watching other people do it on TV. It seemed more like a sure cure for insomnia.

Lily grabbed Sunny's nose as if it was a new toy.

"Hey, you little stinker."

Lily grinned, showing two tiny front lower teeth. Sunny laughed.

"This is the only time you're going to be cute with only two teeth."

Her dad snorted. "Don't let Elmer Fisk hear you say that."

"How old is he now?" Elmer Fisk was one odd bird who'd held more jobs in Sunny's lifetime than he had teeth in his head, even for a short time as one of the hands on her family's ranch during calving season.

"No one knows, but he did finally retire. Now he just hangs out around town and talks to whoever will stop long enough to hear his opinions on anything and everything."

Sunny could imagine Elmer doing exactly that, the same as she could imagine almost every one of the four hundred and ninety-nine current residents of Jade Valley doing things that were uniquely them. Being able to do that for the more than thirteen million people who lived in the LA metro area was literally impossible.

She tried not to think about the other reason she'd come home. Trying to convince her dad to sell the family ranch and move himself and the twins to LA with her wasn't a conversation for her first night back. She was too tired from traveling, and she wanted some nice, heartwarming family time before the inevitable disagreement. It was going to take all the finesse she possessed to get her dad to see the wisdom of the move.

But she had to get him to agree. Taking care of the twins and the ranch, even though he had ranch hands for the latter, was a lot to handle without a broken leg. Right now it was too much for him, no matter how he claimed otherwise. Maybe if the twins were older and didn't require constant care, it would be a different story. But they weren't. Lily and Liam couldn't even communicate with words yet, let alone feed, clean and clothe themselves. If they lived with her or even nearby, she could help with them while still being able to work. And she'd be able to spend time with her dad that didn't require taking vacation days, air travel and rented cars.

Even knowing the change would be for

the best, the thought of selling the ranch hurt her heart. It had been in her family since her great-grandfather started out with a few acres and gradually added to it, and each successive generation continuing to do the same. Her entire family loved this land, but sometimes life dealt you blows that necessitated unexpected change. Sunny hoped her mother and Jason would forgive her for what she had to do.

After catching up with her dad a bit, she made her way to the kitchen to see what Judy had fixed for dinner. As soon as she stepped into the other room, delicious scents greeted her. Lily wiggled in her arms, making Sunny smile.

"Smells good, huh?"

Lily grinned and waved one of her little arms as if to agree.

"You are just too cute for words, little Miss Lily." Sunny planted a kiss on her niece's forehead then approached the stove to find mashed potatoes, green beans with bacon and a meat loaf that looked and smelled as if it would convert even avowed meat loaf haters.

She headed back into the living room to return Lily to the playpen to free up both hands for setting the table. A knock at the door surprised her and it was comical how

Lily and Liam looked toward the sound in unison. They had twinning down.

"You expecting someone?"

"Nope."

Lily still perched on her hip, Sunny crossed to the front door. When she opened it, Dean Wheeler stood there, hat in hand, somehow looking taller than when she'd last seen him. Grown men didn't grow taller past their teens, did they?

"Hey, Dean, it's nice to see you," she said. "Is something wrong?"

Dean hesitated for a moment before responding. "Oh hey, Sunny. Uh, no, nothing wrong. Some of your dad's mail was just in my box."

"That substitute driver has been delivering mail to the wrong people all along this route," her dad said.

Dean extended a stack of envelopes and junk mail toward Sunny.

"Thanks."

"How was your trip?" he asked.

"Tiring, as usual. Glad to be home, though I could have done without the old man trying to break himself in two."

"Sorry about that," Dean said.

"Pretty sure you didn't put that snake there, or push him off his horse."

"How about you two stop talking in the open doorway," her dad said behind her. "Come on in, Dean. We're about to have dinner, and I'm pretty sure Judy made enough for half the valley."

"I don't want to intrude on your family time," Dean said, making as if he was going to step back and leave.

Sunny made a *pfft* sound. "Don't be silly. Come on in."

As if to add her agreement, Lily leaned forward and stuck her arms out toward Dean.

"Well, I'm already being abandoned," Sunny said.

Dean smiled at his little admirer then glanced at Sunny. "You don't mind?"

"About you eating dinner with us or you stealing my niece, who I haven't seen in six months?" Outside of video calls that her dad had finally figured out, that was.

Sunny relinquished her squirming niece and Lily immediately laid her head against Dean's shoulder as if it was the most natural thing in the world. Sunny experienced the oddest little flutter in her middle at the picture they painted.

"Both, I guess," Dean said with a little chuckle.

"Dinner, I didn't mind." Sunny pointed toward her niece. "Now this, I'm crying betrayal."

Dean moved as if to hand Lily back to her, but Sunny waved him off. "Oh no, you've got babysitting duty while I get the table set."

"That's okay with me," he said, looking down at Lily as if she was the most precious being in the world.

Well, Sunny couldn't argue with that.

DEAN WAS 100 PERCENT certain he needed to smack some sense into himself. Honestly, why hadn't years and distance eradicated his crush on Sunny Breckinridge? It was pitiful how the sight of her still made his heart thump a little faster, and yet that was exactly what started happening the moment she'd opened the front door with her niece on her hip.

"Dean?"

He glanced across the table at Sunny, realizing he'd spaced out and missed what she'd said.

"I'm sorry, what did you say?"

"I asked how your parents are doing."

"Oh fine. Dad likes to joke about how comfortable retirement is when I've been stuck out in the rain, heat or snow all day."

"Yeah, right," she said. "I bet he misses being out here every day."

It was amazing how well Sunny could peg people. He supposed that came in handy with her business consulting job. And yet she'd never managed to figure him out. Either she was blind to the possibility of his attraction to her because they'd grown up together or he was really good at hiding it.

"I think it's probably a little of both. There are days when I'd rather be inside than soaked to the bone too."

"Wanna trade spots?" Jonathon asked, tapping the full-length cast on his leg that was propped up with pillows in the adjacent chair.

"No offense, but I'll take a pass."

"Kids these days," Jonathon said. "So rude."

Sunny laughed at her dad. "It's been a while since we've been kids."

"If I can remember when the two of you were running around in diapers like the twins, then you're kids."

"Okay, Dad."

Dean pressed his lips together so he wouldn't

laugh at Sunny's eye-rolling, faux-annoyed teenager tone. But she pointed her fork at him to let him know she'd caught him.

"How long are you here for?" he asked.

"Not sure."

Dean expected her to offer up some additional teasing comment directed at her dad, but she didn't. In fact, he noticed she quickly lowered her gaze to her plate as she cut her slice of meat loaf into increasingly smaller pieces. Something was bothering her. Was it concern about her dad and how easily she could have lost him too?

The Breckinridges had suffered more loss than any family should.

"Come down to the barn tomorrow," he said, wanting to divert her thoughts away from her sudden mood change. "One of the cats had kittens not long ago. I bet the twins would like them."

"Sounds like a good idea."

When Sunny smiled at him, that problematic jittery feeling he often had around her kicked into high gear in his middle. This time he was the one who needed to lower his gaze to his dinner.

Think about kittens. Think about kittens. Think about kittens.

It didn't matter how darn cute those barn kittens were, they were never going to be enough to shove thoughts of Sunny Breckinridge's smile out of his mind.

CHAPTER TWO

THOUGH SUNNY HAD fallen asleep almost before she had fully crawled into her bed the night before, she awoke bright and early. The combination of fussy babies across the hall and a particularly enthusiastic rooster made sure of that. Neither babies nor roosters cared about her body clock being out of whack because of her recent travel.

The moment she heard a thump that sounded like crutches from her dad's room, she tossed back her covers.

"I've got them, Dad," she called out.

"You should rest some more," he replied as she reached her bedroom door, which she'd left open so she could hear if Lily and Liam needed her in the night. Either they hadn't or she'd slept through their cries.

"I'm good. Remember, I'm here so you can get some rest."

And convince you to sell your life's work. Our family's legacy.

She mentally shook off the scolding her conscience was giving her.

"I'm not an invalid, you know."

She walked up to her dad, placed her hands on his shoulders. "I'm fully aware. I would never think of suggesting you are. However, facts are facts, and those facts are that you are not as young as you once were, bones take longer to heal the older we get and caring for two toddlers is quite an undertaking even when you have two fully functioning legs."

Her dad narrowed his eyes at her. "I hate when you use logic against me."

Sunny laughed. "I'd think you'd be happy that my logic got you out of changing a few poopy diapers."

"You have a point."

She pointed down the hallway. "Go on into the kitchen. There should be coffee ready."

Once he was pointed in the right direction and thumping toward caffeine, she shifted her attention to her unhappy niece and nephew.

"Now, what's all this fuss about?" she asked as she entered the nursery.

With sunshine streaming in through the windows, the room was a level of cheerful that didn't match the twins' current mood. Amanda had liked bright colors and had decorated the nursery with eye-popping color that she'd been convinced the babies would like.

The familiar pang of loss squeezed Sunny's chest when she remembered how Amanda never got to see how Liam seemed particularly drawn to red and Lily was an equal-opportunity lover of color. One of the most wrong things to ever exist in the universe was children not being able to grow up knowing their mother's embrace and smiles. Or a mother who had carried those babies with love and care being robbed of the chance to watch them grow.

She pushed the sad thoughts aside, knowing that she had a right to them but not wanting to communicate her sadness to the babies.

Two new diapers and fresh, baby-scented clothes later, she toted brother and sister into the kitchen that still looked exactly as it had when her mother was alive except for a couple of appliances that had been replaced when their predecessors bit the dust.

The way her dad's face lit up at the sight of the babies, as if he hadn't seen them in months, made Sunny smile.

"What?" he asked when she laughed a little under her breath.

"Grandpa is totally head over heels for these two."

"Guilty as charged." He reached out and shook Liam's little hand as Sunny placed him in his high chair.

When the twins were both secured in their chairs, Sunny set about making breakfast that included fresh eggs from the coop out back where the noisy rooster resided. She found herself whistling as she worked in the same space where her mother had once done the same. Despite the losses they'd all endured there was still a lot of love to be had in this cheery room.

She paused in placing bacon in a pan and took in the scene before her. And knew today wasn't going to be the day she brought up selling the ranch either. She couldn't put it off too long, but she simply couldn't bring herself to throw a bomb in the midst of the happiness that her dad had been able to scrape together after the accident that had claimed his son and daughter-in-law.

"What are you planning to do today?" her dad asked a few minutes later when she put a plate of scrambled eggs, bacon and toast in front of him.

"No definite plans. Anything you need me to do?"

"Take a piece of mail back to Dean. A bill of his got stuck inside some of my junk-mail flyers."

"You two are playing hot potato with your mail."

"I don't know what's up at the mail-sorting center but I got something last week that was supposed to be delivered to someone in Cody."

Sunny took a couple of bites of her own food before turning her attention to feeding the twins.

"You three should get outside today," her dad said. "I haven't been able to do that since my fall."

"Maybe we'll go see those kittens Dean mentioned."

For some reason she imagined Dean holding a tiny kitten with as much tenderness as he'd held Lily the night before. The image caused the strangest sensation that she couldn't quite describe, kind of like a flutter of anxiety mixed with the enjoyment brought by indulging in a decadent dessert.

What a strange thought.

After breakfast, she settled the twins in the

playpen with a healthy variety of toys, then set about some housekeeping chores and handling a few things for work, mainly conveying information that Heidi, her colleague who was filling in for her on a trip to Singapore, would need for the upcoming meetings.

"You still enjoying your job?" her dad asked from where he'd been reading the latest issue of the *Valley Post*, the local paper her best friend, Maya, managed to keep afloat on a shoestring budget.

"I am." Maybe she could gradually ease into the idea of him moving to LA. "I often wish you were with me on some of the trips. Lots of beautiful places to see."

"Can't imagine any place more beautiful than what's right outside my front door."

She couldn't argue that this valley was indeed beautiful. Still…

"True. I sometimes forget all that my own backyard has to offer because I'm traveling so much."

"I'm sure the weather is nice, but you couldn't pay me to put up with that traffic."

Okay, this was not going well. Time to retreat and plan a new method of approach.

"I guess every place has its pros and cons."

Her dad just grunted in reply.

When his best buddy, Tom Rifkin, came by, Sunny left them to chat and took the kids outside. Holding their hands, she allowed them to walk beside her but not toddle off into possible danger. At the rate their little legs could carry them it took forever to reach the barn.

Sunny glanced around to see if Dean was nearby, but neither he nor any of the other ranch hands were visible. Instead, she greeted the couple of horses that were standing in their stalls, swallowing a lump as she rubbed the forehead of Copper the bay that had been her brother's. She followed the sound of kitten mews to an unoccupied stall.

"Aww, look at the kitties." She squatted between the twins and pointed toward the six kittens and their mama.

"Ki," Lily said, making Sunny smile.

Lily was more vocal than her brother, though neither of them had much of a vocabulary. Another of her heartstrings got tugged at the fact that babies' first words were usually *mama* and *dada* but Lily and Liam had neither. What would be their first clear words without those usual family figures in their lives? It'd probably be some version of *grandpa*, which would be both sweet and sad.

A fluffy little orange kitten approached them on wobbly legs. Mama cat kept her eyes on her little one but must not have deemed the newcomers a threat because she didn't move to intervene. Likewise, Sunny kept part of her attention on the mama cat. She wanted the twins to enjoy playing with the kittens but not get scratched in the process.

"You have to be gentle with them." Sunny demonstrated care in petting the kitten, hoping that the combination of words and actions would allow the twins to understand what she meant.

The orange kitty was soon joined by one of its black-and-white siblings, allowing each of the twins to have a little fluffball to pet. When Liam started to pet too forcefully, Sunny took his hand and showed him again the proper way of handling a creature so small. When the kitten he was petting rubbed its little head against his palm, he giggled.

"They sound like they're enjoying themselves."

Sunny looked up to find Dean standing outside the stall. Had his voice always been that deep? Had she officially been away from Jade Valley long enough that she was forgetting traits of people she'd known her entire life?

"They're not the only ones. Kittens are adorable at this age."

"Yeah, I admit to sitting and playing with them probably more than I should."

The image of tall, lanky Dean Wheeler sitting in a stall with kittens crawling all over him made her smile.

"I can imagine they're hard to resist."

"Yeah, but the guys like to tease me about it."

"Well, I for one think it's sweet."

"Don't let the guys hear you say that or I'll never hear the end of it."

"Dean Wheeler, afraid of a little good-natured ribbing, what is the world coming to?"

He rolled his eyes at her, and she laughed in response. Her laughter drew Lily's attention, and when she noticed Dean with his arms draped over the top of the stall door she held out her own.

"How is it that my niece has a crush at barely over a year old?"

"What can I say? Kids seem to like me for some reason."

Maybe because kids were excellent judges of character, and Dean had always been a fundamentally good person. A good friend when she'd needed one. When her mom had died, Maya had been the ever-supportive best friend. But it had been Dean who'd been there to listen to her in her most fragile moments when she'd been on the ranch, surrounded by memories of her mom but trying to hide most of her sorrow from her devastated dad.

Dean had seen her cry. Not many people had.

Dean opened the stall and the moment he lowered himself to sit beside her, Lily crawled up into his lap.

Sunny huffed out a little laugh and shifted her attention to Liam, who was still transfixed by the fluffy kitten he was now petting with exaggerated care. The image filled her heart with love. Because she lived so far away, she wasn't able to see the twins that often. But that didn't make her love them any less, and not only because they were all she had left of her brother. They were sweet and lovable on their own. Even at such a young age she was able to distinguish their personalities.

If everything went as planned, she'd get to see them all the time and really be able to watch them grow up. She'd be able to do what Jason and Amanda couldn't.

"You okay?" Dean asked.

"Yeah. Hard to escape memories, I guess."

"I miss them too."

Sunny hated that she hadn't thought of how Dean might be faring. Even though he wasn't technically family, he'd now lived on this ranch longer than either she or Jason. He'd gone to school alongside both of them. While she'd been at college and then working in LA, he and Jason had worked together every day. They'd been about as close to being brothers as two guys who didn't share parentage could be.

"Thanks for being here for my dad."

"Where else would I be?"

Though he hadn't meant that as a criticism of her any more than her dad had, it stung nonetheless.

"I'm not like you," he said. "I didn't have the intelligence to do anything different."

"Don't say that."

He glanced over at her with a slight smile. "I seem to remember you saving me from failing senior English."

"Everyone has things they're good at and things they're not. I, if you remember, am squeamish with touching fish. Something that you and Jason used to exploit much to my displeasure."

Dean smiled. "I don't know what you're talking about."

"Don't lie in front of the babies. I have vivid memories of the two of you chasing me, threatening to put flopping fish you'd just caught down my shirt."

"That was Jason's idea. I was only going along with it, him being the boss's son and all."

Sunny made a *pfft* sound of disbelief. "I don't believe you for a second."

Liam tried to pick up the kitten and it squeaked, causing mama kitty to tense. Sunny quickly pulled Liam onto her lap and soothed the kitten with her hand and its mama with her voice.

"You're good with them," Dean said.

"Kids or cats?"

"Both."

"Well, I've always liked animals, and I'd protect these two with my life." She hugged Liam to her and reached out to smooth Lily's soft hair, which had grown a good bit in the six months since the last time Sunny had seen her.

Dean looked at Sunny with an intensity that surprised her, but it was gone in the space of a blink.

"Let's hope it never comes to that."

When the mama kitty appeared to have had her fill of the human invaders handling her babies, Sunny placed the kitten that Liam was petting closer to its mother.

"I think it's time we made our exit."

Lily and Liam disagreed, crying when she and Dean got to their feet, each carrying a twin.

"The downside of playing with cute kittens, having to leave cute kittens," she said.

"You can come back tomorrow," Dean said to Lily, wiping a fat tear off her cheek.

Lily responded by crying harder.

"Well, I guess her crush on you has worn off."

"I knew I couldn't compete with kittens."

Something about the way he said that made her wonder why he wasn't married with kids and pets of his own. She had a reason for not being married—a crazy overseas travel schedule and long hours at work. But while Dean no doubt worked long hours too, he was always here. Was he dating at least? Not that the pool of potential romantic partners was extensive in Jade Valley, especially once you graduated high school and almost everyone who stayed in town was paired up.

As they exited the barn, Sunny looked around, trying to figure out some way to get the kiddos to stop crying before they returned to the house.

"How about we take them for a walk down by the river?" Dean said. "The sound of running water is calming, right?"

She looked up at him, squinting since the sun was behind his head.

"Were you a nanny in previous life?"

He snorted. "I seriously doubt that."

"I don't know. I'd say odds are at least fifty-fifty."

Dean shook his head and started walking toward the river. Sunny smiled and followed, pointing out everything from cows to birds flying in the air to Liam in an attempt to cheer him up.

It took a few minutes but after they reached the rocky riverbank and Dean showed the twins how to stack little flat rocks that had been smoothed by the continual flow of water, Lily's and Liam's tears ceased.

"Yep, you were definitely a magical nanny in a previous life."

"Careful or I might catch a fish and chase you with it."

Sunny leaned down next to Lily and pointed at Dean.

"See that man, Lily?" she faux whispered. "Don't trust him. He has nefarious intentions."

They joked a bit more before falling into companionable silence. Sunny leaned her head back, closed her eyes and inhaled deeply of the fresh air with tinges of pine, sunbaked earth and river moisture.

"Looks like the twins aren't the only ones enjoying this spot," Dean said.

Sunny opened her eyes and took in the picturesque scene painted with the river in the foreground and the mountains in the distance.

"I always thought it would be nice to have a gazebo here overlooking the river."

"Did you wish for that all those times you sat down here doing homework or reading?"

She nodded. "I imagined it having a table where I could eat or work, a comfy chair, a hammock."

"That's one crowded gazebo."

She smiled. "True."

They were quiet for a few moments before Dean pitched a pebble into the river.

"I told your dad I bet he could bring in

some more income if he built a few cabins along the river and rented them out."

"That's a great idea. Diversification is helping a lot of ranches survive when they might otherwise fold."

"Unfortunately, your dad doesn't agree with you."

She couldn't say she was surprised. Jonathon Breckinridge was the definition of *set in one's ways*. The task ahead of her seemed even more monumental now that she was back on the ranch than she'd allowed herself to admit while in LA.

"What's wrong?"

Sunny turned to sit facing Dean.

"Can you keep a secret?"

"If you ask me to."

Sunny fiddled with some pebbles in front of her, unsure how to approach the topic. If she was this agitated telling Dean about her plans, how was she going to broach the subject with her dad?

"I have another reason for coming back for a visit other than helping Dad out with the twins."

"Oh?"

Was it her imagination or was there hesitance in Dean's response, as if he wasn't sure he wanted to hear anything further?

"I think it's time for him to sell the ranch and he and the twins come to live with me in California."

She glanced up from where she'd been stacking her own little pile of stones and was surprised by the look on Dean's face. If she was forced to describe it, she'd say he looked as if he'd taken a powerful jolt from an electric fence.

CHAPTER THREE

DEAN WAS SO stunned by Sunny's revelation that he didn't know how to respond. He couldn't imagine the Breckinridges not owning the Riverside Ranch. Well, yes, he'd imagined it, and him being able to make it his own, but those were just pie-in-the-sky thoughts whenever Jonathon shot down one of his ideas for improving, updating or diversifying the ranch.

He honestly couldn't believe Jonathon would ever agree to leave this land while he was still breathing. There were too many memories here, too much family legacy. Had Sunny been away so long that she'd forgotten what her father was really like? The incredible stubborn streak?

But what if for the sake of the twins Jonathon agreed with her? Dean might never see her again.

He mentally scolded himself because he didn't have the right to miss her if she left for good. After all, he'd never done anything about his crush, never told her, never given her the opportunity to say whether she could feel the same way about him. First his concern for his father's job had kept Dean's mouth closed about his feelings. Then how excited she'd been to go to college. And finally the fact that she had made a life she obviously enjoyed a thousand miles away. If she hadn't stayed in Jade Valley for family, she certainly wouldn't stay for him. And so he kept his feelings to himself, not wanting to potentially ruin the friendship they had even if they didn't talk that often anymore.

Maybe if all of the Breckinridges left for good, he'd finally be able to let go of what had started as a youthful crush. Perhaps that's all it continued to be now, a holdover from when they were still kids.

Sunny waved her hand in front of his face.

"Have I shocked you into incoherence?"

"You could say that."

She sighed and fiddled with the rocks scattered on the ground between them.

"I know he's going to be resistant."

"More like as movable as those mountains," he said, pointing toward the impressive peaks in the distance.

"I have to find a way to get him to agree though. It would be a full-time job to keep up with the twins as they grow, and Dad isn't getting any younger. Add the limitations caused by his injury and the fact that I have to get back to work, and selling and moving is the only thing that makes sense."

"Selling this ranch, is that what you really want?"

"No, I want my brother to still be alive. I want things to be like they were before the accident, but I can't have that no matter how much I want it."

Before he thought, Dean reached out and took Sunny's hand.

"I'm sorry. I didn't mean to upset you."

She shook her head. "You didn't."

"I think I did."

"No, it's this whole situation. None of my options are perfect." She paused, as if gathering scattered thoughts. "Dad's fall scared me. What if he'd been more seriously injured… or worse?"

Dean squeezed her hand, reminding himself that he was offering her comfort when she needed it and nothing more.

"He's fine. Sure, a bit banged up, but your dad is the toughest guy I know."

He'd had to be because he'd been left to raise two teenagers alone while all three of them were grieving. And to lose his son and daughter-in-law as well was more than anyone should have to bear. But bear it he had. Sometimes Jonathon's stubbornness served him well.

But it wasn't going to make Sunny's goal easy to reach. Might even make it impossible.

"You know I'm here to help out. So are other friends like Maya. And your dad can hire someone else now that Judy is leaving."

Sunny shook her head.

"This isn't your or anyone else's responsibility. They're my family, the only family I have left. This is for me as much as them. I want to be close to my dad in case he needs me. I want to watch the twins grow up each day, not in six-month intervals when I can take vacation time."

He couldn't argue with her reasoning because it all made complete sense.

"How are you going to approach him with the idea?"

"I don't know. I can't keep putting it off, but I want to enjoy my visit a bit first."

Trying to shift his focus in a more positive

direction, Dean decided to put forth a possible win-win scenario.

"Something that might help is him knowing the ranch would go to someone who loved the land and wouldn't divide it up, who would keep it as a working ranch."

"That's a good idea," she said, nodding. "Do you know of anyone who fits that description?"

He took a breath and sat up a bit straighter.

"Me."

Sunny's eyes widened.

"You? You want to buy the ranch?"

"Why is that such a surprise? You know I love it here."

"I…I mean, I knew you seemed to enjoy the work."

"I don't want to be a ranch hand my whole life," he said. "I respect that my father was a good foreman for this place, but I want more. I don't want to depend on someone else for my paycheck. I want to be in charge, make the decisions."

Sunny tilted her head a fraction as she looked at him, as if she was seeing a person who looked familiar but whom she didn't actually know.

"Don't look so surprised. I might be offended."

"I'm sorry. It's just…you know we'll have to get a good price for the ranch so that Dad and the twins are set financially, right?"

Dean released her hand and crossed his arms. "My receiving a paycheck doesn't mean I'm living paycheck to paycheck. I've been saving since you left for Laramie."

"Really?"

"Yes. I might not have been as good in school as you were, but I had plans too."

"Dean, I'm sorry. I didn't mean to offend you. But you can understand why I'm surprised, right? You've never said anything about being a ranch owner, a businessman."

The fact was he could understand. When the two of them had last seen each other every day, she'd had to help him pass English so he could graduate. That didn't exactly scream future business owner.

"A lot can change over the course of a decade. I didn't imagine seeing you post to social media from Helsinki or Brussels or Tokyo back when we were in school either."

"I guess that's true. Those places might as well have been on a different planet back then."

Liam started to crawl toward the river, but before Sunny could reach for him Dean had already grabbed him and placed him in his lap.

"Good reflexes," she said.

"Comes from years of dealing with cows and horses." One hesitation or wrong move could be disastrous when dealing with animals of that size. While babies were tiny in comparison, he wasn't about to let anything happen to them. Granted, he was no relation to the twins, but they'd grown on him nonetheless.

"Or maybe it's that past-life nanny thing."

He shook his head. "You're impossible."

Sunny smiled and the sight of it did inconvenient things to his heart.

"So, when do you think you'll bring everything up with your dad?"

"I probably should do it no later than tonight. Like you said, he's going to resist and I'm probably going to need the rest of my time off to convince him."

"Want me to go with you?"

She shook her head, and Dean wasn't sure if he was relieved or disappointed.

"If you change your mind, call or text me."

"Thanks. Well, I better get these two back

to the house for diaper changes and maybe a nap."

Dean stood and extended his hand to her. She didn't hesitate taking it the same as how she'd not reacted when he'd held her hand a few minutes before. That, perhaps more than anything, told him that she didn't think of him in a romantic way. It obviously hadn't even occurred to her.

Before she could retrieve both babies, he picked up Liam.

"I can take them both," Sunny said as she lifted Lily to her hip.

"I'm going back anyway."

And so they walked side by side, each with a twin. Thankfully the babies didn't cry at leaving their little rock piles as they had when they'd left the kittens.

As they approached the house, Dean spotted Jonathon and Tom sitting on the front porch.

"Would you look at that," Tom said, pointing toward Dean, Sunny and the kids. "Jon, you remember when we were that young and good-looking?"

"Speak for yourself, old man," Jonathon said. "I'm still a looker."

Dean smiled at the familiar back-and-forth between best friends.

"I see you two haven't changed a bit," Sunny said as she climbed the couple of steps up to the porch.

"Why would we change when we're perfect?" Tom extended his arms. "Give me one of those babies."

Dean handed over Liam, and Lily toddled on shaky legs to her grandfather, who scooped her up with an enthusiasm that would make the unknowing think he hadn't seen her in months rather than about an hour.

"What have you all been up to?" Jonathon asked, directing his question toward Dean and Sunny rather than the twins.

There was something a bit off about Jonathon's expression, as if he was actually asking something he wasn't. That was odd. The elder Breckinridge typically said exactly what he was thinking with no filter.

"We played with kittens then stacked little rocks down by the river," Sunny said, evidently not detecting anything off about her dad's expression.

Maybe she was too wrapped up in figuring out how to approach him about selling the ranch. She might as well accept that no matter how she framed the idea, it was going to be received with about as much welcome as a swarm of hornets.

"I should get back to work," Dean said, feeling for some reason that he should make a quick departure.

"Oh, before you go, a piece of your mail was stuck inside Dad's." Sunny headed inside before he could come up with the words to say he'd pick it up later, preferably when Jonathon wasn't giving him strange vibes.

"Must be good to have her home," Tom said to Jonathon.

"Yeah, maybe I should have broken my leg sooner."

Dean stared at his boss, wondering what was going on. Jonathon had always been proud of everything Sunny had accomplished, had even been mad when she'd suggested coming home for good after Jason's and Amanda's deaths. He and Sunny's mom had always encouraged her to make the most of her intelligence and hard work, so why did it feel as if Jonathon was in the middle of an about-face? Was he realizing how difficult it was to raise two toddlers at his age?

If that was his line of thinking, Sunny was going to meet more resistance than she'd planned for—just not the type she'd imagined. Instead of her dad being opposed to a move to California, was he going to reverse his opinion on her moving back to Jade Valley?

While he could understand why Jonathon would want that, it wouldn't be any fairer to Sunny to ask her to give up the life she'd chosen than it would be to ask the same of Jonathon. Like Sunny had said, there really was no perfect solution to their situation.

Jonathon shifted his gaze to Dean. "It's good Sunny has someone her own age to talk to here. Someone between babies who can't speak yet and her old codger of a dad."

Dean didn't know why Jonathon was making that point, as if Dean was some new, welcome arrival on the ranch. Not to mention that Sunny would get along perfectly fine even if Dean wasn't a regular fixture on the ranch.

"You're far from an old codger," he said. "Anyone could have taken that same tumble from a spooked horse."

Thankfully, Sunny stepped back outside and extended an envelope to him.

"Hopefully, we've got all the mail properly sorted this time." When she smiled, it was all he could do to not let his face reveal how much he liked the sight.

Instead, he bid his goodbyes and forced himself not to run away from beautiful Sunny Breckinridge and her suddenly out-of-character dad as fast as his booted feet would carry him.

FOR SOMEONE WHO had a lot of experience in being persuasive and getting the bigwigs at large corporations to implement changes they might initially oppose, Sunny logically shouldn't feel sick at the idea of enumerating to her father the advantages of selling the ranch and moving to sunny Southern California. And yet her stomach was in knots throughout the rest of the afternoon, as she then prepared dinner and as they all sat down to eat. Her atypical anxiety accompanied her as she gave the twins their baths and put them to bed.

"Either of you have any great ideas of how to make this go more smoothly?" she asked her niece and nephew but only received baby gibberish in response.

"Yeah, that will probably work as well as anything I've thought about saying today."

After soothing the babies to sleep with

tummy rubs and a lullaby, she took a deep breath and ventured out of their room. The time for putting off the inevitable had come to an end.

"What's on your mind?" her dad asked as soon as she stepped into the living room where he was kicked back in his recliner.

She noticed the TV remote was next to his hand but he'd not turned on the TV.

"You've been wrapped up in your own thoughts all day," he continued, "and you pushed your food around your plate at dinner as if you didn't know what it was or what to do with it."

Resisting the need to place her palm against her stomach in an attempt to calm the upset there, she sat on the end of the sturdy coffee table facing her dad.

"I have a proposal and I want you to hear me out before you say anything."

"Well, this sounds serious."

She didn't confirm or deny, rather dove into one of the many spiels she'd rehearsed in her brain ever since she'd first had the idea of the move for her family.

"Since your fall I've been thinking that maybe it's time for a change that lets us all be together instead of so far apart."

Was that a positive light in her dad's blue eyes? Maybe this wouldn't be as difficult as she'd feared. If he'd been thinking that ranching and raising two babies alone were too much as well, perhaps this transition wouldn't be too painful.

"I'd love to spend more time with you and the twins, not depending on my vacation schedule to see you all. I know despite your fall that you're still in great condition for your age, but the fact is that the twins are a lot for an adult of any age to handle. It's easier with more people to take turns and help out."

Her dad nodded but didn't interrupt.

"Plus, I bet you'd enjoy the warmth of California when Wyoming is under a ton of snow and the wind feels like it's blowing off an iceberg."

"Wait, hang on a minute," her dad said, holding up a hand and the earlier light gone from his eyes. "You want us to move to LA?"

The tone of his question made it sound as if she was asking him to move to a domed existence on Mars.

"Yes," she said, trying to inject a generous amount of enthusiasm into her response. "The weather's great. We can share taking care of the twins. When they get old enough, there

are great schools. All kinds of cultural opportunities."

"You know I can't live in LA."

"Why not? Just think, no more brutal win-
ters."

"My life is here. My work is here."

"Not if you sell the ranch."

Her dad jerked as if she'd slapped him. "I
cannot have heard you right. Are you actually
suggesting that I sell our family's heritage?
The twins' future?"

"Our heritage doesn't change just because
we live somewhere else. And don't you think
the twins should be able to choose their own
futures the way you and Mom allowed me
to?"

"Well, they won't even have the option of
following in their father's footsteps if we sell
the land out from under them."

The turmoil in Sunny's stomach increased
right along with her father's agitation.

"I want to give them lots of opportunities,"
she said. "As much as you have loved ranching, you know it gets harder to make a living
at it every year."

"We do just fine." He lowered the footrest on the recliner with more force than was
required, but if he'd hurt his broken leg he

didn't show it. "I refuse to see this land your mother and brother loved divided up so rich city folks can play at ranching."

Okay, bringing her mom and Jason into this felt like a really low blow, but Sunny reminded herself that even the idea of this life transition was difficult for her dad. She'd known it would be.

For the moment, she chose to ignore his words about the family they'd lost. She didn't want to get too emotional when she needed to be practical.

"You wouldn't have to worry about the ranch because Dean wants to buy it."

"Dean? You talked to him about this?" Now it sounded as if her father believed she'd betrayed him on another level.

"It happened to come up when we were playing with the twins by the river today."

Her dad stared hard, and she would swear she could hear multiple gears spinning in his head. Then he grabbed his crutches. "Let me tell you something. The only way Dean Wheeler is going to become owner of this ranch is if I die and you abandon your family's legacy entirely. That or he marries you."

Sunny was so stunned by the idea of both of those options, in entirely different ways, that she wasn't able to form a response and sat in silence as her dad shoved himself out of the chair and thumped along at impressive speed to his room.

The thought of him dying caused a pain in her chest that robbed her of breath. But when she tried to shove that possibility aside, she was left with an option that was so preposterous she had a hard time figuring out why her dad had even thought of it.

Married to Dean Wheeler. Of all the crazy ideas.

Or…was it?

CHAPTER FOUR

NOT WANTING TO interact with her dad the next morning, allowing him more time to calm down and hopefully think about her suggestion in a more logical, less emotional way, Sunny got up extra early. It wasn't as if she'd slept well anyway. She checked on the twins to see they were still sleeping, made her dad a simple breakfast and left it on the table for him along with a note that she would be back soon. Because she needed some fresh air and distance to think about what to do next.

She exited the front door as quietly as possible then headed toward the barn. Taking a ride while the day was still in the process of waking up should help her relax and let go of the lingering frustration that resulted from the altercation with her dad the night before.

After saddling Copper, she headed toward the river. If she was seeking some peace, the river that inspired the ranch's name was where she always found it. If she could convince her dad to move, she'd miss these rides. This stretch of water. But it wasn't as if she'd never come back. Maya was here, and despite the distance between where they lived they'd stayed best friends ever since third grade.

Besides, in California she had easy access to the Pacific Ocean. Even in the midst of winter, she could walk along the shore and not freeze half to death. She imagined the twins learning to build sand castles, going to theme parks, exploring all the museums. She wanted to provide a full and rich life for them that Jason and Amanda couldn't.

Sunny bit her bottom lip as a pang of grief hit her. She lifted her gaze to the sky, being lit more each moment by the rising sun. Why had Jason and Amanda picked that weekend to go hiking, their first time away from the twins? Why had that RV driver chosen that exact moment to come around that particular curve a bit too much over the center line, causing Jason to swerve?

She wiped at a tear. Her brother had been gone a little more than a year, and random thoughts of him could still cause her eyes to well up. She didn't think that would ever change judging by how sometimes the loss of her mother still felt as raw as it had fifteen years ago.

Sunny reined Copper to a stop and slipped from the saddle. She led the gelding to the edge of the river, and Copper began to drink. Perched on a small boulder, Sunny watched as the sun touched the snow at the top of the mountains with its orange glow.

The approach of hooves had her looking over her shoulder. Somehow she wasn't surprised to see Dean. Like all ranch hands, he was an early riser, as well. He dismounted and let his horse loose to graze alongside Copper.

"Are you okay?" he asked as he approached her.

She could tell by the look on his face and tone of his voice that he'd probably surmised that the conversation with her father hadn't gone well.

"I'm not quite sure how to answer that question."

"How upset is your dad?"

"Let's just say that I'm probably not his favorite person right now."

"To be fair, I think the twins have that spot permanently locked up."

"You're not wrong about that. And it's as it should be."

Dean sank onto an adjacent boulder. "Want to talk about it?"

Sunny remembered the crazy thoughts she'd had after her dad's parting comments before he'd retreated to his room. She couldn't even believe she'd entertained them, and yet here she was thinking them again. Wondering if she was desperate enough to voice them. Most likely Dean would think she'd taken leave of her senses.

"A bit of warning, I might have brought you up in the conversation."

"Me?"

She spun to face him. "How much do you want the ranch?"

His eyebrows moved closer together. "I would love to have the opportunity to run it." He looked south, toward the pasture where a few cattle from the herd were visible.

"What would you be willing to do for that to happen?"

"Well, nothing illegal or anything that would hurt your family."

"Obviously. How would you feel about a little harmless subterfuge?"

"Is subterfuge ever harmless?"

"When it's done for the greater good?" She posed it as a question, hoping he would validate her possibly insane idea.

"Yeah, I'm not answering that question until I have more specifics."

Sunny took a deep breath, trying to calm the sudden riot of butterflies in her stomach. She felt as if she was acting out a scene in some romantic comedy. Only this was real life with real consequences.

"Dad said he didn't want to see the ranch divided up, so I told him that you would be interested in buying it. He…well, he was understandably already upset at the idea of selling, but then he said that the only way you'd become owner of this ranch is if he died and I sold it to you or…"

Sunny hesitated, not sure she really wanted to reveal the rest.

"Or?"

She intertwined her fingers and squeezed so tightly she was sure the circulation had been cut off.

"Of if you married me."

Dean jerked at the same time his eyes widened and his mouth opened slightly.

"I… What…?" Dean shook his head as if to

realign his ability to think and form coherent sentences. "He actually said that?"

She nodded. "Trust me when I say I was as stunned as you are. In fact, I was speechless and that's how our conversation ended."

"Had he come to his senses this morning?"

Why did his question sting?

"Hey, the idea of marrying me isn't that horrible, is it?"

"No, no, that's not what I meant." Dean looked so flustered that she couldn't help but laugh at his efforts to pull himself out of the hole he'd dug.

"I'm kidding. But to answer your question, I don't know. I left before he got up."

"Ah. You came out here to see if inspiration struck?"

"Yeah. It's always easier to think outdoors."

"Says she who works in an office."

"Yes, but it's not a twenty-four-seven job like ranching. And more stable." She met his gaze as she experienced a measure of guilt for trying to transfer the trials and tribulations of ranching to Dean. "Are you sure you want to take on this kind of responsibility? Your whole life would revolve around this ranch."

"It already does and I love it. I can't imagine doing anything else."

Just like her dad.

"Then… I have what is going to sound like a completely crazy idea that might help us both get what we want."

"Okay." He drew the word out as if he was afraid to let it end.

She leaned forward. "What if we…" Was she really going to suggest this? "What if we faked a relationship? Pretended to date, then maybe even got married temporarily?"

The look of disbelief on Dean's face was pretty much what she'd expected, but she'd started this and rushed ahead before he could shut her down.

"I know it sounds absolutely irrational."

"You're right about that. I can't believe what I'm hearing."

"Listen, this is not my preferred way of getting around my dad's stubbornness and bringing my family together again. I wish I'd never been put in this position, but I can't stop worrying about something happening to Dad or the twins with me being so far away. At least if they were in LA, even when I'm traveling they would have quick, easy access to excellent emergency care. What if Dad had been alone when he fell? What if he'd lain out there for hours?" Her voice broke at the mere idea of that possibility.

"But he wasn't alone, and he's fine."

"He's not fine. He's got a full-length cast on his leg and two toddlers depending on him. How can I go back to work and leave them behind?"

"So your solution is a whirlwind, fake courtship and marriage in what…a couple of weeks? Your dad isn't going to buy that for a second, especially when he's the one who mentioned marriage in the first place. Besides, how does that convince him to sell the ranch and move if you're married to someone who lives here?"

"Maybe he'd be willing to sign over the deed as a wedding present to the two of us?" It sounded insane even as the words left her mouth, but the idea of being so far from her family made her sick to her stomach. And she made enough money that she could support them all. "Maybe we even have to have a long-distance marriage until he's convinced it's real, then after a believable amount of time we could quietly divorce and I could sell you the ranch. I don't know—I haven't worked out all the details."

Dean looked at her as if she not only had

grown a second head but had rather sprouted a Medusa-like head of snakes.

"Do you hear yourself?"

"I know it sounds bonkers."

"You think? Not to mention…"

"If the word you're looking for is *deceitful*, I truly don't mean it that way. At least not in the worst sense. I just think that it might help ease Dad into coming to the decision to sell and move himself. You know how he is. He's resistant to change. You have to plant a seed of what you want from him, let it germinate long enough that he eventually thinks it was his idea."

"And you think all that is going to happen during your short vacation time?"

"I can probably extend my time here by working remotely."

"Sunny, I understand why you want your family together, but this plan seems too outrageous."

She sighed, knowing he was right.

"I'm sorry. I didn't mean to pull you into all this without even asking if you're in a relationship already."

"I'm not but that's not the point. Like you said, your dad needs time for ideas to marinate. Wait a couple of days and try to talk to him again."

She nodded despite the fact that she didn't think a couple of days was going to make any difference in her dad's stance. Probably not even a couple of months.

DEAN RODE ALONGSIDE Sunny as they headed back toward the house even though he wanted to spur his horse and race to the far side of the ranch. Their entire conversation about fake dating and fake marrying seemed like something right out of one of those wild dreams you had when you were super tired or ate something you shouldn't have right before bed.

She obviously didn't have the first clue that he'd long harbored feelings for her. Otherwise, she wouldn't have suggested such a plan, which would take advantage of those feelings for her own benefit. She wasn't that kind of person. The fact that she was willing to go to such lengths to protect her family was evidence of that, even if her idea of how to accomplish it was stretching the limits of rational thought.

He tried to ignore how for a few seconds when he'd first heard her idea, he'd been tempted. But he'd quickly realized he couldn't pretend to date her and not want it for real. That was simply asking too much when he knew that her endgame would take her away from Jade Valley and him for good.

The fact that he'd been tempted at all told him he should keep his distance for the duration of her visit. With that in mind, he started to veer toward the barn. But then Sunny jerked in her saddle and a moment later he realized why. Wailing coming from the house had her spurring her horse, and he was quick to follow.

Sunny dismounted even before Copper came to a complete stop. She'd raced up the front steps and into the house before Dean was able to rein in and follow her.

Lily was screaming louder than anyone with her size lungs should physically be able to. Fat tears streamed down her reddened face.

"What happened?" Sunny asked in a frantic voice as she dropped to her knees in front of Lily.

"I was trying to get them into the playpen and she lost her footing and bumped her head on the coffee table," Jonathon said.

Dean looked over at the playpen where

Liam sat crying as well, likely only echoing his sister.

"Why didn't you wait until I got back?" Sunny said as she checked the red spot at the edge of Lily's hairline.

Dean winced at Sunny's tone, as if she was scolding a child who had been repeatedly warned about certain behavior. He knew she was upset, but Jonathon hadn't hurt his granddaughter on purpose.

"I handle them just fine every day," Jonathon said. "It's only a bump. Babies get them all the time when they're learning to walk."

"You don't know it's only a bump." Sunny lifted Lily in her arms, holding her close. "I'm taking her to the hospital."

"You're overreacting," Jonathon said.

"Maybe I am, but I'm going to make 100 percent sure."

The heat in Sunny's words right before she headed for the door had Dean stepping into her path.

"Not you too," she said with a tone that said she saw his blocking her as betrayal.

"You're too upset to drive. I'll take you."

She shook her head. "I need you to stay here with Liam."

"I'm right here," Jonathon said, plenty of hot frustration in his voice, as well.

Dean held up his hands toward both of them, trying to calm them down before their words went too far. He met Sunny's gaze.

"Liam is fine and he isn't going anywhere," he said, pointing at the playpen. "I'm taking you to the hospital so that your mind can rest at ease that Lily is fine."

Sunny opened her mouth, obviously to object, but he steered her through the front door before she could say anything.

"We'll call when we know something," he said to Jonathon. "I'll tell Carlos to come by to see if you need anything."

The ranch hand had at least some childcare experience, being a father himself.

Dean grabbed Jonathon's truck keys off the small table by the door since he didn't want to take the time to move one of the twins' car seats from one vehicle to another.

By the time they reached the end of the ranch road, Lily had calmed down to sniffles. Even so, Sunny didn't look any less frightened. She continued to sit half-turned in her seat, watching her niece as if something dire might happen if she looked away for a split second.

"I think she's fine," he said as he turned onto the highway and headed toward Jade Valley's little hospital.

"I have to know for sure."

It wasn't until he squeezed her hand in reassurance that he realized he'd reached across the truck and taken Sunny's hand in his. He told himself she didn't appear to mind that he'd captured her hand yet again because all her thoughts were focused on Lily's wellbeing. But when he started to release her, she didn't let him. She squeezed back, latching onto him as if he was a safe port in her panic storm. Willing to be that for her, he held her hand all the way to the hospital.

As soon as he pulled up to the emergency room, however, she released her tight grip and rushed to get Lily out of her car seat and into the ER to see a doctor. By the time he parked and followed her inside, Lily was already being seen by Dr. Allen.

Dean resisted the urge to hold Sunny's hand again or put his arm around her shoulders in support. In a small town like this, the news would be misunderstood and spread faster than a spark on parched grass. Instead, he stood nearby in case she needed him, listened as Sunny questioned Dr. Allen's assessment that Lily was fine but was going to have a knot on her forehead.

"Are you sure? Don't you need to run tests?"

Dr. Allen smiled despite the fact that his medical degree and years of experience were being questioned by someone who had neither. It likely wasn't the first time he'd encountered a freaked-out relative.

"Sunny," Dean said, capturing her attention. "Dr. Allen wouldn't send Lily home if he thought she was in danger."

Though she still looked as if she might fly Lily off to a specialist in LA, she finally nodded and thanked the doctor. By the time they walked out of the hospital, Lily was already smiling and tugging on her aunt's ear. Sunny still looked as if she might break down in tears at any moment, so as soon as she had Lily buckled into her seat and had given her a stuffed penguin she'd found in the truck's back seat, Dean pulled her aside and shut the back door. He turned Sunny to face him.

"You need to calm down. Everything is fine. You can't freak out every time one of the kids falls or manages to bruise themselves. It's what kids do."

"I know."

She sounded so mentally exhausted now that the rush of adrenaline had been spent that he couldn't help pulling her into his arms. Again, she didn't resist his comfort. When she hugged him in return, placing her palms against his back, he had to close his eyes and take a deep breath. Remind himself that to her, this was nothing more than a friend comforting a friend.

After a few seconds, Sunny stepped out of his embrace and gave him a shaky smile.

"Sorry I seem like a deranged person."

"It's okay. I've always known that you were."

Her expression of shocked disbelief preceded her smacking him on the arm. He laughed as he backed away from her, glad to have been able to shift her away from her residual panic.

But as he drove back toward the ranch and listened to her give her dad an update, Dean realized how much of what remained of the Breckinridge family needed to be together. He understood the lengths to which Sunny was willing to go in order to bring them together. Some people might say she was being selfish by not coming back to Jade Valley instead of uprooting her family, but that wasn't fair to her. She'd worked hard to accomplish what she had, and she could provide the kind of life for the twins that wasn't feasible in rural Wyoming.

Not that there was anything wrong with the vast open spaces with more cows than people, but there were no big art museums, no symphonies, no cutting-edge health care, no top-notch higher education in or anywhere near Jade Valley.

But was he willing to go along with her ruse in order to help her? He mulled that question as the familiar pastures and cattle herds sped by his window. Maybe it wouldn't have to go very far, maybe not even to the marriage part. Jonathon might very well see things from Sunny's point of view, especially after Lily's injury, and change his mind.

The possibility evaporated as soon as they got back and Jonathon pulled an "I told you so" regarding Lily's fall. The look of frustration mixed with worry on Sunny's face, like she wanted to scream at her dad and hug him close at the same time, finally made Dean's decision for him.

When the two of them stepped outside, leaving the twins safely in the playpen, he looked out toward the mountains.

"I'll do it," he said.

"Do what?"

He slowly turned his gaze toward her. "Let's date."

CHAPTER FIVE

SUNNY'S PULSE LEAPED like a startled rabbit, only this surprise was welcome.

"Really?"

Dean nodded, and she had to resist the urge to hug him. Or maybe she should. That would point toward their sudden dating being real, right? Still, something stopped her. She'd already hugged him once outside the hospital, and she didn't want to make things weird.

Well, no weirder than fake dating would be.

"I can't believe we're going to do this," she said.

"Me neither. But, hey, I could use a little excitement in my life."

She laughed. Dean was a great guy, a good friend, had been popular when they were in school, but he'd never been Mr. Excitement. Thrill seeking wasn't his thing. He obviously was the type of man who just wanted to live a good, honest, hardworking life, and she admired him for that. She was a big proponent of knowing what you wanted from your time on Earth and going for it.

"Thank you."

Again, he nodded.

"So, how does fake dating work? Do I obviously come to the house at some point and ask you out? I have no experience with grand gestures, just so you know."

"Let's try for a bit more subtlety," she said, smiling at her lifelong friend. She owed him big for this, and she planned to repay him by helping him achieve his dream. Sunny had to admit it eased the ache in her heart at the thought of losing the ranch that she would be leaving it with someone who loved it every bit as much as her family did. In a way, Dean and his parents were family.

"So…?"

"How about we do a picnic with the twins down by the river tomorrow?"

"Is the aim to have your dad come along or not?"

"I don't think he can manage that on crutches, do you? I'll say it's a thank-you for helping with Lily today but maybe, I don't know, act a little differently somehow while mentioning you."

She'd seen enough romantic movies to be able to come up with something.

"Okay, plan for lunchtime so I know when to be available?"

"Sounds good."

With a nod, Dean headed off to resume whatever work was on his to-do list. He'd spent a lot of time with her today, so she felt bad that it had likely put him behind. But she was asking him to continue to carve time out of his schedule for her, and with only a possibility—not a certainty—that he'd be able to buy the ranch as a reward. She needed to find other ways to make this undertaking more beneficial to him during the process in case things didn't work out how she wanted.

As she turned to head inside, the first idea of how to pay him back for his generosity came to her. Since they were going to have a picnic anyway, she'd bake him his favorite cake. That seemed like something that someone who was smitten with a guy would do as well, so bonus.

The sound of an approaching vehicle caused her to pause and turn to see who it was. She smiled when she saw the little cobalt-blue hatchback, remembering the giant smile Maya had worn in her "Here's my new car" post a couple of months back.

Maya Pine skidded to a stop next to Sunny's rental car and got out with her hands on her hips and a lifted eyebrow.

"I finally decided that if I wanted to see my best friend, I was going to have to come to her," Maya said.

"You're scolding me? It's not like I've been here a week or something."

"You have been in town twice."

"Once, I hadn't even been home yet. And today I was at the hospital."

"Okay, fine. Details, details. I heard about Lily's fall. Is she okay?"

"Thankfully, yes. Though I think I aged ten years." Sunny pointed toward her hair. "I'm sure I have a nice patch of gray now."

"You do not. You're as beautiful as ever, darn you."

Sunny laughed and opened her arms. Maya abandoned her scolding and hugged her as if they hadn't seen each other in years instead of only six months. It didn't matter that they texted literally every day. Being able to hang out in person was so much better.

When they went inside, Maya cooed over the babies like another adoring auntie. Truth was she got to see the twins more often than Sunny did. Guilt punched her that she had hatched her plan to move her family to California without telling Maya. They shared everything. But Sunny also knew that her bestie was likely going to tell her that she'd lost every last one of her marbles when she found out. If she didn't let her in on the secret soon, however, Maya wouldn't forgive her.

Maybe she'd give it a few days, see if she and Dean could actually stick to the plan, before revealing the truth. No sense telling Maya about her really-out-there plan if she or Dean decided that they couldn't go through with it.

After they fed and diapered the babies and got them to fall asleep, she and Maya retreated to the kitchen, leaving her dad in his recliner reading the Casper paper and probably on his way to a nap of his own.

She poured two glasses of lemonade but didn't sit across from her friend. Instead, she started searching the pantry to see if Judy had stocked up enough to allow Sunny to bake Dean's favorite carrot cake with cream-cheese frosting.

"Are you baking me a cake because you

missed me so much and feel guilty for not coming to see me sooner?"

Sunny shot her friend a "you're pouring it on thick" look before shaking her head. *Time to commence Operation Make Dad Think Dean and I Are Dating.*

"It's for Dean."

"Dean? His birthday isn't until December."

"It's a thank-you for today. He helped me out with Lily. Took us to the hospital, helped me calm down."

"Oh, that was nice of him."

What was that tone in Maya's voice? It almost sounded as if she was insinuating something romantic between Sunny and Dean when the entire cake-baking undertaking was aimed at making her dad think that way, not her best friend. No, that couldn't be it. Sunny simply had those types of thoughts running through her head and was hearing intent that wasn't there. The three of them had been friends for ages.

But there had been the one time in high school when Maya had commented with obvious disdain on the fact that Dean had briefly dated Holly Vinson. Sunny distinctly remembered Maya saying that Dean could do better. She hadn't thought much about it at the time because she'd agreed, mainly because Holly was way too full of herself. Thank goodness she'd moved with her family to Idaho their junior year, meaning their senior year was blessedly Holly-free.

Maya didn't have a thing for him, did she? No matter how much Sunny wanted her family together, she wasn't about to take anything away from her best friend. Surely with her personality, Maya would have made her interest clear to Dean if there was any.

"Yeah, it was," Sunny said, realizing that she'd let a lengthy pause stretch after Maya last spoke. "I might have been a bit of a mess when Lily was crying so hard she could hardly get her breath."

A snort from the living room told her that her dad could hear their conversation just fine. Would he think twice about the cake though? After all, it was the kind of gesture her mom would have made for someone who'd done a good deed too.

"I bet it scared Lily more than hurt," Maya said. "Mom always said that when Ethan or I fell. Said we'd cry like someone cut off a limb but five minutes later we were giggling and trying to ride the dog or something."

"I'm pretty sure I did see Ethan ride the

dog once." When Maya had left for college, the kid was still only ten years old, an oopsie baby for Maya's parents. Now he was the one attending college in Laramie.

"So, are you going to make me a cake too? I like cake."

"I don't have the ingredients for a pineapple one."

"What kind are you making?"

"Carrot. It's Dean's favorite."

She glanced at her friend in time to see a curious expression on Maya's face.

"What's that look?"

"You remember Dean's favorite cake?"

"Um, yeah. How long have I known him? I remember once he shared some of the birthday cake his mom made for him when I was tutoring him. He mentioned it was his favorite."

"That's a random thing to remember."

"Why? I have lots of dessert-centric memories. Sugar, glorious sugar!" Sunny made a dramatic gesture with the mixing spoon in her hand.

This time it was Maya who snorted at her.

"So, what's the latest valley gossip?"

"Since we last talked, let's see… Oh, Mrs.

Lacey is retiring from teaching after eight hundred and fifty-three years."

"Be nice."

"What? She made biology miserable for me. Science is not my forte, and yet she seemed to want to make everyone into the next Louis Pasteur."

"Actually, her class was more Darwinian."

"See!" Maya jabbed her finger in Sunny's direction. "You're not as saintly as you want everyone to believe."

"I'm far from saintly." She was pretty sure none of the saints faked romantic relationships to get their fathers to do what they wanted.

"Well, as long as you know."

Sunny glanced at Maya as she started mixing ingredients. "Tell me why we're friends again."

Maya smiled and cupped her cheeks in her upturned hands. "Because I'm adorable."

Sunny rolled her eyes. "Whatever."

"Okay, what else is new? Alma and Trudy are reportedly both scheming how to outdo each other at the Fall Festival, but then that's not exactly new."

Sunny smiled as she recalled the competing signs on the way into town. The two ladies' feud went back as long as Sunny could remember so, no, not new.

Maya shared a few more random tidbits.

"I dream of one day having something really exciting to put in the paper."

"You better specify good exciting. You don't want the other kind."

"True. At least I'm still in business, barely. A lot of papers can't say the same."

"As long as there are hunters and fishermen who want to show off their outdoorsman prowess to their neighbors, and kids' sports to cover, I think you'll be okay."

But in reality even that might be in danger with the proliferation of social media among every age group.

Maya sighed and lowered her chin to her crossed arms on the table. "A lifetime of publishing photos of sixteen-point bucks and Millie Compton's recipe column, will I ever survive the excitement? Sometimes I want to trade lives with you."

Sunny shrugged. "You're the one who chose to come back here after college."

"I know, but it's home."

Maya, who had family scattered from Jade Valley to Worland and all across the Wind River Reservation, had never been destined for living in a city. She might whine about the lack of excitement, but she was good at what she did and made the most she could out of the *Post*. If she didn't run the paper, it would probably cease publication and local residents would have to depend on gossip at Alma's or Trudy's for their news.

"You should bring the kiddos and have lunch with me tomorrow. I know Trudy would love to see you. She still says you're the best waitress she's ever had."

"I can't tomorrow. I have plans."

"Plans?"

"The twins and I are having a picnic with Dean."

"With Dean. Is this part of the thank-you, as well?"

Sunny nodded as she poured the cake mix into two circular pans.

"And getting the twins out of the house while Dad's not able to get around, as well. You have to enjoy the warm weather here while it lasts."

"I know you're all California girl now, but I don't think mid-July is on winter's doorstep."

Sunny slid the cake pans into the oven then leaned her hip against the counter while facing Maya.

"No, but time flies. I want to enjoy my visit, and that means not being stuck inside all the time. You know that even when I travel I spend as much time exploring outdoors as I can."

Maya scrunched up her face in a "something's off" expression before slowly replying, "That's true."

"But the next day, we're totally on for lunch. I can taste Trudy's cooking now."

"You better bring me something when you come back," her dad called out from the living room.

"If you didn't fall off horses, you could go yourself."

This was more like it, the normal teasing she and her dad tossed back and forth. She did not like being at odds with him. It didn't happen often, but when it did she always felt as if she'd taken a wrong path even when she was in the right.

Thumping from the other room preceded her dad opening the front door and going outside. He, like her and every other member of her family, was an outdoor person and could only stand being confined within four walls for so long before he got antsy. If he did nothing out there but watch the occasional bird fly by, he'd feel more at peace than stuck in his chair. There was enough of that during the winter months when cold, brutal winds kept everyone inside except for when they had to do essential ranch tasks to ensure the care and safety of the animals.

Surely her dad would grow to appreciate not having to deal with working in the snow once he got used to California. Humans were resistant to change, but often came to enjoy what they initially resisted.

She and Maya talked a bit longer before her friend said she had to go conduct an interview at the school about a custodian who had an impressive collection of coins he'd found on school grounds over the past twenty years. Sunny had to smile because while that might not be breaking national news, it was 100 percent a Jade Valley sort of story. The guy would probably be the front-page feature if nothing earth-shattering happened before Maya sent the next weekly issue to press.

After checking on the still-sleeping twins, Sunny accompanied Maya outside.

"Take care, old man," Maya said with a salute to Sunny's dad.

"Don't forget this cast won't be on forever and I know where you live."

Maya laughed. "You don't scare me."

After Maya left with a wave of her arm out her window, Sunny's dad shook his head and chuckled.

"That girl has more sass than one person should."

"But you love her like your own."

"That I do."

Sunny sank onto the edge of the porch with her feet on the front steps. She stared out at a view that was as familiar as the reflection of her own face in the mirror each morning.

"So, baking a cake for Dean, huh?"

She nodded as if it was no big deal. "Seemed the least I could do."

Her dad nodded. "He's a good man."

He didn't have to elaborate for Sunny to know that. Dean would probably never truly comprehend how thankful she was to him for being there for her dad when she couldn't be. Dean deserved more than a cake, and that's why she hoped that their plan worked out so that everyone was happy in the end. Including Dean.

She looked up at the wide blue sky and thought that her mom and Jason would be happy that the land that was a part of their blood would be staying with someone who loved it. They might not approve of her methods, but hopefully they could see that she only wanted to do what was best for everyone.

DEAN SWORE HE could hear the minutes ticking down to lunchtime as if each second was being marked by a mallet to a large church bell. He'd started his morning by checking a stretch of fencing at the far southern part of the ranch, then gone into town for a new tire for the utility vehicle they used to haul equipment around the ranch and check on cattle when they didn't ride horses. Now he was waiting for chatty Dr. Parsons, the local vet, to finish up with a round of vaccinations in the barn.

Even though the picnic with Sunny wasn't a real date, he didn't want to keep her waiting. He tried to convince himself it had nothing to do with wanting to see her again. He sighed. If he couldn't even fool himself, how was he supposed to fool others? He wasn't an actor, after all.

But shouldn't pretending that he was falling for Sunny be the easiest acting job ever?

The moment Dr. Parsons stepped out of the stall, Dean knew if he didn't send the man on his way he'd launch into another of the seemingly endless stories he always had at the ready.

"Thanks for coming out, Doc."

"No problem."

"If you want to stay and visit with Jonathon for a while, head on over to the house."

"Maybe next time. I best make my way over to the Stevens place."

Dean didn't even wait until Doc was in his truck before he jumped in his own and headed for his house. Sure, this wasn't a real date and he wasn't going to dress up for a picnic, but he didn't want to show up sweaty and dirty either.

One quick shower and a change of clothes later, and he was headed back up the road to the spot where he was supposed to meet Sunny and the twins. When he arrived, he saw her trying to carry picnic supplies while also holding firmly to Lily's and Liam's hands as they toddled along beside her.

He parked in the gravel pull off and hurried to help her. He scooped up Liam and relieved her of the wicker picnic basket, which was heavier than he'd anticipated.

"Thanks," she said, picking up Lily. "This would have been easier if there was a stroller path from the house down to here."

"Probably best that it's not easily accessible to them as they become better at walking."

When he saw Sunny's eyes widen at the idea of the twins managing to reach the river alone, he felt like smacking himself.

"Forget I said that."

"Another reason to sell the ranch."

"Every place has its hazards." He didn't point out that the crime rate in LA was astronomical compared to Jade Valley's. He was supposed to be helping her, not scaring her even more. "But we can't live our lives being afraid of what might happen. You don't think about that every time you get on a plane or go adventuring in some other country, do you?"

"Well, no. Not often anyway."

"And isn't life way more fun when you're not worrying than when you are?"

Sunny stopped and stared at him.

"When did you become a positive-thinking guru?"

"Oh, you didn't know? I even go on speaking tours."

She huffed a laugh, causing Lily to giggle.

"A tour of the pasture talking to the cows, I bet."

"Ouch. You make me sound pitiful."

"Hey, there's something to be said for an audience that can't talk back."

When they reached a flat grassy spot, Sunny carefully checked the area to make sure it was free of snakes before setting Lily down and spreading out the blanket she'd brought.

"What did you put in here anyway?" Dean asked as he placed the picnic basket on one corner of the blanket. "It feels like you included several rocks along with lunch."

"Not quite." Sunny started pulling out sandwiches, chips, containers of pickles, olives, cherry tomatoes. Next came cold sodas and bright plastic containers that obviously contained the twins' lunch.

"Does that basket not have a bottom?"

"How did you know? It's the infinite picnic basic."

"Patent that and you won't ever have to work again. Maybe I'll marry you for real and live a life of leisure." He leaned back on his arms and stretched out his legs, crossing them at the ankle.

"Yeah, right. You're the type who would get bored of a life of leisure in less than a day."

"You're probably right about that."

"I know I am. Even on summer vacation from school, you were still up and working alongside your dad every day."

"That's how I started saving up the money to one day have my own place."

"You knew even back then what you wanted?"

"Didn't you?"

"I knew I liked learning and wanted to go to college. And after studying abroad, I knew I wanted to travel more. But I was probably halfway through school before I started getting an idea of what kind of career I wanted."

"How does one decide on business consultant? I mean, it's not one of the careers school counselors try to guide you toward like doctor, lawyer, engineer."

"We had a project in one of my business classes where we had to look at a failing company and figure out ways to turn it around. I got really into it, and my professor told me that I had a natural talent for seeing issues and innovative ways of fixing them."

He let Liam grab his finger and wave his hand up and down.

"Your dad may not believe this whole relationship thing just because it makes no sense for someone as smart and successful as you to fall for someone like me."

"What does that mean, someone like you?"

"I'm not well educated or well traveled. I don't even own my own home."

"Well, neither do I. My apartment is pretty small, so I'll have to move to a house if this all works out."

He tried to ignore the part of him that wanted to say there were two homes on this ranch and thus plenty of room here.

They spent the next few minutes feeding the twins while munching on their own food, laughing when both Lily and Liam ended up wearing more of their lunch than eating it.

"It's a good thing you two are cute," Sunny said as she wiped their faces, which for some reason they thought was hilarious.

Dean smiled. There was no bad mood that baby laughter couldn't cure.

"You should have a couple of these to help fill up all this space out here when we leave," Sunny said, pointing at the twins.

He had a flash of having those children with her, their own kids in addition to Lily and Liam. He forcefully shoved that thought deep into a vault where he couldn't think about it, especially not when he was sitting this close to Sunny.

"I think having a wife should come first. And I don't even have a girlfriend, thus why I'm able to pretend to be wooing you."

"Wooing?" Sunny laughed a little. "Sometimes you sound very old-fashioned, Dean Wheeler."

If he thought she'd welcome real advances from him, he'd pull out all the chivalry and wooing he could muster. But what they'd be sharing over the next however long was merely an act for their mutual benefit. He shouldn't have to keep reminding himself of that.

"What can I say? I'm a classic catch."

When Liam tried to crawl off the blanket, Dean quickly picked him up and pointed him in the opposite direction. Sunny was right about the twins being a handful. Now that he thought about it, he was surprised that Jonathon had managed them even before his fall.

"So, you mentioned before, you'd floated ideas for changing things around here to my dad without success. Tell me about what you'd like to do."

He plucked a blade of grass and fiddled with it.

"Just an occasional idea of how we could diversify so that all of the ranch's income doesn't depend on animals and weather."

"Such as?"

He glanced up at her. Did she really want to hear about his ideas when she wouldn't be around to see whether any of them panned out?

"My thoughts are kind of all over the place. Whenever I think of something I write it down in a notebook and sometimes mention one or two to your dad. Everything from greenhouses to cabins along the river."

"The cabins make sense. Lots of people who vacation out here like to stay in places that have better views than the hotels. A more authentic Western experience."

"I know there's lots of competition, but there should be ways to differentiate from the others. And there's good money to be made. I've seen the rental rates on some of these places."

"If you want, we could go over your ideas sometime. I could maybe offer some unique angles from other places I've seen in my travels that you could apply here."

"I feel like this is where I should toss out something about not putting the cart before the horse. There's no guarantee this whole crazy act is going to work."

"Well, not with that attitude, it won't," she said as she swatted him on the arm.

Dean stretched out on the blanket, one arm behind his head, and using the brim of his hat to shade his eyes from the sun—but not so much that he couldn't still see Sunny.

"So, exactly how do you want things to progress? Because we can't go from zero to married without your dad calling foul. It's going to take longer than you probably have off work."

He tried not to think about how he wouldn't mind stretching out and spending time with her as long as possible. Or how he'd lain in bed the night before wondering if there was any possibility that her dad might not be the one to change his mind.

He closed his eyes while telling himself he was nine kinds of a fool. If Sunny thought moving back to Jade Valley was the better option, she would do it. Instead, she was going to great lengths to gather her family together in Los Angeles instead. And it wasn't because she was selfish. He could tell she truly believed it was the best option, so he'd be the selfish one for trying to stop her. So here he was discussing how best to trick a man who'd been like a second father to him.

Yeah, sometimes the world made zero sense.

CHAPTER SIX

SUNNY LOOKED THROUGH the photos she'd taken during her picnic with Dean and the twins, trying to choose one for a new phone lock-screen image. If she didn't know better, she'd believe they were a young family on an outing together. A strange warmth filled her at that thought.

She'd been so busy with work and its associated travel over the past few years that she didn't have much time to even casually date let alone think about settling down and having a family of her own. That was another area where she and Jason had differed. He'd married his high school sweetheart and gotten down to the business of being a husband and father. That his life had ended so soon, when he had other lives depending on him, was a cosmic injustice. Sunny owed it to her brother to make sure his children never wanted for anything, that they were always safe and knew they were loved.

Another swipe of her images brought up one of Dean taking a huge bite of the cake she'd baked for him. She smiled at how he'd nearly shot cake out of his nose in the next moment when Lily had grabbed a fistful of cake in her little hand. Sunny had barely stopped Liam from imitating his sister and leaving the cake totally mangled.

"What's so amusing?"

Sunny looked up to see her dad standing in the doorway to the kitchen. She'd been so focused on the photos that she hadn't even heard his distinctive approach.

Time to plant some more seeds.

"Your grandchildren attacking a cake. Want to see?"

"Of course." He used his crutches to maneuver himself into the chair next to her. Then he swiped through all the pictures she'd taken during the picnic, chuckling at the ones of the twins with the cake, first on their hands and then all over their faces. She noticed when he paused a little longer on the one of her with Dean, each of them with a twin on their lap.

"This is a good picture."

"It is, isn't it? I think I'm going to make it my lock-screen image." She took the phone back from him and set the image as her lock screen as if there was absolutely nothing strange about it. She pretended not to realize they totally looked like a husband, wife and two kids.

She sensed her dad was staring at her, but she pretended she wasn't aware of that fact.

Her phone rang right as she finished setting the image.

"It's my boss."

When she answered, Mike didn't waste any time getting straight to the point.

"We landed the account with Romtech, so we need you to be in Brussels the day after tomorrow."

They'd been trying to convince Romtech to go with PTG Consulting's services for a couple of months, so this was great news for the company. The timeline, however, did not work for her.

"Mike, you know I'm on vacation, back home in Wyoming. Someone else will have to make the trip."

"Can't you finish up your vacation after this trip?"

"Considering my dad can't unbreak his leg long enough for me to jet to and from Brussels, no."

She had logged a lot of long hours before

leaving LA so that no one was put in a bind by her absence. Mike was a decent guy, but he didn't have much of a life outside work and didn't seem to comprehend why others did.

After she finally agreed to at least look over the account again and send back some notes about how to conduct the consultation, Mike finally hung up.

"Your boss seems demanding," her dad said.

"He is, but it's how he's helped to build such a successful branch of the company. He needs to get out more though. Pick up a hobby. Maybe go on a date or something."

"What about you? Are you seeing anyone?"

The more-curious-than-normal tone of her dad's voice told her that the seeds she'd been planting with the cake and the picnic might be beginning to sprout. So she tried to imagine herself blushing and not meeting his gaze as she shook her head.

"As you could probably tell from that call, I don't have a lot of free time."

"Then you should enjoy your days off while you're here. You don't have to babysit me."

"I'm not. I'm babysitting the actual babies."

"But you should visit with Maya more. And your other friends."

She suspected that last *friends* meant one friend in particular.

"I'm actually having lunch with Maya tomorrow. I'll take the twins and you can relax, guilt-free."

"You don't have to take Lily and Liam." A tinge of annoyance in his voice told her he didn't like being seen as unable to take care of himself and anything else that needed doing.

"Are you kidding? If I show up without them, Maya will disown me. Give her half a chance and she will spoil them absolutely rotten."

"That's because she can give them back when she's done playing with them."

"Don't try to fool me, old man. I know you do your fair share of spoiling them too."

Sunny knew that was the way of grandparents with their grandchildren, but she also suspected it had more to do with her dad missing Jason and holding on to his babies with all his might. She couldn't blame him for either being protective or spoiling them. Her own freaked-out trip to the hospital with Lily proved she was even more overprotective than her dad. And the way she'd overdone the Christmas presents for two kids who didn't know what Christmas was spoke to years of auntie spoiling ahead.

Though she worked late into the night on the Romtech account prep, when she tried to go to sleep her mind would not settle. She tried listening to music on her phone, relaxing one muscle at a time, every trick she could think of to cure the sudden onset of insomnia, but nothing worked.

Giving up, she slipped out of bed and made her way quietly outside. After a minute or so of sitting on the top step, her eyes adjusted to the darkness. She'd heard the phrase *blanket of stars* many times in her life, more than once on travel brochures from around the world. But she didn't think she'd ever been anywhere that the description fit more than here on the ranch. She'd gotten so used to light pollution in LA that she'd somehow forgotten how stunning a Wyoming sky could be when there was no visible moon or clouds. If she sat in the same spot the entire night she wouldn't be able to count all the visible stars.

She lowered her gaze from the sky to the surrounding landscape shrouded in varying shades of black. No doubt there were various critters out there living their nocturnal lives, perhaps even watching her. When she noticed a pinprick of light in the distance, she realized that she wasn't the only person who was awake.

For someone who got up when stars were still visible on the other end of night, Dean should be asleep already. She hopped up and eased the front door open. Glad the house didn't have any squeaky floorboards, she retrieved her phone before returning to her outside perch.

She pulled up Dean's number and started a text message.

Shouldn't you be asleep?

It took him so long to respond that she thought perhaps he actually was asleep and had just left one of the lights on. As she started to place the phone on the porch beside her, it buzzed and lit up.

I could ask you the same thing.

I tried and failed. Decided to come outside to stargaze a bit.

Want some company?

No, get some rest.

Instead of going to sleep, however, Dean texted her again.

So what's our next step?

She thought about it for a moment. It struck her how odd it was to be talking about when to see each other again and how much affection to show as if they were scenes in a play. She supposed in a way they were. And yet, the fact that they were basically alone in the night right now, only a stretch of dark field separating them, was sort of intimate in a way. It could be seen as romantic if there was actually anything between them.

I'm meeting Maya for lunch tomorrow, but I could invite you to dinner.

Sounds good. But anything sounds better than my own cooking.

Ha ha. I'm totally making frozen pizza.

Oh, so just like home.

Though Dean's texts made her smile, she experienced a little pang of sadness too, thinking of him eating frozen pizza all alone in his house at night after a long day of work. He could easily go visit his parents, of course, but when he came home it was still to an empty house.

She didn't know why that seemed so sad to her when she went home to an empty apartment after work whenever she wasn't traveling. Maybe because despite living by herself, she was surrounded by neighbors. Other than her dad and the twins, Dean was surrounded by wide-open space for miles in every direction. If her dad agreed to move to LA with her, Dean would be even more alone.

But that's what he wanted. At least until he found a real wife.

Sunny stared at the light in the distance. She hoped by him helping her, his own romantic prospects weren't hurt in any way. Laughing a little at herself, she shook her head. Dean himself had said he wasn't seeing anyone, and the fact that he wasn't already married like so many of their former classmates seemed to indicate he wasn't in any hurry to be permanently tied to someone else.

Her phone buzzed with another text, lighting up the photo of her with Dean and the twins. All of them looked so happy, with no hint of the sad events that had led them to have that picnic.

No, she couldn't think of Jason and Amanda now or she really wouldn't see a wink of sleep. Instead she tapped on Dean's message.

I'll see you then. Good night.

Good night.

She looked toward Dean's house in time to see the little square of light disappear. Even after it was gone, she continued to stare at the same spot. And wondered if Dean was lying in his bed questioning how in the world he'd allowed himself to get talked into her crazy plan. Regretting it.

Hopefully any regret would blow away on the wind whenever she handed over the deed. When she tried not to cry that the Breckinridges would no longer be the owners of this land, this majestic view of the Wyoming sky.

HER WISTFUL MOOD of the night before, one tinged with sadness, thankfully disappeared as she finally slept. By the time Sunny had the twins fastened into their car seats in preparation for their trip to town she was mostly back to normal.

That's how grief tended to work. You gradually managed to resume your life, even going stretches without thinking about the loss, but then it hit out of the blue and for a while you wondered if you'd ever be happy again. Thankfully, those bouts were shorter and less intense now than they'd been a year ago, when her tears were never so far away that an instance of being cut off in traffic or seeing a sentimental ad couldn't cause them to appear.

Her job had helped. Not only occupying her mind with necessary work but also the traveling. Something about being in a different country allowed her to distance herself emotionally as well as physically from the sorrow. Over the winter, when holiday images of family were attacking her from all directions, a trip to Australia to consult with a marine products company had been exactly what she needed. Not only was she in a different country but also a different hemisphere and the completely opposite season. The heat of the Australian summer had helped to burn away some layers of her sadness.

She checked that both car seats were secure

one more time before waving to her dad, who sat on the porch.

"We'll be back sometime this afternoon. Try not to break your other leg while I'm gone."

"I don't know when you became so sassy."

Sunny laughed as she got into the driver's seat of her dad's truck and started the engine. She listened to the twins babbling to each other in the back seat, wondering if they were actually trying to communicate specific thoughts or only imitating all the adults they heard speaking.

They were still deep in baby conversation when she parked alongside Main Street a few minutes later.

"Okay, kiddos. Time for lunch with Auntie Maya."

As she was hauling the double stroller from the bed of the truck, she thought it looked more like an all-terrain vehicle.

"Let me help you with that."

She turned her head at the unexpected sound of Dean's voice.

"What are you doing here?" He couldn't be planning to join her and Maya for lunch, could he? They hadn't discussed him making an appearance.

But he shook his head. "I had a couple of errands to run and saw you pull in."

"What a handy coincidence." She allowed him to carry the stroller to the sidewalk and begin to unhook Liam from his car seat while she retrieved Lily.

"Dean Wheeler, I'm surprised you know what to do with one of those."

They both looked up to see Maya pointing at the twins.

"Not all that different from wrestling calves."

Sunny swatted him on the upper arm. "Don't you dare compare my perfect niece and nephew to cattle."

Dean smiled, and for a moment she couldn't look away. He really was a good-looking man. Why wasn't he at least dating someone? Lucky for her plans he wasn't, but still a burning question.

"I didn't know you were joining us for lunch," Maya said, her reporter's inquisitiveness evident in the comment.

Dean shifted his attention, perhaps a bit slowly, from Sunny to Maya. Why did the way his gaze had lingered on Sunny for those couple of seconds leave her breathless?

Had to be because she hadn't been prepared to act out a scene in front of her best friend, at least not yet.

"I'm not," Dean said, answering Maya's question. "I happened to be at the right place at the right time. I best get back to work." He looked at Sunny again. "See you tonight."

She nodded, not quite trusting her voice not to give her away to Maya. Not trusting it to not sound as off-kilter as she suddenly felt.

"Okay, I have questions," Maya said as soon as Dean was out of earshot.

Sunny smiled at her friend.

"When do you not have questions? It's literally your job to have questions."

"What was that all about?"

Sunny feigned ignorance. "What was what about?"

"First you make the man a cake. Then I see you two looking like you are doing a photo shoot for *Young Marrieds* magazine."

"I'm almost certain there is no such magazine."

"Not the point."

"What do you want me to say? Dean and I have been friends forever, even longer than you and I. Also, don't forget that I've made you cakes before."

"For my birthday. Never as a random thanks for doing you a favor."

Sunny had to be careful how she played this. Too much denial and her friend would know something was up. Too little and she'd also know something was a bit on the fishy side.

"He's a good guy. I'm thankful for all he's done, both before I arrived and since."

"Handsome too."

"He is." No use in denying what was obvious.

A sudden fit of crying from Lily ended the interrogation. Sunny stooped down to her niece's level.

"Hey, what's the matter?"

"I think she hit her hand on the edge of the stroller," Maya said. "She was waving her arms around."

"Did you get an owie?" Sunny asked in baby speak, then planted a kiss on Lily's little hand. When Sunny booped her nose, Lily abandoned her tears and giggled instead. "You, little miss, need to stop bumping into things."

Sunny rubbed Lily's soft curls and stood.

"I think I'm going to have to wrap these two in Bubble Wrap for my own peace of mind." Before Maya could launch into interrogation part two, Sunny turned the stroller and headed toward lunch.

When they stepped through the front door of Trudy's Café, Sunny inhaled the familiar scents of fried chicken, yeast rolls and what she thought was chocolate cake. Her mouth watered, and she wondered if after she ate she should order take-out meals for dinner instead of cooking.

No, takeout did not convey the same kind of "I'm falling for my friend" vibe that she needed her dad to observe.

After they claimed a table and two high chairs, then placed their orders, a yelp startled both babies as well as Maya. But Sunny had spotted Trudy Pierce a moment before the older woman's eyes went wide and her ensuing sound of surprise.

"Girl, it's good to see you again," Trudy said as Sunny stood and was enveloped in Trudy's arms.

"It's good to see you too."

Trudy shifted her love to the twins.

"And how are the cutest little boy and girl in the county doing?"

"Be careful," Maya said. "Or all the young

moms in the valley will be flooding Alma's dining room."

"Well, if they want inferior food, they can go for it."

Sunny wasn't able to hide her snort of laughter. This must have been the height of hilarity for the twins because they both busted out laughing and swatted their chubby little hands against the trays of their high chairs.

"I thought older people were supposed to be good examples of proper manners and moral behavior," Maya said once she had herself under control.

Trudy snorted. "You mean old people like me are supposed to be boring and stodgy. No, thank you."

A wide smile stretched across Sunny's face. "You are exactly the same as when I worked here, though I saw while driving into town that the sign war has gone nuclear."

"Well, I wasn't the one who started that," Trudy said with an annoyance that had Sunny biting her bottom lip to keep from laughing. "And she had hers put up while I was out of town. When I was coming back from Casper, I almost drove off the road in shock when I saw it."

"So, of course you had to reciprocate."

"That woman isn't going to outdo me. She keeps trying, thinking I'll give up. Ha!"

No one really knew what had precipitated Jade Valley's somewhat tamer version of the Hatfields and McCoys, and neither woman ever said. Their mutual dislike was older than many of the town's residents, which meant there were all kinds of rumors about why two otherwise nice older ladies did their best to outpromote and outsell each other. Most residents knew the best policy was to make absolutely certain that they didn't eat at either Trudy's Cafe or Alma's Diner more than the other. A strict adherence to equal patronage was rule number one in the *Jade Valley Residents Handbook*.

The waitress arrived with their lunch, and Trudy took one of Sunny's hands between hers.

"How long are you staying?"

"I'm not certain, but probably a couple of weeks."

"I guess some of that depends on how stubborn your dad is being."

"Bingo."

"Well, come see me again before you leave. I want to hear all about your latest travels."

"I will."

By the time Sunny sat back down, her stomach was audibly grumbling.

Life in Jade Valley seemed to flow now pretty much as it had when she'd been waiting tables here as a teenager. Though the faces had changed some, the snippets of conversations she heard from nearby tables told her it was still the same types of conversations that had happened more than a decade ago.

Still, some predictable things in Jade Valley were perfect. Trudy's fried chicken was near the top of that list. The recipe had been passed down from her grandmother, who'd grown up in Georgia, and it was so good that customers drove from as far away as Cody and Greybull, a distance of nearly three hundred miles, to indulge their taste buds.

Maya's phone dinged with a text. Sunny noticed her friend grumbling under her breath as she read it.

"What's wrong?"

Maya shook her head. "Just my boss. He keeps telling me I have to get the income from the paper up, either through advertising or circulation. I keep telling him I can't magically make more businesses or residents appear."

"Anything I can do to help?"

Maya stuck a crinkle-cut fry slathered in ketchup in her mouth and chewed while she appeared to be thinking of an appropriate response.

"Actually, how about you write a series of first-person travel pieces about the places you've been? That's different content that might bring in more readers. I could promote it a little farther afield."

"In case you've forgotten, I'm not a journalist. Or a travel writer."

"You got the top grade in our English class. And it's not like I'm asking for Pulitzer-level investigative reporting here. Just tell readers about different places that take them out of this valley for the amount of time it takes them to read the articles."

After some more pleading and a remarkably pouty face from Maya, Sunny finally relented.

"Awesome. When can you get me the first one?"

Sunny pointed at her half-full plate.

"Can I at least finish eating my lunch?"

"Sure. I might even give you time to tack on dessert."

Sunny had only managed to take a couple

more bites when it was her phone that dinged with a text, also from her boss.

"What is it, Annoying Bosses Day?"

Mike had looked over the notes she'd sent him, but he had some things he thought she should revise. Why the person who would actually be making the presentation couldn't do the final adjustments, she had no idea. After texting back a simple Fine, she set her phone aside and returned to her lunch.

In the next moment, Maya had snatched up Sunny's phone and was pointing at the photo on the screen.

"Explain."

"Explain what?"

"You are playing dumb with me. What is going on between you and Dean?"

"Do you think you could say that a little louder? I don't think the residents of Montana heard you." She pointed at her phone. "It's a good picture. I mean, look at the twins' smiles. They're so cute I get a sugar rush simply by looking at them."

"What I'm noticing are the smiles on your and Dean's faces."

So her idea that she should wait for a bit to tell Maya the truth wasn't going to work. She should have known that. Maya Pine would have made one hell of an investigative reporter or detective if she'd decided to live somewhere larger than Jade Valley.

"I don't want to talk about it here." Too many ears attached to gossipy mouths nearby. Sure, the news about the "relationship" would get out at some point, she needed it to, but she'd like to maintain control of who knew what when. Sunny didn't want things to potentially spiral out of control. The romance might appear whirlwind in nature, but it also had to be believable.

"Fine, but you're not wiggling out of a full explanation by trying to say the twins are fussy or something like that." She shifted her gaze to Lily and Liam. "Isn't that right?"

Sunny held up her hand as one would while being sworn in for before giving testimony in court.

"I solemnly swear to tell the whole truth when we get to a more private place."

After they finished eating and laughing at the twins' messy encounters with mashed potatoes and banana pudding, Sunny purchased the meal her dad had requested. After hugging Trudy goodbye with another promise to visit again before she left for California, she drove to the town park. Sunny placed the twins in the sandbox to play then joined Maya at a nearby picnic table.

Time to spill all the beans.

Sunny sped through the explanation of what she and Dean were doing and why, not giving Maya a chance to interrupt. When she was finished, Maya was staring at her with her mouth partly open.

After a long pause, she asked, "Have you lost your mind?"

"Quite possibly." It wasn't as if she hadn't wondered the same thing.

"You literally let something your dad said when he was upset inspire this whole bananas plan?"

"In a word, yes."

Maya was uncharacteristically quiet. She turned so that her side was facing Sunny and watched the kids play for several seconds.

"Are you sure this is the best thing for your family? Don't you think losing the ranch would be one blow too many for your dad? And what if he likes having Dean as a son-in-law and then you two end things?"

Sunny had asked herself those same questions over and over. But when she wavered, her next thought was always how losing the ranch was a million times better than losing another family member or not being able to spend enough time with what little family she had left.

"I wish I could lay out the pros of moving to California before my dad and he'd agree, but he won't. I keep thinking about how he's there alone with the twins. What if something happened to him when no one else was around? There would be no one to call for help. No one to take care of Lily and Liam."

"But Dean is right down the road. He or one of the other hands would notice if your dad went missing."

"But how long before they noticed? Would it be too long?"

Maya looked over at her. "You're going full worst-case scenario."

"That's because my family is intimately acquainted with worst-case scenario."

Sunny's core personality fit her name. She typically had a positive outlook on things, but that attitude had taken repeated hits. Maya's silence was evidence that she couldn't argue with what Sunny had said.

Still, Sunny wanted to create a bright future for the twins, her dad and herself. Even for Dean. She was a fan of win-win situations. When she consulted with business clients, she often told them that the best way to create both profits and goodwill among customers was to create those types of win-win situations.

Maya sighed and looked at Sunny.

"If you succeed in this and don't come to visit me, I'm never going to forgive you."

Sunny smiled.

"You know that won't happen. And you can come to California too, you know? Planes go both ways."

"When it's colder than a deep freeze here in the middle of the winter, I might just show up without warning."

"And I'd be thrilled to see you. So would Dad and the twins."

Maya huffed.

"More like you'll all forget me. Out of sight, out of mind."

"Now you're being ridiculous. Me messaging you from the literal other side of the world proves I'll never forget my bestie."

Maya pointed at her and narrowed her eyes.

"You better not. And for me not trying to talk you out of this madness, I expect a travel piece from you each week for the next three months."

"What? That's extortion," Sunny said in mock outrage.

Maya gave her an evil grin.

"Yes, yes it is."

Sunny stared at her dearest friend for a couple of seconds before bursting out laughing.

"Fine, I'll pay your price."

"And I'll help you get your man."

Sunny didn't even bother to remind Maya that this was all an act. Let her friend have her fun. Let this situation be a win-win-win-win-win. The more wins, the better Sunny would feel about a little necessary deception.

CHAPTER SEVEN

DEAN STOOD STARING in his bathroom mirror, a little-used bottle of cologne in his hand. His mom had bought it for him a couple of Christmases ago on the recommendation of a fragrance-counter clerk in Cheyenne. She'd said it would smell nice when he went on dates.

It had been a not-at-all-hidden desire on the part of his mom to see him married and giving her grandchildren. It didn't matter that his dad had told his mom countless times to *Let the boy live his own life. He'll get married when he's ready.*

His mom always responded by saying she just wanted Dean to be happy, that she was worried he was lonely out on the ranch by himself. That might be partially true, but he also knew that she really wanted grandkids to spoil absolutely rotten. By only thinking of how his and Sunny's ruse would affect Jonathon, the twins, Sunny, even himself, he'd neglected to fully think about how this was going to affect his parents when he and Sunny split up and she left Jade Valley for good.

And how were they going to handle the timing of things? They couldn't believably start dating and get married and divorced during her current vacation. Were they going to do a long-distance relationship with her traveling back and forth to Jade Valley when she could? Was he supposed to fly to LA? That would cut into the funds he'd saved for the purchase of the ranch. Even with a possible loan he'd discussed with Ben Jorgenson at that bank earlier in the day, he still needed to be frugal.

It wouldn't matter anyway if he and Sunny didn't iron out some more details.

He stared at the bottle of cologne. Would wearing it send up a red flag to Jonathon that Dean was trying too hard to sell this relationship? Or would it actually make him believe the budding romance was real?

Dean sighed. Maybe a little wouldn't hurt. Plus, maybe Sunny would think he smelled nice.

Yeah, he shouldn't have those types of thoughts, but he couldn't seem to help himself.

After a quick spritz of what he'd been told was a woodsy, manly scent, he stuffed the bottle back in the medicine cabinet where it spent the vast majority of its time and headed out so he wasn't late for dinner.

He tried to ignore the little buzz of nervousness that inhabited his middle as he stepped into the Breckinridge home a few minutes later.

"Boy, why do you smell like you're going on a date?" Jonathon joked when he greeted him at the door.

As sure-footed as Dean was, the question nearly made him trip over his own feet.

"I figured if I didn't have to eat my own cooking tonight, then I shouldn't show up smelling like the herd."

Jonathon's quick laugh revealed that he didn't buy it for a minute, and Dean fought the urge to try again to convince his boss that it wasn't what he might be thinking. Because the plan was to actually make the man think exactly that.

Everything was so much more complicated because Dean was pretending to feel things that he actually felt without letting Sunny know he wasn't pretending at all.

"What are you all talking about in here?" Sunny asked as she came up the hallway carrying Lily.

"About how Dean here felt the need to break out the cologne."

Sunny gave Dean a startled look before she seemed to deliberately turn her back to her dad as she put Lily in the playpen with her brother.

"What's wrong with wearing cologne?" she asked as she turned back around, any hint of her surprise gone. "A person doesn't have to be going out for a night on the town to want to smell good. It's why I buy the floral shampoo I do. Isn't it nice?"

Dean pressed his lips together to keep from laughing as Sunny brought her head suddenly under her dad's nose.

Jonathon made the audible equivalent of an eye roll, as if to say he didn't understand young people and their strange need to smell like the various flora.

"I much prefer the smell of dinner."

Sunny smiled.

"You act as if you're starving when I know you didn't leave a bite of the lunch I brought you."

"I haven't had anything from Trudy's since I broke this stupid leg."

Despite staying busy on the ranch, Jonathon never missed his regular Sunday morning breakfast with his core set of friends while enjoying hearty meals that likely didn't do good things for their cholesterol levels.

"You mean Dean didn't tote you into town so you could shoot the breeze with the other old geezers?"

"Someone has to take up the slack around here," Dean said, joining the teasing.

Jonathon pointed at him then his daughter then back to Dean.

"I don't know what has gotten into the two of you, but I don't like it."

Sunny laughed then planted a smacking kiss on her dad's cheek.

"You know you love us. And it's not like you don't give as good as you get when you have the chance."

"Yeah, you should remember that."

When Sunny glanced at him, Dean tried not to wonder if their ruse would include her kissing him on the cheek like that at some point.

"Uh, you need any help?" he asked her, hoping he didn't sound as flustered as he felt. His face felt as hot as if he was standing out on the range under the midday sun without a hat.

This time, her amused smile was directed at him.

"I'm not sure I want help from the guy who has on multiple occasions proclaimed that he has no cooking skills."

"I think I can manage to set the table without incident."

He almost made a liar of himself when he nearly fumbled a glass onto the floor a couple minutes later.

"What's wrong with you?" Sunny asked in a whisper as she leaned close. Too close for his comfort.

"Nothing."

Sunny thankfully put some distance between them again.

"Dad was right. You do smell nice," she said.

Dean really wished she hadn't said that because she didn't mean it in the way he wanted. It was all part of the act, evidenced by the fact that she'd said it loud enough that her dad could hear her if he was listening from the other room. He reminded himself that he'd agreed to this, and that he needed to contribute as much to the selling of the narrative as she did.

"Don't get a lot of opportunities to use cologne. Pretty sure the cows don't care what I smell like."

"I doubt the hands do either."

Dean laughed. "They have no right to, smelling no better themselves."

When he heard Jonathon get up in the living room, Dean went to stand next to Sunny as she chopped tomatoes for the tacos she was making. As he heard the crutches coming closer, he leaned close to Sunny's ear.

"Think this will help?" he whispered.

Sunny startled, and for a moment he was afraid she'd accidentally cut herself. He reached out on instinct to protect her and ended up with his hand atop hers right as Jonathon reached the kitchen.

Dean removed his hand in a flash. From Jonathon's perspective it probably looked as if they were trying not to get caught flirting, which was good for Sunny's plan. Dean hoped Sunny believed that was why he'd reacted that way as well, and not because it had felt as if he'd stuck his fingers in an electric outlet.

DEAN WAS A better actor than Sunny had given him credit for because for a moment earlier he'd made even her believe he was actually flirting with her. But that made no sense. They'd known each other literally their entire lives. If there was any sort of attraction between them, wouldn't it have made an appearance when they were hormonal teenagers?

Maybe it was precisely because they'd seen each other all the time then that it hadn't. It wouldn't have occurred to them to be attracted to each other. Right?

Why in the world was she even having those kinds of thoughts? She'd had to push them aside all throughout dinner.

"How do you think it's going?"

"Huh?"

Dean stopped walking toward his truck and turned to look at her, then pointed back toward the house.

"Do you think your dad is beginning to suspect what you want him to?"

"Oh," she said, wanting to smack herself for letting her mind wander in odd directions. "I don't know. Maybe. I caught him watching us a couple of times during dinner. Then again when you were helping me put the twins to bed."

"How quickly do you think we should move and have it still be believable?"

"I wish I knew the answer to that question." She continued walking until she was next to his truck then turned to lean back against the cool metal. "Maybe we should go somewhere beyond the ranch and do something together that looks more like a date. I can get Maya to babysit. Oh, by the way, she knows everything."

"I figured."

"Actually, I was going to hold off telling her, but you know how Maya is."

"A bloodhound in human form."

"Precisely."

Dean leaned against the truck bed next to her. "What about the rodeo at the fairgrounds tomorrow?"

She nodded. "Sounds like a good option, nightlife being what it is in Jade Valley."

"Except that your dad will want to go too."

"And there's a fifty-fifty chance that Maya will be covering it for the paper." Seeing as how the paper only had one other staff member. "Is this why you're not dating anyone? Lack of options both in dating partners and places to actually go on a date?"

"Among other things."

She wondered what those other things were, but they weren't her business unless he decided to share them. They were good friends, but not the kind who shared in-depth discussions about their romantic endeavors or lack thereof—except for the current fake one.

"Let's do the rodeo anyway," she said. "Bring the whole entourage. It's still an outing away from the ranch. I'll even let you buy me something I shouldn't eat from the concession stand."

"Ah, romance in funnel-cake form."

"Hey, don't knock the romantic possibilities of a good funnel cake."

"If we keep eating sweets at this rate, our teeth are going to be as fake as this relationship."

"I'll make sure I make a giant salad the next time you come over. And we'll drink water."

"Who said romance was dead?"

Sunny swatted him on the arm with the back of her hand.

"Good night, Dean," she said as she stepped away from him then started walking backward toward the house. "Be sure to brush and floss before you go to bed."

"I might even get fancy and use mouthwash."

"Oh," she said, making it sound as if she was truly impressed.

Dean laughed and shook his head. "See you tomorrow."

When Sunny reached the porch, she stopped and turned to watch Dean's taillights disappear. For some reason she waited until she saw his headlights pulling into his driveway in the distance.

Dean wasn't only a good guy, a hard worker. He was also funnier than she remembered. Too bad none of her real dates were as easy and relaxed as these fake ones with Dean.

DEAN RETURNED TO the bleachers where he'd left Sunny, Jonathon and the twins, armed with two funnel cakes, a bag of popcorn and three sodas. He smiled when he thought about their dental discussion the night before. He couldn't remember the last time he'd had so many sweets in a short amount of time. Probably over Christmas when his mom went full tilt on baking.

First had been the cake Sunny had made for him when they picnicked by the river. Then apple pie with vanilla ice cream the night before. And now funnel cake and sodas. Good thing their pretend relationship wouldn't last long or they were going to end up with diabetes as well as cavities.

When he rounded the corner at the end of the bleachers, the smile dropped off his face. Ryan Taylor was sitting next to Sunny, and both of them were laughing. Ryan wasn't originally from Jade Valley, but he'd moved down from near Billings to help run his grandparents' ranch. And even Dean had to admit the guy was good-looking. Just about every unattached woman between the ages of sixteen and seventy-six had taken notice of that fact since his arrival in town last summer. Dean was surprised there hadn't been a county-wide arm-wrestling contest yet with Ryan as the prize.

"Oh good, you're back," Jonathon said when he spotted Dean.

Dean handed his boss the popcorn and funnel cake he'd requested.

"Didn't you get anything?"

"I'll share this with Sunny," Dean said, barely resisting emphasizing her name while staring hard at Ryan.

"I introduced her to Ryan," Jonathon said. "Said he should come over for dinner sometime since Sunny's been cooking so much that she's going to make the two of us have to buy bigger pants."

Dean wanted to swat Ryan away like a pesky fly even though he actually liked the guy. He didn't, however, like the way Ryan was looking at Sunny—the same way the local female population looked at him, like they could gobble him up with a spoon.

"Thanks," Sunny said as he climbed up to the spot next to her on the level above Jonathon and handed her the funnel cake and her drink.

"Good to see you," Ryan said with a nod.

"You too." Dean tried not to sound as unenthusiastic as he felt, but he was pretty sure he didn't succeed based on the look Sunny shot him.

"How long are you visiting for?" Ryan asked Sunny.

Dean reached over and ripped off a significant piece of funnel cake and took a big bite.

"I'll have to go back to work soon."

Dean resisted the urge to smile.

Lily started to fuss where she sat beside her brother in the double stroller.

"What's wrong, cutie?" Ryan asked as he leaned over and attempted to tickle her, which only made her start crying.

"I evidently don't have a way with kids," Ryan said.

Dean knew he was being petty, but he made quick work of retrieving Lily. As soon as she was sitting on his lap, she not only stopped crying but grinned wide up at him. Everyone else temporarily forgotten, his heart moved for this sweet little girl. She'd been through so much already but didn't even remember it. He would literally protect her and Liam with his life, same as Sunny would. Of course, he'd protect her with his life too.

"She seems to like you," Ryan said, an annoying smile on his face as he nodded at Lily.

"Yeah, she's my little buddy, aren't you?" Dean let Lily grab his finger and babble something that sounded like "E" before she gave his finger an enthusiastic shake. He had no idea if she associated the sound with his name or it was only random babyspeak.

"If you have time while you're here, we should go out and do something," Ryan said, speaking to Sunny again.

"Great idea," Jonathon said. "She works so much and now thinks she has to babysit me as well as the twins. You should go out and have some fun when you have the chance."

"What do you think I'm doing now?" Sunny asked her dad.

"You're hanging out with an old man, two babies and the person you wrangled into helping you tote us around."

"Dad," she said in a scolding voice that also sounded embarrassed. Then she looked at Dean. "Ignore him."

"I didn't mean to make things awkward," Ryan said, drawing her attention away from Dean. "Especially if you're seeing someone."

Ryan's gaze met Dean's, full of curiosity.

Jonathon scoffed. "She's free as a bird."

Ryan was still watching Dean.

This was the moment. Sunny hadn't known how to take the relationship to the next step and make it believable, but Dean was more interested in putting an end to any advances Ryan might make toward her. And not for the sake of their ruse. He reached over and took her hand in his.

"Actually, she's not."

Sunny looked at him with wide eyes, but then she must have remembered that she wasn't supposed to be surprised by his declaration because she smiled and squeezed his hand.

"Sorry, didn't mean to overstep," Ryan said.

"It's okay," Sunny said, returning her attention to him but not letting go of Dean's hand. "It's all very new."

Ryan nodded then made his departure.

"I thought something was going on with you two," Jonathon said, then ate a piece of popcorn while looking at them as if what Dean had revealed was an interesting twist in a movie. "You are not good at hiding the truth, neither one of you."

"Sorry, Dad. It was just so unexpected. I mean, we've known each other forever."

Sunny gave Dean a shy look that didn't really match her personality but nevertheless caused a fluttery, vibrating sensation in his chest.

"I've liked her for a long time but never said anything."

He had no idea why he'd let that truth tumble from his lips, but there was no way to call it back now.

When one of Jonathon's friends showed up and drew his attention away, Sunny gave Dean a thumbs-up. She'd obviously taken his confession as a further embellishment of their whirlwind romance story.

In the next moment, she slid her hand out of his grasp and ripped off another piece of funnel cake. He was still feeling the loss of the weight and warmth of her hand when she lifted the piece of funnel cake to his lips.

He sucked in a breath before he could think about how that might look, but then he opened his mouth and accepted the treat. And he refused to break eye contact with her as he did so. She was the first to look away, and he was glad she did because he'd begun to wonder what she'd do if he leaned forward and kissed her right there in front of half the town.

SUNNY CONTINUED TO stuff funnel cake in her mouth to try to forget the breathless, unsettled feeling that had hit her when Dean had held her gaze moments ago. She should not have those kinds of feelings when this was all an act. But, man, was Dean selling it. She'd almost believed what he said about having liked her for a long time. Never would she have imagined that he could act that well. Maybe he should move to LA too. Movie studios could cast a real cowboy in some Western projects if they had a resurgence.

Though her plan had been to convince her dad she and Dean were in a relationship, she'd never been so glad to see Frank Tillson show up and capture her dad's attention. She needed a few minutes to pull herself together.

"You want another funnel cake?" Dean asked.

"Huh?"

He pointed at the paper plate, now empty except for some leftover powdered sugar.

"You devoured the first one."

She shook her head. "No, I'm good. Actually, I'll probably regret this later."

"Regretting the consumption of junk food, a tale as old as time."

She laughed, glad he was back to his normal self.

"Now I have that song from *Beauty and the Beast* in my head," she said.

"I dare you to start singing it out loud."

"Don't tempt me or you'll be known as the guy with the embarrassing girlfriend."

Dean shrugged. "There are worse things."

He smoothed a few strands of fine hair off Lily's forehead as she drifted closer to sleep. The gentleness with which he did so caused that weird feeling behind her breastbone again. It oddly felt as if she was playing with an open flame.

Sunny startled when someone suddenly sat beside her.

"So, about thirty seconds ago I heard an interesting rumor," Maya said.

"Oh? What rumor?"

"That the two of you are dating." Maya checked to make sure Sunny's dad was facing the other direction before she gave Sunny and Dean an exaggerated wink.

"I think you must have something in your eye," Dean said, humor in his voice.

Sunny swatted him lightly to keep him from ruining the progress they'd made tonight in the mission to have all of her family together again.

"So?" Maya said softly while leaning close to Sunny and surreptitiously pointing at her dad's back.

Sunny responded with an expression she hoped conveyed that she thought her dad had bought the revelation.

"Well, lovebirds," Maya said a bit too loudly. "When did you first know the other was the one?"

It took everything Sunny had not to pinch Maya until she begged for mercy. Instead, she stared hard at her, trying to telepathically ask, "What in the world is the matter with you?"

For her part, Maya looked quite proud of herself.

"You know what they say about paybacks,"

Sunny whispered so that only Maya could hear her.

"What was that? I couldn't quite hear you."

Sunny reached back, as if preparing to slug her best friend. Maya hopped up, laughing.

"Well, I'm off to take some exciting pictures of people falling off horses."

Frank had settled in next to her father, both of them giving their assessment of each bronc rider as they entered the dirt arena.

Dean leaned over and whispered next to her ear, "You okay?"

"Yeah."

Though as they watched the competitors in the arena, added hot dogs to the oh-so-healthy foods they'd consumed and fed the twins baby-appropriate food, she was strangely aware of him sitting next to her. Or maybe it was more that she felt the eyes of those around them, imagined she could hear the news that they were dating spreading through the crowd. By the time the bull riding was over, she'd bet the entire balance in her bank account that everyone in the stands had heard the news.

"You're such a lovely couple," Mrs. Winslow, the local librarian as far back as Sunny could remember, said as she stopped in front of them at the end of the night. "I always thought you two should get together. You're perfect for each other. Does this mean you're going to be moving back to Jade Valley, dear?"

Though she understood where that assumption might come from, it annoyed Sunny. Why was the first assumption never that the man would change his life to further a relationship?

"Sunny has a great job in LA," Dean said as he settled his arm around her shoulders. "She's worked hard to get where she is."

Mrs. Winslow's brows came together as if she was trying to understand nuclear physics.

"You're going to have a long-distance relationship? Those hardly ever last."

"Now, Sharon, you know that's not true. You and Joe did fine when he was overseas," Sunny's dad said.

"That was different. He was serving his country."

"Well, last time I looked, Vietnam was a lot farther away than Los Angeles."

"It's all new," Sunny said, trying to cover up for her dad's lack of tact. "We're taking it a day at a time."

"Well, I wish you all the best." Mrs. Winslow headed after the rest of the crowd making for their vehicles parked in the field behind the grandstand.

"I don't think she believes we'll make it," Dean said, watching the older woman disappear around the end of the bleachers.

"Ignore her," her dad said. "She's been nosy and opinionated as long as I've known her."

Sunny was surprised her dad didn't have a few questions of his own, but he seemed to take the news of them dating in stride. As if it was not a surprise at all. Though it was possible he was planning to interrogate them both separately.

By the time they all made it to the truck and everyone was safely buckled in, Sunny realized how tired she felt. As Dean drove them back toward the ranch, she felt her eyes drifting closed. She kept forcing them back open but finally gave up and leaned her head against the window. The twins were already completely out, and she was going to be joining them momentarily.

She woke with a jolt and quickly realized it was because Dean had pulled off onto the gravel road that ran along the edge of the ranch, flanked on one side by the river and the other by acres of pasture as well as first Dean's house and then her father's.

"I don't want to see her hurt," her father said. "She's lost too much already."

It took Sunny a foggy moment to realize he was talking about her and another moment to realize that the situation had become unexpectedly serious. She almost spoke up, though she didn't know what to say. Would she really put an end to the plan to bring her family together when it had barely gotten underway?

"You know I'd never do anything to hurt Sunny."

Right then Liam let out a sudden and ear-piercing cry, effectively putting an end to the conversation as well as Sunny's eavesdropping on it.

"Hey, hey," she said, acting as if she'd been awakened by her nephew's unhappiness. "The world is not ending, little man."

"That sounds like a diaper cry," her dad said.

Indeed it was, which she discovered once they arrived at the main house. After Dean helped her get the babies into the nursery, he went back outside to make sure her dad didn't tumble backward down the front steps.

When she had both twins freshly diapered,

changed into their pajamas, fed and tucked into their bed, she expected Dean to be long gone. Instead, when she entered the living room, her dad pointed toward the front door.

"He's still out there."

She heard the distinct note of teasing in her dad's voice. This was not how she'd expected him to react at all, and she wondered why he was acting so differently about it around her than he had been with Dean earlier. She'd expected a litany of questions, but maybe he only intended to grill Dean.

Poor guy.

When she went outside, Dean was sitting at the top of the steps.

"Sorry about earlier," she said as she sat next to him, their shoulders barely an inch apart. When he looked at her as if he didn't know what she was talking about, she nodded behind them. "With Dad. I heard him grilling you on the way back."

"That was to be expected, don't you think? You're his only daughter, after all."

"But you're not some random guy he's never met. He knows you every bit as well as he does me."

"Maybe that's even more concerning for him."

She started to ask him why but then remembered a thought that had occurred to her right before Liam's "I went poo in my diaper" wail.

"He's probably thinking that if this doesn't work out, not only will you be hurt but he'll have to find a new foreman," Dean said.

She really hadn't thought all this through, but now it was too late to back out of the story they'd put in motion. The whole county probably knew they were dating by now. She wouldn't put it past Maya to literally make it front-page news. Everything had to work out how she'd planned now, not only for her family's sake. She refused to be the reason Dean lost his job and his spot on this land he loved.

"I won't let that happen," she said. "No matter how our plan turns out, I won't let him blame you. I dragged you into this without taking the time to think through all the possibilities. I'm sorry about that."

Dean reached over and patted her hand but didn't remove his after doing so. Instead, he left it lying atop hers, the warmth of his palm soaking into her skin.

"There's nothing to apologize for, okay?"

She nodded though she still felt like a terrible friend for roping him into her scheme, even if the success of that plan would also get him what he wanted.

CHAPTER EIGHT

DEAN COULDN'T TAKE back anything he'd done or said the night before, but the situation with Sunny had taken a serious turn when he'd let his jealousy get the better of him. After leaving her the night before, he'd sat on his own front porch for a long while, long enough that his eyes adjusted fully to the dark. The sound of the river would have lulled him to sleep if his mind hadn't been so full of questions about how to best proceed. He had to strike a balance between being believable and not falling so far into the ruse that he let his true feelings tumble out again.

He'd finally settled on simply having fun with the whole situation. If he didn't think about its eventual end and kept things light and easy, he'd make it through. After all, he and Sunny had been friends before he'd one day looked at her and realized his feelings had changed.

He reined in at the top of a rise overlooking the river, noting the dark clouds gathering over the mountains to the west. The weather forecasters were calling for a wetter-than-normal July into August. He'd take it after the fires the summer before had filled the valley with thick smoke on more than one occasion, making it hard to breathe when outside. And with his job, he was always outside. It had been so bad that his parents had gone to visit his aunt Ginny in Nebraska for a couple of weeks so the smoke didn't trigger his mom's asthma.

His horse's ears flicked at the faint rumble of thunder.

"I agree, time to head back." He used the reins to turn Pecan around, keeping his eye out for any sign of the mountain lion that had cost Junior Blackwell a calf on his ranch a few days before.

Dean wasn't of the mindset that all predators should be eradicated. After all, they'd been in this part of the world before any of his ancestors had been. He just wanted them to stick to the mountains and avoid any unwanted interactions with humans that would lead to either's demise. His wasn't a popular opinion in some circles, but he wasn't going to abandon it to fit in more comfortably. Some of the old-timers thought he'd been infected by *newfangled ideas*.

Wait until they saw how he planned to diversify a ranch that had only run cattle and a few horses during its entire century-long existence.

When he reached the barn, he didn't expect to see Sunny coming out. But there she was looking more beautiful in a pair of jeans and a T-shirt than any runway model could ever hope to be. Models probably paid small fortunes to get the kind of wavy blond hair with a hint of red that Sunny had naturally.

"How's the herd?" she asked, shading her eyes as she looked up at him before he dismounted.

"All seemed well. Maybe the lion decided domesticated dinner was too much of a risk."

He slid from the saddle and led Pecan toward the barn door. While loosening the cinch so the horse could breathe more easily, he noticed the front of Sunny's T-shirt had a print of some historical looking building. He pointed at it.

"Where's that?"

"Gyeongbokgung."

"Afraid I still have no idea."

"Gyeongbok Palace in Seoul, South Korea.

It's where the kings of the Joseon Dynasty lived for hundreds of years."

"Well, now you're just showing off."

Sunny laughed. "You know I always liked history."

"And every other subject in school."

"I did *not* like trigonometry."

"You got not only straight A's but an A+ in every class." He started removing the saddle and the rest of the tack.

"That doesn't mean I liked it, only that I worked hard for those grades."

Dean gave Pecan some water and set about feeling the horse's legs and checking his hooves for any trapped stones.

"You've been to some interesting places." No wonder she wouldn't want to give up her job if it allowed her to travel all around the world on someone else's dime.

"I have. Not all of them so grand or important to history, but every place has its charms and beauty. I mean, if I were to ask someone on the streets of Seoul where Jade Valley, Wyoming, was, they likely wouldn't know either. But it doesn't lessen the beauty here."

He nodded at the truth of her words.

"So, did your dad hit you with a barrage of questions after I left last night?"

"Oddly, no. He seems to be taking this all very much in stride, which was not what I expected."

"Me neither. Do you think him being so accepting will make it harder when we end this?" He remembered Jonathon's words the night before, that he didn't want to see Sunny get hurt again, and how he'd responded that he'd never hurt her.

But she wasn't the one emotionally invested in this pretend romance.

"Or he expects it to not last long so isn't making a big fuss," she said.

Dean smoothed his hand down Pecan's back.

"Maybe we should follow his lead then and not stress over any of this, just have fun with it."

"That sounds like a great idea." She shoved her hands in the back pockets of her jeans. "So, you up for a real date tonight?"

He knew that by "real date" she likely only meant going somewhere without the twins or her dad being third, fourth and fifth wheels, so he nodded.

"Sure. What do you have in mind?"

"Maya said they're still doing the outdoor

movies this summer and that she'd babysit. I might have already told Dad we were going."

"Good to know I have a say in this relationship."

Sunny stuck out her tongue at him.

Dean laughed. "Some things never change."

SUNNY MADE A sound of appreciation and closed her eyes as she savored the delicious pulled-pork barbecue sandwich. Beside her on the blanket they'd spread out at the small town park, Dean chuckled.

"Don't laugh," she said. "This is top-tier barbecue."

"Be careful or you might get disowned by your father for eating that before we can even get hitched."

The way he so casually referred to their plans to get temporarily married caused her to suck in a breath and subsequently choke on the bite she'd taken a moment before. Dean beat her on the back then handed her the large cup of lemonade he'd brought back for her from the circle of food trucks at the edge of the park. Movie in the Park night always increased the dining options in Jade Valley threefold.

"If he didn't toss me out for saying I preferred pork chops to steak when I was a kid, I think I'm safe now. Besides, this is ambrosia." She held the sandwich up to him, offering him a bite.

"I think I'll stick with beef, thanks." He wiggled his hamburger then took a bite so big she couldn't help but laugh at him.

"I still can't believe it's true."

Sunny looked up to see Olivia Redmond staring at her and Dean, her arms crossed.

"Olivia," Sunny said, trying to keep her voice as neutral as possible. Which was a feat since Olivia caused her jaw to clench on a good day. Her parents owned the only bank in town, and she suffered fully from "big fish in little pond" syndrome. She also thought everyone's business was hers.

"Seems to me you'd want to date someone who actually lived here," Olivia said. "At least in the same state."

The way she said those words and looked Dean up and down made it abundantly clear who she thought that someone should be. A heated dislike flooded Sunny's body and she deliberately reached over and placed a possessive hand on Dean's knee. Even if they weren't in a pretend relationship, she'd do this to save him from Olivia's manicured claws.

"I'm actually surprised you still live here," Sunny said before Dean could respond. "But maybe I shouldn't be. You have a pretty good life here."

"Not all of us run away from our families."

Sunny felt as if she'd been stabbed right in the center of her heart. She'd known Olivia wasn't the nicest person ever, but she hadn't counted on her being hateful.

"Olivia," Dean said, his voice hard and sharp.

"What? She started it."

"No, you did. Plus, how old are you?"

Dean took Sunny's hand and threaded his fingers with hers then squeezed. Thankful for his support, she looked up at Olivia. If she was successful in moving her family to California, she would not miss Olivia at all.

"Whatever," Olivia said, tossing her long blond hair over her shoulder as she walked away.

"When did she get so nasty?" Sunny asked.

"Probably about the time I told her once and for all that I had no interest in dating her."

"Oh, that explains a lot. Though I don't think she's given up based on how she was looking at you like I've been looking at this barbecue sandwich."

Dean laughed and his smile was prettier than she remembered. Though she didn't have a lot of experience seeing it this close.

"I assure you she has zero chance."

Sunny wasn't entirely sure why his saying that made her happy, but it had to be because the thought of him with Olivia...well, she wouldn't wish the woman on her worst enemy let alone a good friend.

When he released her hand, she had the craziest urge to not let him go. But then the movie started and she focused her attention on the screen and consuming the rest of her food before it got cold.

A few minutes in, Dean leaned over and spoke next to her ear.

"Olivia is watching us, so I'm going to put my arm around your shoulders, okay?"

Chills ran down her extremities. Had Dean's voice always been that deep? She managed to remember he'd asked her a question, so she nodded.

When his arm settled on her shoulders, he also slightly tugged her next to his side. She was glad night had fallen because otherwise Olivia and anyone else in the vicinity might very well see how startled Sunny was by how nice the contact felt.

She really needed to make time for actual dating when she got back home. Though if she had her dad and the twins to consider then, she'd have even less free time than before. And real dating was way more awkward and uncomfortable than pretending with Dean.

Sunny shook her head at that thought. She couldn't get caught up in her own charade.

"What's wrong?"

"What? Oh, just a mosquito." She fanned her hand in front of her face and next to her right ear as if to shoo away the nonexistent little bloodsucker.

Sunny split her attention between the movie and the people around them, about an equal number of families, friend groups and couples obviously on dates. The park was so full that it would be easy to believe half the population of the town was there. And they were all seeing Dean Wheeler with his arm wrapped around her. They weren't only deceiving her dad, but also the entire town of Jade Valley.

She was about to pull away from Dean out of guilt when he shifted and she found herself way too easily letting her head ease onto his shoulder. Dean didn't seem to mind. In fact, after a few seconds he leaned his cheek against her head and rubbed his hand gently up and down her arm.

This *felt* like a real date. Her heart fluttered in response to that thought.

She nearly shook her head to dissipate that strange thought but stopped herself in time so that she didn't have to repeat her mosquito excuse.

"You feel tense," Dean said so that only she could hear him.

"This feels weird, doesn't it?"

"You're thinking about it too much. Remember, we're just going to go with the flow and have fun with it."

"Do you not question what we're doing every day?"

"We can quit whenever you want to."

She lifted her head from his shoulder and looked him straight in the eye.

"No, we made a deal. I don't want you bearing the brunt of the fallout."

But wouldn't he have to anyway if he was the one left behind? Either he'd be blamed for running her off for good, along with her family, or he'd be pitied that she'd abandoned him.

She thought of Olivia's words earlier.

"Do you think other people view me like Olivia does? That I abandoned my family?"

"Why are you giving what she said a second thought?"

She looked down and picked at a loose thread on her shorts.

"Maybe because I've thought it about myself on more than one occasion."

"Don't."

"I almost came back right after Jason and Amanda's accident. When I went back home, I fell apart. I was so afraid that something would happen to Dad or the twins."

"But he told you to stay, didn't he?"

She looked up and saw understanding in Dean's face.

"He told you?"

Dean nodded.

"I guess I shouldn't be surprised. You're about as close to Dad as a person can be without sharing DNA."

"You know he's proud of you, right?"

"Yeah. He's said that over and over, and I know Mom made him promise to let Jason and me follow the paths we wanted to, even if that took us away from the ranch and Jade Valley. Still, I can't help feeling guilty sometimes, like despite what he says, he wished

I'd made a different choice. Stayed here like you and Maya."

"I can't say that he wouldn't have liked that, but he's never resented you finding your life elsewhere. He knows the opportunities are limited here. He's always telling me and the rest of the guys, really anyone who will listen, about your latest travels. I'm fairly certain I've seen every postcard you've sent from all over the world."

Sunny smiled. "I know postcards might seem old-fashioned, but I've always liked them."

"They're nice because people don't use them as much anymore. It shows extra effort and thought. Maybe if I make the ranch a big tourist destination someday, I can have Riverside Ranch postcards."

Sunny smiled. "I'll buy the whole set and frame them."

"Pretty sure I'd just send you a set."

"Maybe you can hand deliver them." She liked the idea of taking Dean around and showing him all the places in the Los Angeles area he might actually like—the Griffith Observatory, the Angeles National Forest, Solstice Canyon and of course the beach.

He met her eyes and smiled.

"Maybe I will."

Someone nearby shushed them, so Dean pulled her back against his side as if it was the most natural thing in the world.

"I feel like a naughty teenager getting shushed at the movies," he said quietly so no one else would hear.

She swatted his jean-clad leg.

"Watch the movie."

She needed to do the same and not think about being naughty teenagers at a movie together. This was her friend Dean, the guy she'd known her entire life, and not a real date no matter how much they were trying to convince everyone around them otherwise.

They must be doing a good job of it judging by the smiles sent their way at the end of the night as they walked toward Dean's truck hand in hand. It was almost enough to convince her.

"So, how was your first official date?" Maya asked when they arrived at her house to pick up the twins.

"We got shushed for talking too much during the movie," Dean said as he lifted a sleepy Liam in his arms as if the kid's twenty-three solid pounds were no heavier than a taco.

"For talking? You should have at least been scolded for smooching."

"Maya!" Sunny said it so loud that both twins startled. She'd deserve it if it now took her half the night to get them back to sleep.

"What? You want people around here, people who have nothing better to do than gossip about you two, to believe you're a real couple, then you're going to have to do some public smooching at some point."

Sunny couldn't look at Dean, and her face felt as red as a chili pepper.

Tacos, chili peppers. She must be craving Mexican food.

"She might be right," Dean said.

Sunny jerked her attention to him, her mouth falling open. But when she saw the huge, teasing smile on his face, she swatted him on the arm.

"I think I'm done with the both of you for tonight."

"Not if you want to go home, you're not." Dean sidestepped another smack, chuckling.

Sunny rolled her eyes but was grateful the strange feeling she'd had with him earlier was now gone. It had simply been a combination of him listening then telling her what she needed to hear, the realization that she'd not been held or shown affection by a man in a long time and sinking perhaps a little too far into the role she was playing. She was grateful to him for a lot of things, nothing more.

When they reached the ranch and Dean helped her once again carry the twins to bed, he for some reason stayed while she sang them to sleep.

"You're good with them," he said, looking at her across the top of the crib in the room lit only by a small table lamp shaped like a carousel. It had been Sunny's gift to Amanda at her baby shower.

"It's easy," she said. "Sometimes it startles me how much I love them."

"Do you want some of your own someday?"

"I honestly don't know. Sometimes I think yes, but then I start worrying about if something happens to me and I leave them alone." She looked at the twins and resisted the urge to rub her hand gently over them. "And I think maybe raising these two will be more than enough, like what I'm supposed to do instead of having my own."

"You could do both."

She looked at him and huffed out a quick laugh.

"I do have to work and sleep at some point, you know?"

"You'd have someone to share the work-load."

If she didn't know better, she'd swear he was volunteering to be that person. But in reality he was speaking of some hypothetical husband who'd be the father of the hypothetical children.

"Speaking of workloads, I need to address some of mine before I go to bed." She eased toward the door of the nursery and Dean followed.

"So, I heard you two were cozy at the movie," her dad said when she and Dean entered the living room.

"I don't know how Maya manages to keep the paper afloat when news travels so fast between issues."

Her dad looked at her then Dean.

"When the two of you going to get hitched?"

Sunny's mouth fell open.

"Did you fall again while we were gone and break your brain this time? What kind of question was that?"

"Don't act so surprised. You two obviously like each other, and dating is about getting to know each other but you have known each other your entire lives. Plus, you're not getting any younger."

"Yes, please, I'm on the verge of collecting Social Security." She looked at Dean. "I'm sorry—my dad seems to have temporarily misplaced his sanity."

Dean shrugged. "He's not wrong."

Had everyone in the world been affected by some sort of weird mind-altering event to which she was immune? She was literally without words to respond.

But this was what she'd wanted, right? She'd never imagined that it would be so easy though, so easy it was suspicious. She shifted her full attention to her dad.

"Are you saying that you wouldn't mind if we went and got married tomorrow?"

"Why would I? Dean's the only person I wouldn't have to worry about if you were getting married. I know this boy as well as I know you."

So his outburst about Dean not getting his hands on the ranch unless he married her hadn't been anything against Dean but rather the strength of her dad's resistance to the idea of selling the ranch.

"So you wouldn't mind if I stole your ranch foreman and took him home with me?"

Her dad laughed. "Dean would fit in where you live about as much as I would."

"But that's where my job is."

"You can do it from here. Isn't that what you've been doing sitting at the kitchen table with your computer? And if you need to fly off somewhere, Wyoming has airports."

Had Dean been right when he'd said her dad would love to have her living back here in Jade Valley but didn't want to steer her from her chosen path? Did he see her "romance" with Dean as a way to get what he wanted without having to say so? Who was playing who now?

"If she said yes, I'd marry her tomorrow," Dean said, almost causing her to suffer from whiplash. The ride her life was on sped up to where she was getting dizzy.

"You have my permission," her dad said.

"What!"

They'd both gone crazy. And then Dean had the nerve to smile and wink at her when she met his gaze. She huffed and deliberately refocused on her dad.

"I think the person who needs to give permission is me, don't you?"

"Well, I just assumed you'd say yes, and I was getting the formalities out of the way since I figured Dean's the kind of man who'd ask the father for his daughter's hand in marriage."

This had to be a dream. She was going to wake up any minute and breathe a sigh of relief that it was her subconscious mind—and maybe a guilty conscience—messing with her while she tried to rest.

But nope. A couple of minutes later when she accompanied Dean outside, she realized she was very much awake.

"What was that all about?" she asked as she pulled Dean to a stop halfway to his truck.

"It's what you wanted, right? And you've been worried about how to make it happen quickly but believably, and your dad just made it easier for you."

"Too easy." She kicked a piece of gravel so hard it bounced off Dean's back tire. "He's obviously doing this to get me to move back here. This was the most bananas idea I've had in my entire life."

"Quite possibly."

She pointed at Dean. "You are not helping."

"Actually, I am."

Okay, he had a point there.

"Why don't we go for it?" he asked.

"What?"

"Getting married," he said slowly. "The quicker we do that, the quicker we can get to the other steps."

"You don't sound super thrilled by any of that."

"Well, it's not exactly how I imagined getting married one day."

Sunny looked up at him, stared at his handsome face for a few seconds, his medium brown hair looking darker in the dim light coming from the house.

"I'm sorry," she said.

"You don't have anything to be sorry for. You never have to apologize to me."

Why did his words sound so heavy with meaning?

"You are a great person, Dean. I truly mean that."

She couldn't imagine any other person on the planet going along with her crazy plan, no matter what they got out of it in the end. She hoped none of this ended up hurting his chances of having the happy future he deserved. If it did, she'd never forgive herself—even if their ruse being successful got her everything she wanted.

CHAPTER NINE

DEAN CHECKED OUT a display of rings at Riverside Gifts and Treats, the combination gift store, ice-cream parlor and candy store that attempted to pull in tourists but more often than not was filled with locals indulging in some sweet, sweet calories. There wasn't a proper jewelry store in Jade Valley, and Dean didn't have time to drive to Jackson or any other town that had stores selling actual engagement and wedding rings. It seemed silly to go to the time and expense when his and Sunny's "marriage" wasn't going to be lasting long anyway.

He turned a spinning display filled with an array of copper rings engraved with various designs. One designed with flowers all along the band caught his eye and he pulled it from the display to examine it more closely.

"Hey, Dean."

Maya's chipper greeting startled him so much he dropped the ring and barely caught it before it rolled off the other side of the polished wood counter.

"Why so nervous?"

Dean stared at the teasing look on her face. Maya took a sip of her milkshake then eyed the ring in his hand. She reached out and took it from him, examined the design.

"I think she'll like this. So, when are you popping the question?"

He looked beyond her, hoping no one had heard.

Maya leaned forward. "Don't be so secretive. You want everyone to know, right?"

"Why would I want everyone to know?" he asked, his voice quiet but tense. "We're just going to do this quietly so it's no big deal when it's over."

Maya shook her head.

"Seriously, you have to at least make it look like it's real."

"Why? It's nobody's business but ours. Only Jonathon has to think it's real."

Said the guy who had proclaimed they were dating in public, who had acted very much a real boyfriend at the movie in the park.

"So what happens if one of his friends or, I don't know, everyone in town tells him something is fishy? Then you two would have done all this for nothing and Sunny ends up on the outs with her dad."

He hated the idea of making a big show of a wedding and marriage that weren't real, but more so he hated the idea of Sunny and Jonathon's relationship suffering a break.

"I mean, if you're going to pretend to have a relationship, the least you can do is pretend to be romantic."

"Fine," he said, motioning for her to keep her voice down.

But Maya responded with a grin of victory and quiet little hand claps despite the large foam cup in her hand.

"Awesome! I've always wanted to plan a wedding."

Before he could stop her steamrolling, Maya spun and headed toward the exit. No doubt Sunny was about to get an unexpected visit from her bestie. Thinking he'd better warn her, he pulled out his phone and started typing a text.

I think I perhaps just stepped in it.

While waiting for her to respond, he quickly paid for the ring, slipped it into his pocket and made his way out of the store.

I'd think all these years of walking around in cow pastures would have taught you how to avoid that.

Ha Ha Ha. For that I shouldn't tell you what's likely coming your way.

Why do I now think this has nothing to do with cow patties?

Because it has to do with your best friend being very excited about being your wedding planner.

What!

Before he could respond, his phone rang. No surprise, it was Sunny.

"I think you had best start explaining. No matter where Maya is right now, it won't take her long to find me."

So he told her about his brief but frustrating encounter with Maya.

"Don't worry. I'll rein her in."

He actually laughed. "Because that's a thing that happens."

Sunny sighed. "You're right. She's a bit like a bulldozer when she wants to be."

"I thought steamroller, but bulldozer works too." Dean slipped into his truck but didn't start the engine.

"Do you think she might be right? Should we have a little ceremony at least?"

"Probably." He tried to convince himself he'd said so because it made sense in selling the story, but there was a part of him that wanted to see Sunny walking down the aisle toward him even if it was pretend.

"I'm sorry this whole thing is snowballing."

"What did I tell you about apologizing to me?"

"Still, you didn't bargain for all this."

"Well, we're both navigating new fake marriage waters, don't you think?"

She laughed the smallest bit. "Yeah, I guess so."

When they ended the call, he continued to sit in his parking spot wondering if he was the biggest sap to ever breathe air in the state of Wyoming. He had to make sure no one else ever found out that his and Sunny's romantic relationship wasn't real, for her sake and his own. If he planned to stay in Jade Valley, he didn't relish the idea of all his neighbors thinking him a fool at best or, worse, a betrayer of the man who had always treated him like one of the family.

It took him a moment to realize someone was standing in front of his truck waving at him and another for it to register that it was his mom.

"You seemed to be in outer space," she said as she walked around to his open window. "Thinking about Sunny?"

Her tone and the accusatory look on her face made him realize that in the midst of everything going on, he'd failed to tell his parents that he and Sunny were dating. He imagined the ring in his pocket burning through the denim at the lies that were piling up.

But right now his mom didn't know he'd lied to her, only that she had heard about her son having a girlfriend through the town's gossip network instead of from him.

"Who'd you hear it from?"

"Who'd I not hear it from? But I should have heard it from my dear son." She smiled sweetly but he wasn't fooled.

"Sorry." He didn't say anything more, not wanting to add to the layers of lies and omissions.

"Well, you can make it up to me by bringing her over for dinner tonight."

"That's not a lot of notice."

"Well, you should have thought of that before the entire town knew before your mother. I've always thought you two were perfect for each other, so this makes me really happy."

If their dating made her this happy, how was she going to react when he told her they were getting married? No doubt she'd have a million mom questions about why they were moving so fast. Maybe he and Sunny should do a practice run answering all the questions people might aim at them when the wedding news hit.

"I'll ask Sunny if she's available tonight and let you know."

"Call her now. I'm headed to the store and I need to know if I should pick up some extra things."

A lifetime of experience let Dean know there was no use arguing, so he texted Sunny.

"Why don't you call?"

"Because most people text now, Mom. Plus, I don't want to chance waking the twins if they're asleep and she's near them with her phone."

"Oh, good point. I knew I raised a smart son."

He rolled his eyes as he glanced at his phone when it buzzed.

Sounds great. I haven't seen your parents in a long time.

"Looks like we'll see you for dinner," he said, holding up his phone and wiggling it.

His mom smiled like a megajackpot lottery winner. He hated what his and Sunny's eventual breakup would do to her. He'd just have to help her understand that it wasn't a big deal, that they simply realized they were better as friends.

When he escorted Sunny into his parents' house that night, however, he discovered things were not going to be as simple and clean as he hoped. Not only had his mom cooked a spread worthy of Christmas, but she'd also pulled out the china that her mother had given her for her wedding. He was pretty sure he'd only seen those dishes grace the table maybe twice in his entire life.

And his mom had greeted Sunny as soon as she came in with a kiss on the cheek, as if she was already her daughter-in-law, the one who would produce the long-awaited grand-children.

A jolt went through Dean at that thought, of what would have to happen between him and Sunny for grandchildren to make an appearance. The thing that would not happen between them despite the vows they were going to speak because the marriage wasn't real. Because Sunny wanted her life, a life without him in it, to be somewhere else. Not to mention she didn't feel the same about him as he did about her. Soon he was going to have to have a sit-down talk with himself about how he needed to start erasing those feelings if he didn't plan to truly act on them. Harboring them all these years without ever telling her wasn't healthy for him. He needed to move on.

"I'm so happy to see you two together," his mom said as she led Sunny to a seat at the table. She held on to Sunny's hand as if she was afraid she might run away if she let go.

"I think Sunny's going to need both hands to eat, Mom."

"Oh, of course." She released Sunny but took a moment to pat her gently on the shoulder before turning to put the final couple of dishes on the table.

As Dean took his usual seat at the table, he eyed all the food. There wasn't much space between all the bowls and platters.

"You look like you're feeding the lunch rush at Trudy's, Mom."

His dad chuckled. "I told her she was overdoing it. As much as we love Sunny, I don't think she expects the Queen of England treatment."

Dean's mom scolded his dad by giving him a gentle smack on the shoulder.

"Hush. It's not every day your son brings home someone he's dating." She leveled her gaze at Dean. "But then that's hard when he doesn't date."

"Mom, you make me sound pitiful."

Sunny reached over and took his hand, surprising him. Despite their agreement, he couldn't get used to the moments of feigned affection. Especially when she wore the kind of smile that lit up her face like bright sunshine.

"You didn't have to go to all this trouble," Sunny said, "but it looks scrumptious."

His mom beamed at the compliment.

"So, how long have you two been secretly dating?" his mom asked as she finally took her own seat.

This was what Dean had expected, why he and Sunny had spent the afternoon getting their proverbial ducks in a row.

"We've been talking for a while now, especially after Dad took his tumble," Sunny said. "But even before that."

That much wasn't a lie. Sunny had already thanked him several times for helping out Jonathon until she'd been able to make arrangements for her visit. And they did occasionally communicate with each other before that, though not at the level that would naturally lead to a romantic relationship. But his parents didn't have to know that.

"You two have known each other forever and never dated," his dad said. "Why now?"

Dean had expected a litany of questions from his mom. That his dad had tossed in one, a pointed one at that, surprised him.

Sunny shrugged. "Maybe we knew each other too well before. With the years since graduation mostly apart, I don't know, I just saw him differently."

Dean's heart beat faster at the way she was looking at him as if he was her dream come true.

No, hadn't he told himself he needed to put an end to that type of thinking? To stop being so blasted pitiful if he wasn't planning to tell her the truth.

"When did you know?" his mom asked him.

"Before she did," he said simply. "So, about all this food, how about we eat some of it before my stomach consumes itself."

His dad laughed even if his mom looked like she'd prefer to continue playing romance detective.

Thankfully the conversation veered to more comfortable topics as they ate. He had to bite down on his own laughter when he noticed that Sunny was making a sizable dent in the spread all on her own. But then she'd never been one of those types of girls to pretend she wasn't hungry when she was. And yet her figure was even more attractive than it had been in high school.

As dinner progressed, he relaxed more with each minute. Even when Sunny held his hand beneath the table, no doubt another part of her plan to look like a young couple in love, he found it more pleasant than troubling.

Maybe he'd been making a bigger deal out of the situation than necessary. This time together could end up being a good thing, a way to say goodbye to his romantic feelings for

Sunny once and for all. That sounded like a healthy plan, for both of their sakes.

After dinner, they sat on the front porch talking for a long time. Sunny seemed as genuinely interested in his parents' trips to Nebraska and up into Yellowstone and the Tetons as they were in her travels to places like Peru, Indonesia and Italy. Even though they weren't Catholic, his mom was completely rapt as she listened to Sunny talk about her visit to the Vatican.

He had to admit her travels sounded fascinating, and the way she talked about all the places she'd visited made him understand more why she didn't want to give up her job. Not to mention she was obviously good at it if her company kept her traveling as much as she did. It made him feel somewhat better about his part in the ruse to help her bring her family together in one place. Not that he wasn't without some guilt, but there was no malice in what they were doing.

When they finally took their leave, later than he'd intended, and both loaded up with enough leftovers to feed a football team, he was wiped out but felt as if they'd cleared a major hurdle. As he'd watched his parents, he'd seen no signs that they could detect anything was off about his and Sunny's relationship.

He opened the passenger door of his truck for Sunny, then held her hand as she climbed in. Even after so little time pretending to be a couple, the action felt strangely natural. She accepted the plates of leftovers covered in aluminum foil that he carried and placed them next to her. Instead of stepping back and closing the door, he stood there staring at her until she turned to face him.

"Thanks for tonight," he said.

"No need to thank me. I love your parents—you know that."

He did, and the fact that after her mother's death his own mom had showered Sunny with as much maternal love as she could. He suspected Sunny had gone to his mom to talk about things where her dad would have been a poor substitute for her mother.

"Still, who would have thought my parents would be the Spanish Inquisition instead of your dad?"

"Oh, look at you with the historical reference."

"I wasn't a complete idiot in school." He started to step back then, but Sunny suddenly reached out and grabbed his arm.

"I know you weren't. I'm sorry for teasing you like that."

He placed his hand over hers and smiled. "It's okay."

"No, it's not. I hope you didn't feel like my telling all those stories earlier was… I don't know, making it seem like your life is less in any way."

Dean squeezed her hand. "You're worrying too much."

"You're just being the best about everything and I feel like I'm taking and not giving."

"You do remember what I get out of this if all goes to plan, right?"

"Yeah, but it still feels like a one-sided relationship."

How right she was and didn't even know it.

He assured her again that he was fine, then closed her door before walking around to the driver's side. After being chatty all night, she was unusually quiet on the ride out of town and toward the ranch. Knowing that she was probably letting her worries run wild in her mind, he deliberately pulled off the road halfway back and cut the engine.

"Is something wrong?" she asked.

"Get out." Before she could question him,

he slipped out and walked around to the back of the truck. By the time she exited the truck, he was sitting on the lowered tailgate looking up at the sky.

"You stopped to stargaze? I'm pretty sure the same sky is sitting over your house."

"True, but as soon as we get back you'll be racing off to check on whether one of the twins or your dad has managed to injure themself in the few hours you've been gone."

"Well, I feel like I've been called out," she said, hopping up onto the tailgate beside him.

"It's okay to care, to even be concerned to some extent, but it's also okay to loosen your grip a bit too."

Sunny let out a sigh then lay back to face the sky.

"I know that in theory, but every time it feels as if I've relaxed into life I lose someone. I mean, I enjoy my life but I'm also aware that it can be gone in a moment, without notice."

"That's true of everyone."

"I know. Honestly, most of the time I'm fine. I learned that life goes on after tragedy, more than once. But there's also this part of me that is kind of holding its breath and tries to convince me that if I start breathing again something bad will happen. It's how I've heard some people who are afraid of flying feel, that if they relax while flying it'll tempt fate too much and the plane will crash."

"I wish you hadn't had to deal with so much loss."

"Me too."

The sadness in her voice prompted him to lie back beside her.

"Hopefully after all this craziness is over, you'll be able to relax with your family all together."

"Yeah." She was quiet for a moment, then turned her head to face him. "I hope your plans work out too. I hate thinking about you out on the ranch all by yourself."

He smiled. "Are you worried about me?"

"Sure. Can I not worry about a friend?"

A friend. That's all he'd ever be. Never would he be in the position he was now and be able to reach over, pull her toward him and kiss her the way he ached to do. But if he tried that right now, it would be awkward at best. At worst, it would send her running and end their time together.

Instead, he returned his attention to the sky in time to see a satellite moving across the star-studded background.

"I wonder if that's the space station," Sunny said, evidently having spotted the same object.

"Possibly. Or one of the thousands of satellites floating around up there."

They drifted into comfortable silence watching the beauty of the night sky. There was nothing quite like a clear, moonless night for really seeing everything the heavens had to offer.

"This is one thing I miss living in LA," Sunny said. "Even if I drive out of the city, the sky just isn't the same there."

He suspected she meant due to pollution, of the air and light varieties.

"One of the benefits of only six people per square mile," he said.

"More cows than people."

"And cows aren't driving cars."

"Though if you did have a car-driving cow, that would certainly bring people to the ranch," Sunny said with a little laugh.

"Even I don't want to diversify that much."

This was nice, hanging out joking, pointing out constellations, sharing memories. He would miss this when she left, whether it was with Jonathon and the twins in tow or on her own.

"When do you have to go back to your office?"

"I put in a request today that when my vacation time ends I be able to work remotely for a while. Even with the accelerated rate we're doing things, it simply can't all happen within the space of my vacation time."

"Speaking of accelerating the process, I guess I should faux-propose." He dug in his pocket, trying not to think about why he was still carrying around the ring he bought even though he'd been home and changed clothes since buying it.

"If you get down on one knee on the side of the road, I won't promise I won't laugh."

"Shall we test that out?" The best way through this was to make it as absurdly funny as possible. So he sat up, scooted off the end of the tailgate and dropped to one knee in the dust on the side of the road, holding up the copper ring. "Sunny Breckinridge, will you be my fake wife?"

Getting into the goofy mood, she brought her hands to her mouth and gasped in mock surprise.

"Yes, I will fake-marry you."

He laughed as he got to his feet, determined to ignore the part of him that felt like doing the opposite. He slipped the ring on her finger.

"I can't tell what it looks like." She pulled out her phone and used the flashlight feature to look at the ring she now wore. "Oh, it's pretty."

"I'm glad you like it. I didn't figure going the whole diamond-engagement-ring route was called for despite us trying to make everyone believe this is the real deal."

"Actually, this is more realistic. I'm not really a diamond-wearing kind of gal." She held up her hand and looked at the ring again. "I actually love this. Can I keep it in the divorce?"

He swallowed past the sudden, potato-sized lump in his throat.

"Sure. I don't think I'd have much use for it."

He certainly didn't want it lying around as a reminder when he would need to focus on moving on with his life once Sunny was gone.

CHAPTER TEN

SUNNY FINALLY GAVE up trying to talk sense into Maya. Even though her best friend was in on the truth of her upcoming marriage to Dean, for some reason Maya had insisted on Sunny having a "proper wedding." And thus why Sunny was not only now the owner of a white eyelet dress and would be wearing a crown of daisies on the big day, but half the town had been invited to the outdoor ceremony.

Resigned to letting Maya have her way, Sunny sat on the porch alternating between watching the twins stack blocks then knock them over to uproarious laughter and Maya directing where all the white folding chairs should be placed. Sunny shook her head. She still couldn't believe that her dad had agreed to pay for not only all the hasty wedding preparations but also a big reception with a live band afterward. He hadn't put up any fuss at all, which made her wonder if he'd broken his former personality along with his leg.

Sunny looked down when Lily crawled into her lap and held up a red plastic block, a drooling grin on her sweet little face. She wiped Lily's face then tickled her tummy.

"I think you, your brother and I are the only sane people left around here."

"I heard that," Maya said as she approached.

"It's the truth." Sunny motioned toward where the crew was now assembling a white metal arch where she and Dean would exchange vows the next day. "This is excessive."

"What? It's totally appropriate for a wedding."

Sunny clenched her jaws for a moment before responding.

"Maybe if it was a real wedding," she said.

Thankfully Dean had taken her dad into town for a checkup on how his leg was healing, and the twins were too young to understand what she was saying.

"It is a real wedding. Sure, unconventional and with you both already agreed it'll end at some point, but you bring a minister and a marriage license into the picture and it's real."

"Imagine, a journalist fixating on seman-
tics."

Maya had the temerity to offer a wide,
proud-of-herself smile.

"This will just make everything more difficult to end when the time comes."

"Or maybe it doesn't have to end at all."

Sunny stared at Maya, wondering what had
possessed the woman who usually displayed
good sense.

"What are you even talking about?"

"Listen, it's not that crazy if you think
about it. You and Dean are already good
friends, your dad and the twins like him, he's
good-looking."

All of which was true, but it didn't mean
she and Dean were destined to be a real couple.

"You're forgetting why I'm doing this in
the first place."

"To have your family together and so Dean
can own the ranch. Pretty sure that would be
easier if you stay married and live here."

"Except that my job is in California."

"You said yourself that you've been working remotely lately."

"In a limited way. I can't attend in-person
strategy sessions—"

"Teleconferencing is a thing now."

"And I travel all the time."

"Wyoming has airports."

Sunny sighed. "Why are you pushing this?"

"I like having you here, and I really do think you and Dean make a cute couple."

"Fake couple. He has said nothing to indicate he thinks of me in any way other than friendship."

"Maybe not with words."

"What?"

"Nothing. Just don't be so quick to overlook a good thing when it's right under your nose."

"I feel like I don't know you anymore."

"But I know you better than you know yourself."

Sunny had no idea how to respond, and it ended up not mattering since Dean drove up then with her dad. Since it was nap time for the twins anyway, the next few minutes were spent getting them freshly diapered and settled in bed while Dean made sure her dad made it into the house in one piece. Maya had gone back to her wedding coordinator duties, no doubt with crazy matchmaker thoughts in her head.

By the time Sunny exited the nursery,

her dad was alone in the living room rifling through the most recent mail delivery.

"Amazingly it's all mine today," he said.

She glanced toward the window but saw that Dean's truck was already gone.

"I told him to scoot," her dad said. "He shouldn't see you again until the wedding."

Sunny barely resisted rolling her eyes. But she couldn't hold back her curiosity anymore.

"You seem remarkably okay with this wedding."

"Why shouldn't I be? Dean isn't forcing you to get married, is he?"

"Well, no."

"Then what's not to like? I can't think of a man I'd rather see my only daughter marry."

She should put a stop to this before there was no turning back.

"This is the happiest I've been in a long time."

And with that one sentence, her father sealed her lips. She also realized that she may have walked herself into a situation that she couldn't walk out of as easily as she'd imagined.

DEAN HAD BARELY stepped inside his house when his phone rang. When he saw it was

Sunny, he knew showering off his afternoon of dirty work on the irrigation system would have to wait.

"Hey, you're not getting cold feet, are you?" he teased when he connected the call.

"I called to give you one more chance to back out of this."

He heard tension and worry in her voice. Something had happened.

"What's wrong?"

"Doesn't it feel like this all has gotten way bigger and more out of control than we planned?"

"I don't think there's a normal blueprint for this."

"Still, I thought we'd just go see the judge or have a simple family-only ceremony. Now it feels like no one is going to be in town tomorrow because they'll all be here."

He didn't respond because her silence felt more like a pause than simply an end to what she had to say. His gut was telling him something else had prompted her concern.

"And Dad had to go and say this is the happiest he's been in a long time, and now I feel like the worst daughter on the planet."

He sank onto one of the wooden chairs that had been in his kitchen his entire life.

"What do you want to do?"

"I don't know. One minute I think I should confess everything and the next I can't bear to break Dad's heart like this. But I doubt it will be any easier later." She sighed and he imagined her rubbing her hand back through her hair like she did when she was frustrated. "Breaking up later might be easier, at least from the standpoint of not embarrassing in addition to upsetting him. And he might not forgive me if I admit everything now when the whole darn town has been invited for a wedding tomorrow."

"Hey," he said, interrupting before her worry train kept on rolling, gaining speed. "It's going to be okay. We'll make this work."

"Huh?" She sounded startled by his response for some reason.

"Maybe we'll have to stay married longer than you'd planned, but you can work remotely some, fly back to California or wherever when you need to. I'll make sure that your dad and the twins are checked on frequently when you're not here."

"You'd be willing to do that?"

"Why not? It's not like we ever settled on a time frame anyway."

"That's true. Still, dragging it out—"

"Sunny, stop worrying. Instead, try to enjoy tomorrow. You'll get to see lots of people you know, eat some good food, have a party. And you'll witness the appearance of a rare species—me in a suit."

She laughed. "Well, since you put it that way, how can I resist?"

Glad that he'd apparently helped her past her attack of conscience mixed with a generous dose of freak-out, he made his way to the shower after she said good-night. As he stood under the hot water, however, it was his turn to have his thoughts attack him.

When this whole charade was over, how were his neighbors going to look at him? If Jonathon didn't agree to leave and still held title to the ranch, Dean wasn't sure any of those people would even be his neighbors anymore. Because Jonathon would probably fire him for breaking his baby girl's heart even if Sunny told her father the breakup was her fault.

The truth was Dean would take the heat so that Sunny could have her family together and be happy. If that made him pitiful, so be it. He preferred to think that he was the kind of person who cared about others' happiness. He knew mental health experts would tell him that his happiness mattered as well, and he didn't disagree. But if his happiness came at the cost of someone else's, someone he cared about, then he wasn't willing to pay that price.

After he ate some leftovers, he attempted to watch TV but couldn't find anything remotely interesting. Considering he had a busy day beginning in a few hours, he gave up and went to bed. As he stretched out, it really hit him that tonight was the last night he'd be spending in this house alone—at least until Sunny got what she wanted and left for California. But she would not be sharing his bed.

Instead, she'd be in the master bedroom his parents had once used and which he'd taken over when they moved to town. The larger room made sense for her to use since she'd be putting a crib for the twins in there too. Though there was no firm plan regarding Lily and Liam, they were likely to be doing some back and forth between the two houses on the ranch. He didn't mind sharing his space with the kids because they were cute and sweet, even if they weren't self-sufficient. They'd also be a buffer between him and Sunny when they were together in this small space. She wouldn't need it but he was afraid he might be a different story, that tempta-

202 THE RANCHER'S UNEXPECTED TWINS

tion might overrule his common sense and
his platonic agreement with Sunny. Not that
they'd even discussed that there would be no
physical relationship between them. Rather,
it was simply understood.

Even so, he didn't think it was possible to
prevent his mind from wandering in that direction. But he couldn't act on his imagin-
ings. He'd have to hope that no one noticed
that his and Sunny's public displays of affection never went further than holding hands.

"WILL YOU STOP FIDGETING?" Maya swatted at
Sunny's hand that had been reaching up to
readjust the crown of daisies atop her head.
"I feel like you're going to grab one of those
daisies and start picking off petals while saying, *He loves me, he loves me not.*"

"Don't be ridiculous, and stop making this
marriage something it's not." Sunny kept her
voice quiet so no one outside her bedroom
would be able to hear and spread gossip to
the rather large assemblage of people outside.

"You haven't seen Dean yet. I predict you'll
fall in love before you get halfway down the
aisle."

"As soon as this wedding is over, I'm disowning you and advertising for a new best friend."

Maya laughed, knowing very well that Sunny would do no such thing.

Sunny took one more look at herself in the full-length mirror, wondering if the last time she'd used it this much was before her senior prom. She had to admit that the dress Maya had helped her pick out was pretty. It was a shame it wasn't being used for a real wedding. She felt as if she was doing the dress a disservice.

"Okay, time to get this party underway," Maya said, then gave Sunny a toodle-oo wave before exiting the room to attend to her wedding coordinator tasks.

Since her dad was on crutches, they'd decided to forego him walking her down the aisle. He hadn't been one bit happy about it, but she'd convinced him it was the thought that counted and she'd rather not have to worry about him taking a tumble on uneven ground on her wedding day. He'd relented but only with the promise that he still got a father-of-the-bride dance with her at the reception even if all he could do was sway in place.

She'd agreed and kissed him on the cheek, hoping that he'd forgive her one day if he ever found out about all the lies he was taking part in during this wedding. Forgive her for making Dean a son-in-law he liked and then taking him away.

No, she couldn't think about the end of things today, not when she was supposed to appear happy about beginnings. Fortifying herself with a deep breath, she grabbed the bouquet of daisies and followed in Maya's wake.

When she reached the front door, Maya motioned for her to pause then signaled the cello player who'd driven all the way from Casper to play Wagner's "Bridal Chorus." As the first notes of the song filled the air, Sunny's stomach tightened. She was really doing this.

"Breathe," Maya said, drawing Sunny's gaze to hers. "You look beautiful, Dean looks incredibly handsome, the weather is perfect. Seems like the stars are aligned perfectly."

That would all be great if this was a real wedding, but she pushed that thought as far away as she could. As everyone kept telling her, she should stop fretting and enjoy the day. After all, it wasn't as if she was being forced to marry an ogre.

Far from it. As she reached the back row

of seated guests, she looked toward the now flower-covered arch and almost gasped. Maya hadn't been lying. Dean looked…gorgeous. How could someone she'd known her entire life, someone with whom she'd spent time every day since she'd been back on the ranch, suddenly look so different?

She barely kept herself from shaking her head to dislodge the thought she shouldn't be having as she was minutes away from making legal a fake marriage. Suddenly finding her new husband attractive would make this situation even more awkward than it was already.

She told herself she was simply getting caught up in the wedding hoopla, letting Maya's teasing take root where it shouldn't. Still, she found herself smiling as she approached Dean, and when he smiled back her heart gave an extra hard thud against her ribs.

A fleeting desire to turn and run before she cemented the biggest mistake of her life evaporated when Dean reached out and took her hand in his. She was thankful to be able to turn to face Reverend Reynolds before Dean saw how shaky her smile was becoming.

As the minister said the appropriate words and she and Dean exchanged vows, she slowly managed to get her racing heartbeat under control. Once this ceremony and the reception were over, she'd be able to relax. She and Dean could kick back and laugh about how they'd gotten more than they bargained for with their wedding.

"By the power vested in me by God and the state of Wyoming, I now pronounce you husband and wife." Reverend Reynolds gave Dean a knowing grin before saying, "You may now kiss the bride."

She'd prepared herself for this, knowing that all their efforts would likely be for naught if they skipped at least a chaste kiss to seal the deal. She could manage a peck. Those in attendance would easily believe Dean was too shy or easily embarrassed to really lay one on her, though her skin suddenly heated at that thought.

Sunny smiled as she turned to face him, and for a moment she thought she saw something powerful and real in Dean's gaze. But then he smiled and she realized she must have imagined it. As he lifted his hand and slid it softly along her cheek to cup the back of her head, however, her heart started speeding up again. Then he was lowering his mouth toward hers and she fought an unexpected panic.

At first when his warm lips touched hers, it was the light touch for which she'd prepared herself. Thank goodness. As soon as that thought formed in her mind, however, the kiss turned surprisingly real. The thought that she should ease away appeared for no more than a second before she relaxed and kissed him back.

It's an act. We're selling this to all these onlookers.

Plus Dean looks so handsome.

Why is he such a good kisser?

That thought startled her sufficiently that she uttered a small gasp. Dean's mouth lifted from hers in the moment she heard giggles from the crowd. Evidently her gasp had been more audible than she'd hoped. Even Reverend Reynolds chuckled.

As if he knew she was embarrassed, Dean eased her forehead to his chest and rested his warm, strong hand against her back for a few seconds.

"Ladies and gentlemen, I present Mr. and Mrs. Dean Wheeler."

Mrs.—

Why didn't Reverend Reynolds get the message that she wasn't changing her name? She could pass it off as being a modern, independent businesswoman, but in reality it made no sense to go through the trouble of changing her name only to have to change it back once a sufficient amount of time had passed and they divorced amicably. Whatever "sufficient amount of time" meant. Neither she nor Dean had been able to guess the answer to that. It all depended on her dad and how quickly she thought he'd move with her when she announced she and Dean were calling it quits.

When she and Dean turned to face their guests, her attention went straight toward her father. Guilt slammed into her when she saw how he was beaming with the biggest smile she'd seen on his face since the day the twins were born. And as if they were feeding off their grandfather's happiness, the twins were grinning and kicking their little feet where they sat in their double stroller.

How was she going to take them, all three of them, away from Dean?

No, this was supposed to be a happy day, she a bride in love. She glanced up at Dean, smiled again, and squeezed his hand where their fingers were entwined. As they made their way down the aisle, they were showered with rose petals. Maya really had done a great job making this fake wedding seem beautifully romantic.

By the time they had greeted most of the guests, Sunny's facial muscles ached from smiling so much. Dean placed his hand at the small of her back as if it was as natural as the sunrise and leaned over to whisper in her ear.

"Are you okay?"

She nodded and looked up at him so that she couldn't feel his breath on her ear and neck anymore. Why her hormones were suddenly losing their collective mind, she had no idea. She needed to get through all these romantic traditions of the day so she could collect her sanity from whatever corners to which it had scattered to hide.

"I feel like every time we turn away the number of guests multiplies."

"Yeah, it's a lot. But in a few hours, this will all be over and things can go back to normal."

She laughed at that. "You have a funny definition of *normal*, Dean Wheeler."

"Good point." His crooked grin didn't help settle the jittery feeling that had taken up residence all throughout her body.

But a foolproof cure for that strolled up next. Even if it was fake, Sunny hated that Olivia Redmond had shown up at her wedding. She figured Maya hadn't been able to exclude her from the guest list without doing the same for her parents, and one did not want to offend the owners of the only bank in the county. But did the woman have to show up dressed as if she owned half of Wyoming and was here to snatch away the groom for herself?

Sunny wondered if she'd telegraphed her thoughts because Dean's hand on her back slipped around her waist a moment before he pulled her close to his side.

"Congratulations," Olivia said, sounding about as genuine as a fox telling a hen he wanted to be friends. She glanced at Sunny. "Cute dress. I almost bought that but in a more flattering color."

Olivia shifted her gaze to Dean and, in all honesty, she was about to place her palm on his chest before Dean made a smooth move to stand behind Sunny, wrapping his arms around her waist. Olivia didn't look happy, but she got the message—at least for the moment anyway. When she moved to join her parents at the table they were sharing with another family, Sunny slowly looked back over her shoulder.

"Did you just hide behind me?"

"Um, yes?"

The sheepish look on his face caused her to laugh, and she relaxed more than she'd been all day. Dean moved back to her side, but he held her hand as if he was afraid Olivia would pounce if he didn't maintain some type of contact with Sunny.

"So, is it wrong to smack a guest at your wedding?" she asked. "I'm asking for a friend, and that friend is me."

"It seems bad form," he said. "But if she were to accidentally trip and fall face-first into the wedding cake, who are we to argue with karma?"

"Oh no. Her face better not get anywhere near that cake. Trudy made it and I've been dreaming about biting into it all day."

In between greeting the straggling guests, she and Dean joked with each other the way they normally did. It was almost enough to make her forget the way he'd kissed her. Almost, but not quite. She hoped she could finish forgetting before she had to sleep at his house tonight.

CHAPTER ELEVEN

SUNNY LOOKED AT Dean when he chuckled at her.

"What?"

He grabbed his napkin and reached over to wipe her mouth.

"You are attacking that barbecue like someone who hasn't eaten for a week."

She tried to ignore how intimate his action had felt even though he likely hadn't meant it that way. Rather, she was probably just wearing more barbecue sauce than one should at her wedding.

"Not all week, but this is the first thing I've eaten today if you don't count a lemon muffin Maya brought from Trudy's this morning." What seemed liked three lifetimes ago based on how empty her stomach had felt when she and Dean had finally made it to their reception table and some food.

"Well, eat until you're stuffed then."

"I think you might be the perfect husband."

It wasn't her new husband who laughed this time but rather her best friend on her other side. But when Sunny turned to see why Maya had found the statement funny, Maya had already shoved a piece of roasted potato into her mouth. Sunny gave her a narrowed-eye look, but Maya responded by grinning around her mouth full of potato.

When Sunny finished eating, she and Dean moved to cut the cake.

"I swear if you smash cake all over my face, I'm going to dunk you in the river," she told him.

His grin was full of mischief right before he said, "It'll be worth it," and shoved a slice of cake against her mouth until she probably looked like a baby on her first birthday.

"Well, two can play this game." She ripped apart the piece of cake in her hands and smashed it against both of his cheeks, quite possibly getting the sweet confection in his ears. She couldn't help bursting out laughing at his look of surprise, his eyes blinking above the frosting-covered lower half of his face.

"You're wasting a delicious cake!" Trudy called out from her spot in the crowd, eliciting more laughter from everyone, including Sunny and Dean.

Using his index finger, Dean swiped some of the cake off his face and ate it. Then he looked out at the crowd.

"You're right—it is delicious."

After they'd managed to wipe away errant cake and actually consume a slice each, it was time for the father-daughter dance.

"Try not to let him break the other leg," Dean whispered to her before she headed to the temporary dance floor.

"Don't even put that thought out into the universe."

The way Dean smiled at her, she thought he might actually drop a kiss on her cheek. Thankfully, he didn't even touch her and she fled to retrieve her dad.

Yes, fled. Every time she chalked up her weird feelings toward Dean to getting caught up in the wedding pageantry, he did or said something that made her heart skip a beat. Those reactions had to cease if she was going to make it through this fake marriage with any peace of mind.

"You ready to take a spin, old man?" she asked as she stopped in front of her dad.

"Wait till this cast comes off," he said as he stood.

Sunny laughed and bent over to give Lily and Liam loud smooches on their soft baby cheeks.

"You two go on," Trudy said. "I'll watch these little darlings."

Sunny pointed her finger at the older woman. "Don't you dare sneak them sweets."

"Who, me?" Trudy asked with overacted faux innocence.

"Yes, you."

Trudy held her hand over her heart. "I promise to refrain from giving them sweets until they at least have a full set of teeth."

"Your restraint is noted."

Once Sunny and her dad made it to the dance floor, she let her teasing fall away. Even though her dad didn't know the wedding wasn't real, this moment felt special. She reminded herself that she was doing all this so they could be together, that she didn't have to go months at a time without seeing her only parent and her precious niece and nephew. It would all be worth it in the end.

As the music began and they swayed as much as his broken leg would allow, she found herself smiling.

"I'm so glad you're happy," her dad said. "I've never seen you like this before."

Was he mistaking her guilt for happiness? Those seemed to be odd emotions to get confused for one another.

"Dean's a good guy."

"He is, and it's obvious how much he's in love with you when he looks at you."

Her heart thudded a bit harder for a moment until she told herself that if her dad was mistaking her happiness at being married, then it was likely he wasn't reading Dean correctly either. Odd since her dad was usually a good judge of people. He must be blinded by his desire to see his daughter happily married, seeing what he wanted to see.

Someday maybe she'd be able to give that experience to him for real. Though when she caught sight of Dean she felt a pang that didn't make sense, one that gave her the oddest sensation that she was missing him already when he was sitting only a few feet away. Her dad's words reverberated in her head as she realized Dean was watching her and smiled when their gazes connected. Startled, she looked away, acting as if her dad had said something to her.

Great, now she was basically lying to Dean too through her actions.

The song ended and was immediately replaced by another. Sunny's dad surprised her by giving her a kiss on the cheek.

"I hope you and Dean are as happy together as your mom and I were."

Sunny couldn't seem to move as her dad used his crutches to turn around and head back to his seat. She'd tried not to dwell on what her mom would no doubt think about her lies, but now her dad's words made it impossible to avoid imagining her mom looking down on her with disappointment.

"May I claim the next dance?"

Startled from her thoughts, Sunny looked up to see her new father-in-law standing in front of her with his arms open. She smiled and nodded, then let him spin her around to the lively tune.

"I should officially welcome you to the family," he said as he maneuvered them expertly between all the other couples who had made their way onto the dance floor.

"Thank you, Mr. Wheeler."

He chuckled. "Mr. Wheeler sounds a bit formal now, don't you think?"

"It would feel weird to call you Ken."

"Getting used to something takes practice."

"I suppose so." Though she'd often called

the ranch hands, Trudy, any number of people older than her by their first names, Dean's parents had always been Mr. and Mrs. Wheeler. It was a respect her own parents had insisted she and Jason pay to the ranch's foreman and his wife. Considering calling them Ken and Susan made Sunny wonder if she'd be scolded by her father or even her mother from the great beyond.

To be honest, that would be the least of her transgressions for which her mother would scold her.

"You've made Susan so happy," Ken said. "She's been worrying herself sick that Dean wasn't even dating, that he was lonely, that she might never get grandchildren, and here you've gotten him to the altar in record time."

It occurred to her that the fast pace of their relationship might have spawned some rumors as to why they were getting married so quickly, especially since her job was in California. Maybe everyone thought she'd quit. Or, more likely, they were assuming she and Dean "had to" get married. Time to put a stop to that rumor right here and now.

"The twins are already a lot to handle, so I think more kids are going to have to wait for a while."

A long while, like when Dean and Sunny each actually fell in love and got married for real.

She spotted Dean dancing with his mother and they both smiled at her. More guilt sliced at Sunny, and she realized how much it was going to hurt to sever relationships she'd had all her life.

Because no matter what Dean said when they got divorced, his parents would never look favorably at her again. And she couldn't blame them. From their perspective, she would be the person who hurt their son. Even though she'd never given birth, she understood the protective parental instinct. She felt it with every decision, big or small, that she made about the twins. She couldn't imagine Amanda would have been any more scared than Sunny had been the day she'd rushed Lily to the hospital, because the fear had consumed every cell in Sunny's body.

"You two do things at your own pace. Susan can cool her grandma jets awhile longer, particularly if you let her babysit Lily and Liam every now and then."

"I'm sure that can be arranged."

When the song was over, Ken patted her hand and handed her off to Dean.

"Got one more dance in you?" Dean asked.

"Sure. Not to mention it would look odd not to dance with my husband at our wedding, right?"

She probably imagined it, but she thought she saw his smile falter the tiniest bit before he took one of her hands in his and slipped his other arm around her waist, pulling her close. As he led her around the dance floor, she was tempted to sink into the warmth and strength of him. And she got the feeling he might let her.

Was Dean allowing the "magic" of the wedding-day festivities to get to him too? She remembered her dad's words again, about Dean looking at her like a man in love. Silliness, all of it! Afternoon had faded into early evening, and believing in romantic nonsense was easier at night. That's why she needed the music to end, all these people to go home and to be able to change into something that didn't say *Bride* in blinding white.

The moment the song ended, a scream caused a chill to run down her spine. But it wasn't a human scream that caused a chorus of gasps and the turning of heads but rather that of a wild animal.

She and Dean moved at the same time, but

then he stopped and held her by her shoulders. "Stay here with your dad and the babies."

Nothing else could have prevented her from riding out with him and the ranch hands already headed toward the barn, and he knew that. As he started to move away, without thinking she grabbed his hand.

"Be careful."

"I will." And then he slipped out of her grasp and ran toward the barn.

The sound of a mountain lion way too close for comfort tended to put a damper on a party, and so wedding guests started gathering their things and heading for their vehicles. Sunny's first priority was her family, and so she rushed her dad and the twins into the house, quickly changed into jeans, a T-shirt and sneakers, and hurried back outside to help with the cleanup and the carrying of the left-over food into the house so it wouldn't pose a tempting feast for any critters, big or small.

Maya rushed around alongside the caterers who'd been hired for the reception. Even Alma and Trudy seemed to have temporarily put aside their long-standing feud to help clear tables.

All the while, Sunny kept looking out into the dark pasture where her family's livelihood grazed. But her thoughts were less for the cattle than the men who'd ridden out to protect them. One man in particular.

By the time all signs of the wedding had been cleared away and everyone had left except Maya, Ken and Susan, Sunny was really beginning to worry. Maya, bless her, fed, diapered and put the twins to bed. Ken sat with Sunny's dad on the porch reminiscing about all the times over the years they'd had to battle animals, disease and everything Mother Nature could throw at them to protect the herd. Susan busied herself in the kitchen, used to years as a ranch wife. She was performing some sort of kitchen magic to make all the leftovers fit into the refrigerator. Sunny wasn't going to have to cook for days.

Unable to sit still or coop herself up in the house, she headed toward the barn. Playing with kittens should help calm her nerves.

The moment she looked into the stall, however, she saw that the normally laid-back mama kitty was on high alert and actually hissed at her before it must have registered Sunny didn't pose a threat.

"You heard your much bigger cousin too, huh?"

Even recognizing Sunny, mama kitty stayed

close to her babies, who'd grown an amazing amount in the short time Sunny had been back at the ranch. This time when she sat in the hay next to them, they immediately used her as a jungle gym.

"At least you little guys seem unconcerned." Much like the twins, completely oblivious that danger lurked nearby. It must be nice to exist in blissful ignorance of all the potential hazards and heartbreaks the world held.

She laughed when a little gray fluffball made it all the way to her shoulder.

"Aren't you quite the mountain climber?" She plucked the kitten off her shoulder and placed him in her lap so she could pet him. He lifted his head into her touch. "You like that, huh? Nothing like a good massage."

"Maybe your new husband can give you one."

Sunny startled so much that the kittens went scurrying and mama kitty tensed for battle.

"It's okay, mama. No danger other than my best friend scaring me half to death."

"Your mind must have been elsewhere." Maya's teasing grin was back.

"Or you're being sneaky on purpose. Not a

good time for that considering what sent everyone speeding off in different directions."

Maya sobered. "Sorry. Have you heard anything?"

Sunny shook her head. The night had been eerily quiet since everyone had left. No more indications the mountain lion was nearby, no rumble of cattle stampeding, no gunshots.

"I'm sure he's fine."

"Hopefully, they're all fine," Sunny said.

"Of course."

"You should go on home."

"Had more than enough of me today?"

Sunny exhaled a small laugh. "If journalism finally dies, I think you have a future as a wedding coordinator. You can call it Bulldozer Wedding Planning."

"I like it. You'd know what you were getting with a name like that."

"Maya Pine, the queen of truth in advertising."

Maya grabbed a black-and-white kitten that had meandered her way.

"Hello, you adorable little thing. I may just have to adopt you when you're old enough to leave your mama."

Sunny and Maya turned at the sound of approaching horses.

"Sounds like your man is back," Maya said.

"Would you stop with the teasing already? I mean, you know the truth."

"Yes, yes I do."

Sunny sighed and shook her head. "You can go home now."

"Nope, I'm spending the night here tonight."

"What? Why?"

"One, so you don't accidentally forget you're married and try to go sleep in your bedroom. And two, so you don't have to worry about your dad or the twins tonight."

"Maya," she scolded. "You know nothing is going to happen tonight."

"But your dad doesn't know that. He expects you to go enjoy your wedding night."

"Okay, eww, I don't want to envision my dad thinking about…that."

Thankfully, Maya didn't continue that line of conversation, though the grin on her face told Sunny she was still quite amused by her teasing.

"If nothing else just enjoy a good night's rest while not worrying about your dad falling or changing the diaper of a squalling baby in the middle of the night."

That did sound nice.

"Though I could do without the teasing and how big the wedding got, I do owe you a lot of thanks for helping out today."

"What are best friends for if not to throw you an awesome wedding?"

Sunny didn't even bother mentioning again that the showy wedding had been unnecessary, would likely end up making things more difficult in the end. For today, it had made people happy.

Sunny didn't want to feed her friend's delusions that there was something between her and Dean, but she also really needed to know that he and the others were okay and if they'd crossed paths with the mountain lion. She placed the kitten back in the hay next to the others.

"Here, baby, go to your mama."

Sunny walked out of the barn alongside Maya. When she spotted Dean still in the saddle talking to his dad and hers where they stood on the front porch, she breathed a sigh of relief. The two ranch hands who'd ridden out with him, Carlos and Billy, approached the barn with their mounts.

"How'd it go?" she asked Carlos.

He shook his head. "Didn't see the cat, but the herd seemed fine from what we could tell. Won't be able to be sure until daylight tomorrow."

"I'm glad you're all okay. That's what's most important."

"Congratulations, by the way. I was too busy wrangling my heathen children earlier to tell you that."

She laughed at the image because she'd seen him with his two boys, giving them a good talking-to.

"Easier to wrangle cows, I'd imagine."

"You got that right."

As he moved to take care of his horse, she noticed that Maya had already made her way toward the house. At that moment, Dean used his reins to turn his horse toward the barn.

"This may be a first," she said as he stopped next to her and dismounted. "I doubt too many people ride the range in suits."

He'd actually left his suit jacket behind at the table they'd been sitting at earlier and his bolo tie was nowhere to be seen. Though his white shirt, the top couple of buttons undone, and his dark suit pants were not the right kind of attire for ranch work, he looked good in them. More than good.

Maya's earlier teasing echoed in Sunny's head, and she wanted to somehow vacuum

228 THE RANCHER'S UNEXPECTED TWINS

out those thoughts and dispose of them. She wasn't supposed to think of Dean in any way other than as a really good friend who was willing to do crazy things for her.

"Wyoming's most stylish cowboy," he said as he spread his arms and struck a pose.

Sunny laughed. This was the Dean Wheeler she knew and...well, the one she knew.

"Carlos said you didn't see the mountain lion."

He shook his head. "It's getting bolder though. That was too close for comfort earlier."

She got chills thinking about all the children who'd been at the wedding, especially the twins. If one of the kids old enough to be mobile had wandered off... She didn't want to think about what could have happened.

"We're headed home," Ken called out. Both he and Susan waved, and Dean and Sunny returned the gesture.

"I better let you finish up here," Sunny said to Dean. "I'll go grab a couple of things and meet you at your house in a few minutes."

He nodded.

When she stepped inside her dad's house, however, she spotted her packed bags sitting behind the couch. Maya pointed toward them from where she had parked herself on one end of the couch.

"I packed all your stuff for you."

"Um, thanks."

Maya gave her a mischievous wink, and Sunny promised herself she'd devote time each day to brainstorming the perfect way to deliver payback to her friend.

Not wanting to give her dad any reason to question his daughter's new marriage, she grabbed her suitcase, backpack and laptop case.

"Don't worry," her dad said. "We've got baby duty covered."

Sunny made a noise that indicated she understood then headed out the door, her face on fire. Thank goodness Dean was still busy in the barn. She tossed her bags into the car she'd extended the rental on and headed to Dean's house.

It felt weird letting herself inside with him not being there, but she had to get used to this being her temporary home. She stowed her bags in the corner of the living room and took her laptop to his kitchen table. She had work to do, work she hadn't looked at in two days thanks to all things wedding.

A zing of nerves hit her when she heard

Dean's truck pull up outside, then reminded herself there was no reason for it. They were co-habitating friends, nothing more. She couldn't even believe she had to tell herself that.

When the front door opened, she looked up to see Dean standing there but not shutting the door behind him.

"I can't believe you didn't wait for me to carry you over the threshold," he said.

Sunny's mouth dropped open, which evidently made her look hilarious since Dean started laughing.

"I'm kidding." He closed the door then toed off his boots that had been a lot cleaner and shinier earlier.

"Ha ha, very funny."

He nodded at her open laptop. "I see you wasted no time getting back to life as normal."

"Yes, because pretending to be married is so normal."

"Technically, we are married."

Honestly, she didn't need to be reminded of that because this day had already messed with her brain and her nerves enough.

"Details, details." She sat back and pecked the edge of the laptop with her fingernail. "I'll be as quiet as possible so you can sleep."

He nodded and headed toward the bathroom, most likely to wash the smell of animals and dust off him. Her assumption was confirmed when she heard the shower. But despite staring at the computer, she couldn't concentrate knowing there was a naked man on the other side of the bathroom door. One she was married to. When Maya's teasing about Sunny's wedding night echoed in her mind, she closed her eyes and ran her fingers back through her hair.

She forced herself to focus on the suggestions she'd been typing up regarding a new potential client for the company. Each time her mind wandered to the crazy situation she'd put herself in, what everyone must think she and Dean would be doing tonight or the fact that her *husband* was not currently wearing clothes, she mentally smacked some sense into herself. Or tried to at least.

She'd only just gotten back on track for the umpteenth time when Dean strolled into the room wearing shorts and a T-shirt, with bare feet and carrying a quilt and a pillow, which he proceeded to place on the couch.

"Thanks," she said.

When he looked at her, she noticed his hair was still damp too. He could not possibly know how attractive he looked like that.

Of course, he wasn't used to having to share his space with anyone.

"For what?"

She pointed at the pillow and quilt.

"Those are for me. There are fresh linens on the bed though." He lifted her suitcase and backpack and headed toward his bedroom with them.

Sunny hopped up and followed him.

"Dean, I'm not ousting you from your own bed. You've done enough for me already. I'll stay in the other bedroom."

"Can't. No bed. Mom and Dad took theirs when they moved, and I moved mine in here."

He placed the bags at the foot of the bed in question then turned and walked past her back out of the room. Again she followed him, in time to see him stretch out his tall body on the couch.

"Dean, don't be ridiculous. It makes more sense for me to sleep on the couch. I'm the guest here."

"I don't know what you're talking about. I'm getting the better end of the deal. This is a comfy couch."

Sunny crossed her arms and lifted an eyebrow.

"Are you going to try to make me believe

that you sleep on your couch every night when you have a bed?"

He pulled the quilt over his bare legs and feet and rolled onto his side, tucking the pillow under his head.

"No comment."

"Dean!"

"You're not going to win this argument so you might as well save your breath."

She couldn't very well hoist him onto her shoulder and carry him into his bedroom, so she huffed and spun to retrieve her laptop.

"I feel sorry for your real wife one day, having to deal with your stubbornness."

He lifted to his elbow and propped his head in his upturned hand.

"I could say the same about you, Mrs. Wheeler," he said, teasing thick in his words.

She pointed at him. "Cut that out. I've had enough out of Maya today."

"What did she say?"

"You don't need to know."

Dean was still chuckling at her when she retreated to his bedroom and shut the door.

"Good night, wife!"

She ignored him, which resulted in more laughter from the other room. She felt like smothering him with his pillow, in a nonlethal sort of way of course. He, like Maya, was having one hoot of a time with the whole situation while she was beginning to question her sanity.

Especially when she allowed herself to think about Dean in a way that she'd never expected. When she thought about how he'd kissed her to seal their wedding vows…and how she'd kissed him back.

CHAPTER TWELVE

JOKING, THAT WAS the only way Dean was going to survive his marriage to Sunny. That and pretending he hadn't let his true feelings get the better of him when he'd kissed her at the end of the wedding ceremony. And ignoring that she'd kissed him back.

Maybe she'd thought he was going all in to convince any doubters among the guests and had decided it was a good plan and silently gone along with it. That had to be it because she'd given him no other indications that her feelings might have changed. Whatever the reason, he was pretty sure he was going to be reliving that kiss in his mind when he was rocking away his senior years.

As he lay on the couch, not even remotely close to falling sleep, he could hear her pecking away on her laptop. He wondered what she was working on, for what company in what country. He couldn't fully imagine all the places she'd seen with her own eyes.

Someday she'd probably end up with a guy as cultured and worldly as she was, someone the opposite of her current husband who didn't even have a passport.

His mind wandered, and he found himself wondering if he'd like traveling if he tried it. Where would he want to visit? He'd seen some things about Australia, particularly the Outback, but he wondered if it looked interesting because it was more similar to what he was used to than France or Japan or any number of other places Sunny had probably been. Would he actually like going outside his comfort zone if he tried it?

He shook his head on the pillow. When would he have the time? Ranching wasn't exactly something that could be put on hold for a couple of weeks while you jetted off to some faraway destination. Animals had to be fed and cared for, predators kept away, fences mended, buildings repaired, equipment maintained.

Yes, it was a lot of work, but he loved it. There was nothing like the freedom of not having to punch a clock to sit in a stuffy office all day long. As he stared at the ceiling, he tried not to think that at least now he had something to look forward to when he came home at the end of each day. Though Sunny would be sleeping at his house, most of the rest of the time she would likely be with her dad, the twins or Maya.

He needed to purge the memory of their kiss from his mind, couldn't assign it more meaning than it was due. Even knowing that, it kept replaying in his memory. As he closed his eyes, he remembered how he'd felt in those few moments—free to allow his true feelings to show.

For the first time, he hoped his marriage with Sunny ended quickly. The longer it went on, the more nights she spent under the same roof as him, the more difficult it was going to be to not let those feelings have free rein again.

SUNNY YAWNED AS she exited the bedroom early the next morning. She'd stayed up way too late working after a long day of wedding festivities. When she noticed Dean had already left, she shouldn't have been surprised. He'd always been an early riser, typically hard at work while most people were dragging themselves and their bed hair toward their first cup of coffee.

She'd thought he might stick around the

house a little later this morning for appearances, but she supposed too-real kisses were the extent of his acting.

Why am I thinking about that again? She needed to make like a famous cold-climate princess and let it go.

Her phone buzzed with a text.

No need to hurry to the house. The twins are taken care of, your dad has eaten and now I'm off to interview a man about his collection of shot glasses from around the world. Yes, this is Pulitzer-Prize-winning journalism at work. Remember, you owe me a feature by the end of tomorrow.

Well, Sunny guessed she knew how she was going to spend her day. After quickly showering and dressing, feeling weird doing both in Dean's house, she grabbed her laptop and headed to the main ranch house.

"You're here awfully early," her dad said from his spot next to the coffeepot when she walked in.

"I missed you so much I couldn't stand it." She gave him a big smooch on the cheek before reaching for a coffee mug for herself.

Her dad snorted. "I guess I shouldn't be

surprised to see you since I saw your husband ride out early."

"He's a man who loves his job and this ranch." Might as well remind her dad of that fact whenever the opportunity arose. She'd have to figure out the timing of the demise of her relationship at some point, but starting that the day after her wedding seemed like a bad idea.

After breakfast, placing the twins in their playpen on the porch and making sure her dad didn't tumble going down the front steps because he insisted on going to the barn *before I go crazy in this house*, Sunny parked herself in one of the porch chairs and opened her laptop.

She'd decided to ease local readers into the travel series by writing about a trip she'd taken by train across Australia. As she started writing, she lost herself in memories of the trip. So much so that she didn't even hear her dad's approach until she noticed him at the bottom of the porch steps.

"That work of yours must be interesting because you didn't freak out once watching me walk back from the barn."

She stuck her tongue out at him. "I don't

freak out. Pardon me for being concerned and not wanting you to break any other bones."

"Sassy."

"It's in the genes."

He huffed then climbed his way carefully up the steps. Sunny made the difficult decision to not even get up out of her seat, but she was ready to toss her laptop and fly to his aid if he showed the slightest wobble.

The fact that he didn't seem quite as tired doing so as he had when she first arrived was a good sign. Still, he seemed glad to sink into the chair next to hers and reach into the playpen so Lily could grab his tanned, calloused finger.

"How's the prettiest girl in the world?" he asked his granddaughter.

Sunny gave a dramatic sigh. "I remember when you used to ask me that. Now I've been usurped."

"Yep, you have."

Sunny fake punched her dad on the arm. He laughed, which caused Lily to giggle too.

"You've got someone else to tell you that you're pretty now," he said.

She didn't respond, thankful that at that exact moment Liam tossed his little ball out of the playpen and she had the excuse to get up to retrieve it.

"Toys stay in here with you, little man," she said, then ruffled his fine hair, which elicited some of those delightful baby giggles.

"What are you working on?" her dad asked, thankfully not noticing anything amiss with her not responding to his previous comment. "Where will you be jetting off to next?"

"I'm actually writing a travel article for Maya. She suckered me into doing a series of travel pieces."

"Not sure how many people will read those around here."

"You might be surprised."

He shrugged, and she suddenly found herself hoping that the issues her features appeared in sold in record numbers. But it was entirely possible her dad was right. Oh well, if she inspired one person to travel internationally, it would be worth the effort.

After she finished the rough draft of the article, she tackled a bit more of her work, then made sure the twins were safely inside before heading into town to pick up a few grocery items. Before going to the market, however, she stopped in to see Trudy and grab a strawberry milkshake.

But when she stepped into the kitchen, she was just in time to see Trudy slam a pan against a metal prep table.

"That woman is going to be the death of me." Trudy turned around and startled when she saw Sunny.

"Oh sorry. Didn't realize I had an audience."

"Let me guess. Alma?"

"That obvious, huh?"

"I can't imagine anyone else who would bring out that kind of reaction in you."

"Well, I don't think she'll be satisfied until she runs me out of business."

"Judging by the amount of people in the dining room, I don't think there's much chance of that."

"It looks much different at dinnertime."

"And Alma's doesn't?"

"She somehow got interviewed for a travel magazine, and they said she was the owner of the only restaurant in town."

"Do you think Alma would outright lie like that?"

"Well, she didn't correct them at least. And evidently the magazine editor's nephew is Josh Carlson, and he has a hunting and fishing cabin about an hour from here. I don't know what she said or did, but he's going to be playing there on Friday night."

Josh Carlson was a Wyoming celebrity after he won one of those singing reality shows a few months back. No doubt the whole county was going to try to cram into Alma's dining room because Jade Valley didn't get many celebrity sightings.

"Okay, then we have to think of something even bigger and better."

"A lovely thought, dear, but how can I beat having a rising country star playing in my dining room?"

Sunny gripped Trudy by her shoulders. "You do remember that business consulting is what I do, right? And that I'm very good at it?"

"What do you have in mind? Because I'm all ears."

"I don't know yet, but give me a bit of time to do some brainstorming."

"I don't want to intrude on your honeymoon period."

"You're not. Dean was out working bright and early this morning as usual."

"Well, that man could use some lessons in how to take a break and enjoy himself."

Sunny's face heated.

"Ranch work waits for no one, newly married or not."

"I suppose that's true. Stupid cows."

Sunny laughed and imagined Dean would laugh at Trudy's response too.

"You sure you have time to do this?"

"For you, yes."

Trudy placed her hands on Sunny's cheeks and for a moment she thought the older woman might kiss her. Instead, she walked over to a glass-fronted cold-storage unit and pointed at it.

"Pick whichever dessert you want and you're taking it home to have with that handsome husband of yours."

No matter how many times she heard Dean referred to in that way, it didn't get any less strange.

By the time she managed to leave the restaurant, she had acquired a lemon icebox pie in addition to the milkshake she'd come for in the first place. She'd also promised Trudy not only to come up with a great business plan to compete with Alma's newest venture but also that she'd attend the next meeting of the Fall Festival committee to see if she could give them some winning ideas to bring in more attendees.

She certainly was going to be busier than she'd expected while back in Wyoming. Maybe she could use all this time spent away from Dean as the beginning of the imagined fissure between them.

As she sank into the driver's seat of her rental car, she felt a bit nauseated. She looked at the milkshake but didn't think it was bad, and she wasn't lactose intolerant. But something wasn't sitting right in her middle.

She realized the sick feeling had hit right after she'd thought of the first step toward the dissolution of her marriage. It had to happen, but not before she secured what both she and Dean wanted and ensured that everyone was happy with the end result. She'd started this madness with the best of intentions and would do everything she could so that no one got hurt in the process.

When she left the market, it had begun to sprinkle. By the time she reached the ranch, her windshield wipers were going full speed and she could still barely see. If she didn't know the road from town so well, she would have likely missed the turn onto the ranch road.

By the time she unloaded the groceries, she was soaking wet. She'd planned to take the twins back to Dean's house with her, but her dad convinced her they'd be perfectly fine with him overnight same as they'd been while she'd been in town. Still, she ignored her drenched state long enough to feed, bathe, diaper and clothe Lily and Liam, then place them back in the playpen next to her dad's bed, where he'd agreed to let them stay rather than trying to carry them to their crib. She didn't want to think about how they and her dad might all be injured if he tried that maneuver.

"Call me if you need anything," she said. "Please don't try to carry them anywhere."

"I know, I know. Stop pestering me like I don't have two working brain cells."

"I'm not. You have three."

He lifted one of his crutches as if he was going to hit her in the butt, causing her to laugh as she headed toward the door.

By the time she walked into her temporary home, the rain had slackened to a drizzle again. She didn't even hurry inside because what was the use? The only way she could be wetter was if she was under the surface of the river. She glanced down the road, wondering where Dean was and if he was every bit as soaked.

Feeling chilled, she decided to take a hot shower after depositing Trudy's lemon pie in the fridge. It didn't feel any less weird to be standing naked in Dean's bathroom a few minutes later, letting the stream of hot water drive away the chill. Thank goodness he wasn't home.

Already planning how she'd spend the rest of her evening, she stepped out of the bathroom rubbing her hair with a towel. And screamed when she saw someone an arm's length from her. In the next moment, she realized it was Dean.

"Sorry, didn't mean to scare you," Dean said as he took a step back.

She waved off his apology. "No need to apologize. I'm so used to living alone in LA that it was instinct to freak out seeing someone when I stepped out of the bathroom."

At least she had thought to take clothes in with her and hadn't come out actually wearing a towel.

"I wasn't expecting you back so soon," she said.

"With the rain and nothing really pressing, we called it quits a bit early today."

If they were a real married couple, she'd assume he couldn't wait to get back to his new wife. But they weren't a real couple. Why did she feel a smidge of sadness at that thought? The wedding was over. She wasn't supposed to have these wayward romantic thoughts anymore.

"Guess you probably want the bathroom then. You look about like I did when I got back."

"I've been wetter. I've also been dryer."

She smiled and motioned him toward the bathroom.

"I need to get some clothes first."

She realized he was asking if he could enter his bedroom.

"It's your house, Dean. You don't have to ask my permission to go into your own room."

"I didn't want to assume."

"It's not like I have my unmentionables lying about. If I'm not in there, come and go as you please."

As Dean replaced her in the shower, Sunny distracted herself by warming up some leftovers that had been transferred from her dad's fridge to Dean's and toasting some rolls to go with them. When Dean joined her in the kitchen, she had to try very hard not to notice how the worn green T-shirt stretched across his chest. He should really wear a looser shirt, not one that made her wonder what he looked like without a shirt at all. She wondered if losing her mind was a consequence of lying.

She deliberately turned her back to him to retrieve a glass of water.

"What do you want to drink?"

"Water's good," he said. "Is there anything I can do? I don't expect you to prepare dinner for me, you know."

"Trust me—this was minimal effort. I even brought back a lemon pie from Trudy's."

"I'm going to need you to go back to California soon or I'm going to have to buy bigger pants."

"Somehow I doubt that from someone who works as much as you do."

As they ate, they shared the details of their day like many married couples did over dinner. Sunny had to keep telling herself that if Maya was sitting across from her, they'd be doing the same thing. Only her gaze wouldn't have kept drifting to Maya's chest or her bare arms.

"Be careful if you go to that festival meeting," Dean said, drawing her attention back to something other than his distracting physique. "Give them half a chance and they'll rope you into doing something."

"I'm only going to help them brainstorm a bit. Trudy said that attendance has been down the past couple of years and they're hoping to draw more tourists as well as people who live a little farther afield."

After they'd eaten and Dean had washed the dishes while she put away what they hadn't eaten, Dean retreated to his recliner. But instead of watching TV, he pulled out a spiral notebook and started writing something.

"Don't tell me you have secret aspirations of being a novelist," she said as she sat on the couch with her laptop, aiming to finish up the article for Maya then start brainstorming ideas for Trudy.

"Huh?"

Sunny nodded toward his notebook.

"Oh. My random ideas for what I want to do with the ranch someday."

"Can I see?"

"Don't you have enough to do already?"

"I'm not going to go out and build cabins for you," she said.

He smiled and handed her the notebook. For the next few minutes, she examined all of his ideas and jotted down her own for ways to improve or expand on them.

"This is pretty impressive," she said.

"Really?"

She looked at him. "Why do you sound so surprised?"

"I don't know. Maybe because they've just been ideas floating around in my head for so long."

"But you knew you'd put them into practice at some point."

"Well, no, not if your dad didn't agree to any of them. I even considered leaving and buying my own place, but I'd be starting from scratch and who knows when I'd be able to make any of the things in that notebook a reality."

His admission surprised her, and she didn't like the tinge of defeatism she heard in his voice. It wasn't like him at all.

"Come here," she said, patting the couch next to her.

He stared at her as if not understanding English all of a sudden.

Sunny pointed at him then pointed next to her, repeated the action again until he lowered the footrest on his chair and came to sit beside her. When she felt the warmth of his nearness and could smell the lingering scents of his soap and shampoo, she questioned the wisdom of her request. Also her sanity.

She did her best not to allow those types of thoughts mental space and started going over her ideas for his greenhouse and cabin-rental plans, things that would make the cabins stand out from others in the area and how he should grow organic vegetables and maybe even flowers. He could provide supply to area restaurants as well as the tiny florist in town.

"And you could take advantage of the growing popularity of the farmer's market," she said.

"I thought of that."

He leaned closer to point at something in the notebook, but Sunny couldn't have told anyone what it was because she was too busy trying to remember how to breathe.

"I…uh…" Oh no, she was revealing too much with her inability to speak. "I had another crazy idea, something that would probably need to be implemented even farther down the road."

"Yeah?"

Sunny made the enormous mistake of looking toward Dean at the same moment he looked at her. He was close, too close. And she did not imagine how his gaze dipped to her mouth. The memory of their kiss made her lips tingle.

No, this wasn't right. They were friends, ones who should not let their acting get out of hand so much that they did something that ruined that friendship.

She jerked her gaze back to the notebook, doing everything in her power to not reveal how fast her heart was beating.

"What do you think of a small restaurant beside the river too? It wouldn't have to be anything big because, realistically, there wouldn't be enough business for a large place. But guests would have easy access to meals, and it could become known as a special-occasion place for locals and people in surrounding towns. Have a different type of menu than Trudy's and Alma's so you weren't in direct competition."

"Sounds like a risky investment."

She looked over at him again, but this time she'd prepared herself for the fact that her husband was more attractive than she'd ever realized before. She supposed familiarity had blinded her to that fact.

"I didn't think you were risk averse."

"Just because I have ideas to diversify doesn't mean I can do everything."

"You wouldn't do it immediately. I never advise clients to implement too many improvements at once. You add one thing, then when you feel confident it's going to be a success you add the next one, slightly bigger and more ambitious. The profits from the first steps fund the ones that come after."

Dean sat back and stretched his arm out along the back of the couch. The added distance between them allowed her to breathe a bit easier and her heart to slow a fraction.

"I have other ideas too. Or do you not want to hear them?" she asked.

"Doesn't cost me anything to listen."

And so she outlined how she would implement both his ideas and hers, starting with the greenhouse.

"Not only could you establish a brand for organic vegetables but you could expand that to also include beef. After those things are solid moneymakers, I'd start with a couple of cabins, see what the demand is. Gradually add more. Then come up with advertising campaigns that are themed—group stays for corporate retreats, wedding parties, reunions. Tied in with that could be hosting weddings and other special events. There's plenty of space to add a building that could host all kinds of events. Or you could reverse the order and do the cabins first and use the income from those rentals to fund the organic efforts."

She looked up from her notes and saw Dean grinning at her.

"What?"

"You really like this stuff, don't you?"

"I do. Was I getting carried away?"

He held his thumb and forefinger barely apart. "A little."

"Does any of this appeal to you at all?"

"Everything sounds great, but I'm not sure half of it is possible."

She smiled and tossed out what she'd told so many clients.

"Anything is possible if you want it enough."

Dean's expression seemed to freeze for a split second before he nodded and pointed at the notebook.

"What else do you have?"

As she continued sharing her ideas with him, Dean asked insightful questions that prompted even more ideas. Sunny lost track of time as they continued to bounce possibilities back and forth like an endless tennis match. When she started yawning, she looked over and noticed Dean's eyes looked heavy.

"I'm sorry," she said. "You must be worn out."

When she started to stand, Dean surprised her by clasping her arm to keep her on the couch.

"I'm fine. It's nice to talk these things out. I've not had anyone to share even my initial ideas with who didn't immediately tell me every reason they weren't feasible and that I should stick to what I know. I like ranching, you know that, but I want something more than endless days of cows in my future."

Sunny leaned back on the couch, perhaps overly close to Dean, but she was too tired to think about that.

"I'm sorry no one has given you support."

He shrugged. "It's not like anyone's been awful. I have a good life here."

"But you want more."

"Yeah." He leaned his head against the back of the couch and closed his eyes. "I think you're the first person who's understood why."

"Because I left to find more too?"

He nodded.

And she'd found it, experienced so much, gained a lot of professional knowledge, which she was now able to use to help him fulfill his dreams. A warmth flickered to life in the middle of her chest and grew outward until it filled her entire body. It felt really good to help someone she knew personally.

Dean's arm moved behind her, his hand settling on her shoulder. She wondered if he'd actually fallen asleep. Not wanting to bother him if he had, she stayed quiet. But the lack of conversation added to her own fatigue, and her eyes began to drift shut. She should muster the energy to trudge to bed, but it was so much easier to stay right where she sat.

When Dean sighed as if relaxing into the first stage of sleep, he gently tugged her toward him. Though she knew it was a mistake, she allowed herself to be moved and ended up with her head resting on his shoulder.

As she drifted, her lips lifted at the corners. It was nice to be held, nice to be with someone who understood her without her having to say the words. Even if it wasn't completely real and was only for a short period of time, she couldn't fight the need to indulge in that heady feeling.

CHAPTER THIRTEEN

DEAN WOKE SLOWLY, wincing against the crick in his neck. He started to reach up to massage the ache but became aware that not only was he not in his bed, he also was not alone. He opened his eyes and recognized the top of the head nestled against his chest.

His heart thumped harder, so much so that it'd be a miracle if it didn't wake Sunny. But he was powerless to stop the intensity of his heartbeats. He vaguely remembered her leaning her head against his shoulder as he'd been drifting off to sleep, but somehow in the intervening hours her head had slipped to his chest and her arm was draped across his waist.

They'd obviously both been too tired to move to their separate sleeping spots, and if he was being honest he didn't mind. He wanted to let his arm drift down to wrap around her back, but he didn't want to chance waking her, breaking the spell. Though it was selfish, he wanted these few minutes of having her close. He wouldn't do anything to violate her trust or his respect for Sunny, but these few moments had to be okay.

As if she sensed he was awake, she mumbled something, readjusted her position as if snuggling into her pillow. His breath caught, and he momentarily closed his eyes as he tried his best not to move. But those actions must have made her aware of where she was and with whom because she lifted her arm and sat up, scooting away from him in what she probably thought was a not noticeable way.

"Sorry I fell asleep on you," Sunny said as she smoothed her hair.

"It's okay. Guess we were both more tired than we realized."

"I think I bored you to sleep with all my business talk."

"Not at all. Your enthusiasm is infectious. I can see why you're good at your job."

He noticed that as she spoke Sunny did not attempt to make eye contact with him. She wasn't one to get embarrassed easily, but he thought it was cute. He pressed his lips together so that she wouldn't catch him smiling and he'd have to explain why.

"Oh good. Well, good night," she said as she stood.

Dean started to reach for her, to ask her to stay, but that wasn't part of their agreement. There was no one around they needed to convince of the truth of their relationship. And she was obviously uncomfortable.

"Good night. Sleep well."

She nodded then walked around the coffee table rather than stepping past him as she hurried toward the bedroom. When she closed the door, putting a barrier between the two of them, Dean exhaled a sigh and let his head drop to the back of the couch. He was going to have to guard against anything like that happening again, no matter how nice it felt. He'd mostly restrained himself from expressing his true feelings so far, if one ignored the wedding kiss, but a man only had so much willpower.

Outside, the telltale sound of rain in the distance moved closer until he finally heard it start hitting the roof. He wished he could snap his finger and turn out the light, but it required him pushing to his feet and crossing the room. That done, he stretched out under his quilt on the couch to get two or three more hours of sleep before he had to attack another day of work.

But unlike earlier, sleep proved elusive now. He lay on his back, staring at the ceiling and trying not to focus entirely on how he wished he could join Sunny in the bedroom. Even though they were legally married, he didn't have the right unless she invited him. And judging by how she'd reacted to falling asleep next to him, he didn't see that happening anytime soon. Ever.

Which shouldn't surprise him at all considering his was a one-sided love.

He forced his thoughts in another direction, replaying their conversation about all the various ways to expand the income base of the ranch. The heart of this place would always be cattle ranching, at least as far into the future as he could imagine, but it made good business sense to create other streams of revenue. The fortunes of ranching depended a lot on Mother Nature, and she was notoriously fickle.

His mood dampened like the ground outside when he thought of how none of his ideas or Sunny's would become reality if Jonathon didn't eventually go to California with Sunny and the twins. Dean hated the idea of Sunny leaving. Of Jonathon and the kids leaving, for that matter. Here, in the safety of his own mind, he could admit that he wished things could stay like they were now, all of them living here on the ranch together, eventually making exciting changes together. Only he wanted his marriage to Sunny to be real, for her to feel for him the way he felt about her.

But he'd seen how animated she'd become the more she shared her ideas of how he could create a multipronged business strategy with the ranching operation as the centerpiece. She loved what she did, could help so many more people than just him. He had no right to want to take all that away from her to make himself happy.

Would he even really be happy if he knew she might very well be longing to be somewhere else than this ranch in rural Wyoming? The world was so much bigger than Jade Valley, and her desire to explore all its corners was obvious. He couldn't achieve his professional dream as well as his personal one, especially when Sunny's path was obviously elsewhere and most likely with someone else.

That wasn't an easy truth to accept, but it was the truth nonetheless.

Sunny knew she'd once had the ability to focus, but she must have misplaced it somewhere between Dean's couch the night before and Trudy's dining room. She'd lost count of how many times she'd had to forcefully yank her attention back to the conversation going on around her and respond at the appropriate times. It didn't help that Angela Schuster, the head of the Fall Festival committee, wasn't in attendance and there wasn't a lot of structure to this meeting.

But the last thing she wanted was for any of the people seated around the table to question why her mind was in another universe—the one where she'd woken up pressed up against Dean and it had felt really nice.

After she'd retreated to the bedroom and put the flimsy barrier of a single, unlocked door between them, she had tossed and turned for most of the rest of the night. When Dean leaving for work had woken her only a couple of hours after she'd finally fallen back to sleep, her churning thoughts had returned. Somehow she needed to speed up the timetable on getting her dad to agree to transfer the ranch title, then begin the breakup process with Dean in a believable way.

Who could possibly look at their relationship after it was over and believe anything about it was real?

Except her rapid pulse and the chaotic fluttering in her stomach had felt very real the night before.

"What do you think, Sunny?"

Did someone say her name? She looked up to see five faces fixed on her with expectant expressions.

"I'm sorry, what?" She didn't even know who'd spoken to her.

Eileen Parker, who ran the tiny art center and who had been one of Sunny's mom's good friends, smiled.

"This is what we get by expecting the full attention of someone still in her honeymoon phase," Eileen said.

Heat crept up Sunny's neck, and no excuse she could think of on the fly was going to make things sound any better.

"I'm sorry—could you repeat what was said?"

"I asked what you thought of a cake walk?" Nettie Jones asked. "Those are popular, right?"

"They have been in the past," Sunny said, wanting to steer the conversation quickly away from her so-called honeymoon phase.

"But if you want to draw more people in, you have to be more innovative. Go to any school festival and you'll find a cake walk or something similar. For lack of a better phrase, you need to think outside the box."

"How so?" Johnny Marston, a retired industrial arts teacher at the high school, asked. "Pies?"

Sunny barely kept herself from laughing, instead leaning back in her chair and crossing her arms as she let her creative mind wander. Then one of those light-bulb moments happened.

"What if you had a town-wide scavenger hunt for clues? Like one of those whodunit mysteries where all of the business owners in town who want to participate have to answer the questions of people who come in seeking clues to who the 'killer' is. One of those business owners would be the 'killer' and whoever figures it out first after asking each suspect at least one question gets a big prize of some sort."

"So not cakes or pies?" Johnny asked.

Sunny smiled. "Do you have a sweet tooth by chance?"

Johnny smiled. "Busted."

She laughed. "For the sweets, what if there is instead a silent auction for them?"

"I like that," Eileen said. "We could pick two or three good causes to give the proceeds to."

Much like her conversation with Dean the night before, once the ideas started flowing they came faster and faster.

"I don't think I've ever been so excited about putting this festival together," Eileen said a while later as she tapped the list she'd been keeping with her pen. "You really are a natural at this."

"Thanks. Lots of practice."

"Angela," Eileen said, looking past Sunny.

"Hey, everyone." Angela sounded hesitant as she approached.

"What's wrong?" Eileen asked.

"Nothing really, except I feel guilty for what I'm about to say. Jake got the job he applied for in Cheyenne. We're moving in a week, so I'm not going to be able to chair the festival this year."

Sunny's phone buzzed with a text. She pulled it out to read the message while the committee members dealt with the sudden need for a new chair. Against all common sense, the fluttery feeling returned when she saw it was from Dean.

I'm going to be later coming home tonight, so you might want to eat dinner with your dad.

Though he was only being considerate so she didn't wait on him, it felt way too much like the kind of message a real husband would send to a real wife.

"I think that's a great idea. Don't you, Sunny?"

"Huh? Yeah." Wait, what had Eileen said? Sunny had to stop getting distracted by thoughts of Dean. "What? Sorry, I was reading a message."

When she looked up, the whole committee was looking at her with smiles on their faces.

"Thanks so much for doing this," Angela said as she placed one of her hands over Sunny's atop the table. "I feel so much better leaving the festival in such capable hands. You'll be a hundred times better at this than I've ever been anyway."

"Wait, what are you talking about?"

Eileen and Francis Trenton looked at each other and chuckled before Eileen returned her gaze to Sunny.

"Honey, you just agreed to chair the Fall Festival."

"What? No, I didn't."

"Yes, you did," Eileen said, and everyone around the table nodded.

"I think it's a fabulous idea," Trudy said as she arrived with slices of pie for everyone.

Sunny shook her head. "I can't do that. I won't be here then."

The smiles dropped off everyone's faces, and Sunny realized she'd made a big mistake that she now had to try to explain away.

"I mean, I'm working remotely now but I'll have to go back to traveling soon. I have no idea where I'll be when the festival happens or in the weeks leading up to it."

"I didn't realize you'd still be working for the same company," Eileen said.

"At least for now," Sunny said, hedging a little. "I enjoy my work and there sadly aren't any business consulting companies in Jade Valley."

"What does Dean think about this?" Francis asked.

Sunny only barely kept her instinctive dislike of that question from showing. Francis was a nice lady, but her question smacked a bit too much of misogyny to Sunny.

Eileen swatted Francis's arm. "Times have changed, and for the better. Women don't need their husbands' permission to do what they want anymore."

"That's not what I meant," Francis said.

"Dean is very supportive of my career," Sunny said, wanting to put an end to this conversation. Thankfully, this wasn't a lie.

"Of course he is." Trudy patted Sunny's back. "He's a good man, through and through."

True.

"And quite a handsome one at that," Eileen said with a wink.

Also true, though Sunny would do well not to let her thoughts travel that particular road. Especially when she was afraid she wouldn't be able to prevent her thoughts from playing across her face like a movie-theater screen.

"Any of you would be a better choice for the chair position than me," Sunny said, deciding to not comment on the attractiveness level of her husband.

"Could you do it as an interim?" Eileen asked. "You'd have lots of worker bees to help, but I think you've shown today that you are, in fact, the right person to helm the new direction for the festival."

Everyone around her made enthusiastic

sounds of agreement. Angela reached over and gripped Sunny's hand.

"Please say yes. I'd feel so much better about leaving if someone with your talent and vision was taking over."

Sunny felt as if the vines of Jade Valley were growing around her legs, beginning to make her more of the ecosystem than she could be in the end. Mike was not going to let her work remotely forever, and flying to international destinations from Wyoming was not sustainable in the long term. Already she was probably going to have to go back to California before she managed to complete her entire plan for convincing her dad to move there with her. That she'd even for a moment thought she could reach the endgame both she and Dean wanted in a short amount of time made her wonder if she'd temporarily lost her ability to make rational decisions.

She should continue to say no to this group's requests, and yet she found herself nodding.

"Just as interim chair. Once we have everything decided on and people assigned to head up each area of the festival planning, I'll hand things over to one of you."

"Sounds like a good plan," Eileen said.

"Thank you so much." Angela looked as if she might cry with relief. Sunny wondered if that might be at least partially because she'd been freed from the burden of trying to revive a festival that had been waning.

"I feel really good about this year's festival," Eileen said. "With new blood and fresh ideas, I think it's going to be a success."

"Of course it is," Trudy said, squeezing Sunny's shoulders from where she stood behind her. "This gal has the golden touch. Next up, filling this dining room so full that Alma will be spitting mad."

DEAN LAUGHED SO hard that Sunny had to shush him.

"If you wake the twins, I'm making you stay up all night with them. They were uncharacteristically cranky, and it took me forever to get them to calm down and go to sleep."

"Sorry," Dean said, his voice much quieter than his outburst of laughter had been. "But you have to admit it's hilarious."

"Why is me getting suckered into being the festival chair hilarious? As if I wasn't juggling enough balls already."

"Just the fact that despite how you tell large

corporations around the world what to do, you got bamboozled by a handful of older ladies on a mission."

"It wasn't all women. Johnny Marston's on the committee."

Dean snorted so loudly that Sunny smacked him on the arm.

"Sorry," he said again. "But Johnny's there to escape his wife. He figures the committee is less work than she'd have him doing if he stayed home. It's also probably a good way for them to not end up in divorce court."

Despite her demands that he not wake up Lily and Liam, who were sleeping in the new crib in Dean's bedroom, she felt relieved to be laughing with him without any leftover awkwardness in the aftermath of her falling asleep on him.

"I feel conflicted," she said. "While that is funny, it's also sad that they're in a marriage that fractious."

"It happens to a lot of older couples. Once their kids grow up and leave, they realize they don't have much in common and don't even really like each other."

"Your parents don't seem to be like that."

"Oh no, they are still nauseatingly in love."

Sunny smiled. "Don't try to convince me

you would have it any other way. Your parents are the best."

"Yeah, they're top tier in the parents department."

She glanced toward the closed bedroom door, knowing that her brother and sister-in-law would have fit that description, as well.

"Hey," Dean said as he took her hand in his. "No sad thoughts."

"I can't help it sometimes."

It probably wasn't the wisest move ever, but she didn't protest when Dean pulled her gently to him and wrapped her in a comforting hug.

"I miss them too," he said. "Every day."

She allowed herself to relax into his embrace and placed her hands against his warm back. He smelled like the outdoors, not fresh and clean like he had after his shower the night before but rather like the familiar scents of an honest day's ranch work. Like sunshine, dust, grass, animals and sweat. And yet she didn't mind.

"Sometimes it still doesn't seem real that they're gone. I alternate between trying to convince myself this has all been a long, extremely detailed dream and acknowledging that I have to accept the finality of the truth."

"That's normal, don't you think? Part of the stages of grieving or something."

"Yeah. Doesn't make it any easier knowing that."

Dean held her loosely so that when she was ready she was able to step free easily and without it seeming like a big deal.

"Are you hungry?" she asked as she moved toward the kitchen.

"Yeah, but I'll warm up something after I shower. Or did you not eat with your dad? Did you get my text?"

"I got the text. Sorry I didn't answer, but I was in the middle of the festival meeting."

"The festival you're now in charge of."

The teasing tone of his voice along with the mischievous smile had her grabbing and threatening to toss a loaf of bread at him. Dean laughed and sprinted toward the bathroom and safety from flying carbohydrates.

Sunny smiled and shook her head. She tried not to attribute too much meaning to the fact that Dean always seemed to know exactly what type of support she needed and when she needed it.

As she warmed up a healthy portion of food for Dean's late dinner, she was struck by how comfortable she felt here after such a short time. They'd had their awkward moments, but thankfully there were longer stretches of easy companionship in between. Whether they were brainstorming business plans or having a moment of mutual grief over the loss of Jason and Amanda, the interactions felt more effortless than those in a fake marriage should.

What should concern her more than that was the fact that she found it way too easy to imagine letting the word *fake* start to disappear.

CHAPTER FOURTEEN

SUNNY DIDN'T KNOW why she was dreaming about a baby crying when she didn't have a baby. She was living the single, professional life in sunny, vibrant SoCal. She rolled over and pulled a pillow over her head, hoping to smother the dream.

Lily! Liam!

She sat up fast and tripped over her quilt while trying to get to her feet, sending herself sprawling onto the floor. Wincing at the pain in her knee, which had taken the brunt of the fall, she pushed her sleep-mussed hair out of her face and was getting to her feet when the sound of a knock on the door managed to register in her foggy brain.

"Sunny? I'm coming in, okay?"

"Uh, yeah," she said, her words not totally coherent.

The door opened and Dean hurried in.

"Are you okay?" he asked as he rushed over to her and gripped her upper arm.

She blinked several times, trying to shove away the vestiges of sleep so she could tend to whatever had awakened the babies.

"Yeah." But she winced again when she took a step.

"Sit. I'll—"

"I'm okay," she said as she crossed to the crib to see both twins in full meltdown. Not knowing which one had started crying first, she checked Lily and found a wet diaper. "Let's get you fixed up, sweetie. I'd cry too if I was in your position."

She noticed Dean had stepped up next to her and was checking Liam's diaper.

"In the clear here," he said.

"He's probably just crying because his sister is."

Dean lifted Liam out of the crib with little effort and held him high in the air.

"Hey, little guy, no need for all that fussing."

By the time she was finished diapering Lily and drying her tears, Sunny was more awake. As she lifted Lily out of the crib and soothed her by bouncing her gently and rubbing her back, she noticed that Liam had stopped crying too. Instead, he was actually giggling.

She looked over to find Dean was holding

her nephew and tickling his plump little belly. The sight of Dean holding a baby while wearing a smile of adoration wasn't something she needed to see in the middle of the night because it made her feel things that were decidedly inconvenient.

But who could blame her? It was quite possibly the sweetest, most attractive thing she'd seen in her entire life. That the man in question was someone she'd known since before she could remember made her question if she was actually awake or really dreaming.

Dean glanced toward her and smiled. "Looks like we make a good midnight team."

"Uh, yeah, I guess so."

His expression grew concerned.

"Is something wrong?"

She shook her head. "Sleep hangover, I guess. Not firing on all cylinders."

He nodded toward the bed. "Sit down and I'll leave them with you while I get an ice pack for your knee."

"I'm fine, really."

"Wouldn't it be better to take care of things now instead of tomorrow when you need to be able to walk? I swear you and your dad are two stubborn peas in a pod."

She huffed out a little laugh at that. "We're certainly both klutzy enough lately."

Luckily she hadn't managed to break any bones. But the ice pack probably was a smart idea, so she situated herself against the headboard with Lily in her lap. Dean placed Liam next to her.

"Make sure your auntie doesn't manage to fall out of the bed," he said to Liam as if speaking one man to another.

"I don't remember you being this annoying."

"Maybe I've gotten better with age."

He had no idea how disturbingly right he was.

Ahh, she had to stop thinking like that.

"I thought you were getting me an ice pack." She motioned him toward the door.

He bowed like a courtier before a queen.

"Your wish is my command, dear wife."

Thankfully at that moment Liam grabbed the hem of her pajama top and tugged, demanding attention that she gave him so she didn't have to figure out how to respond to Dean. She knew he was teasing, but it still made it difficult to sit still and breathe normally when he offered an endearment.

She made sure her attention was focused

entirely on the twins when Dean returned to the room with the ice pack.

"Your right knee?" he asked.

"I can do it," she said, reaching for the ice.

"I think you have your hands full already."

That she did. Two unfortunately wide-awake toddlers who were currently using her as a jungle gym.

Dean sat on the edge of the bed and placed the ice pack gently on her aching knee.

"That okay?"

She nodded. "Yeah, thanks."

Now that Dean was close at hand, Lily abandoned Sunny and crawled toward him.

"Well, you look happier than you did a few minutes ago," Dean said to his pint-size admirer as he scooped her up and placed her on his lap.

"Of course she is. She knows she has you wrapped around her tiny finger."

"She does indeed."

Sunny's entire body felt warm and fuzzy watching Dean with her niece. He was so good with her, with both of the kids. If things were different, he'd make a good father figure for them. When she thought about how he might miss them if they moved to California with her, she experienced a pang of guilt and sadness. She found herself wishing Jade Valley and LA weren't so far from each other.

Sunny snuggled Liam close, and he seemed contented to let her. She hated that he would have no memory of his mother doing the same. Lily wouldn't remember her father doting on her the way Dean was doing.

"Even if you convince your dad to come to California, this caretaking in the middle of the night is still going to be a challenge."

"Parents with jobs do it all the time. Dad and I will be able to manage."

Dean shifted his gaze away from her and back to Lily, bouncing her on his leg as if it was a toddler-sized horse. He didn't say anything further, not to her anyway, and it made her curious what he was thinking.

It took about half an hour of quiet, back rubs and some light rocking before they managed to get the twins back to sleep. Dean eased them one at a time into their shared crib. After he covered them with a thin blanket he moved back to the bed, though he didn't resume sitting.

"Would you like some more ice?" He kept his voice soft and quiet so as not to disturb Lily and Liam.

She shook her head. "I'm good. Go get some more sleep. I'm sorry they woke you up."

"It's okay. I fall asleep pretty easily most of the time."

After he left the room and closed the door, she found herself wishing she could fall asleep quickly too. Because the more time she spent with Dean, the more confusion seeped into her thoughts.

DEAN GUIDED HIS horse to the right to steer the edge of the herd in the direction of the new pasture. As he'd spent his morning looking at the back ends of cattle, he'd day-dreamed about being able to freeze time so he could fall into blissful sleep for about a week. Maybe then he'd feel rested and have figured out a way to forget about his wife.

His wife. No matter how many times that phrase ran through his thoughts, he couldn't believe he was married to Sunny. Granted, it was only on paper and not a real marriage in all the ways that counted, but they were indeed husband and wife. He hadn't wanted to leave the bedroom the night before. Even if they didn't consummate their marriage, it would be nice to simply lie beside her, hold her close as she slept.

"You look like you haven't been sleeping much," Carlos said in a tone that left no doubt what he thought was keeping Dean up at night when he should be sleeping.

He wasn't about to discuss his sex life or lack thereof with his coworkers, so he pointed toward a straying calf so Carlos would ride in the opposite direction and hopefully forget about teasing him. Dean didn't want to add any more lies to the load he was already carrying. One more had joined the tally the night before when he'd told Sunny that he fell asleep easily.

Okay, so that used to be true before she'd moved in. But since then? He'd had one hell of a time quieting his mind each night. And when he'd gone to the bathroom in the wee hours a couple of nights before, in his half-asleep state he'd almost entered his bedroom on the way back. Only the closed door had reminded him that his bedroom was already occupied.

But otherwise, living with Sunny had been great. He didn't even mind late-night toddler care. When he'd been holding Lily and had the thought that they almost seemed like a real family, he hadn't been able to look at Sunny, afraid she'd read his thoughts.

His phone buzzed and he hoped neither Carlos nor Billy noticed how fast he reached for it. But the message wasn't from Sunny, who was no doubt up to her nose in one work project or another, but rather his mother.

I just saw Sunny in town with those darling twins.

He didn't have to see his mom's face or hear her voice to know she was itching to go full grandma with Lily and Liam.

Satisfied the herd was heading in the right direction, he reined to a stop so he could text his mom a quick response.

She said she was going to visit Trudy, help her with something to combat Alma's unexpected Josh Carlson appearance.

Those two old women are still acting like teenagers.

Dean laughed out loud at his mom calling Alma and Trudy old women when they were probably only ten years older than her.

"Your wife sending you interesting texts?" Carlos called out to him, causing Billy to chuckle.

"No, my mom being sassy."

"Okay, that I believe too. I miss having her around."

Dean understood. It had taken a while to get used to his mom and dad not living on the ranch after his dad retired and Dean took over as foreman. Though his dad still came out occasionally to chat with Jonathon and the hands, he'd taken to retirement better than Dean had expected. While his mom experimented with new recipes she got from cooking shows and indulged in her craft of the week, his dad puttered in his little wood shop behind their house. To everyone's surprise, he'd developed an interest in making miniatures and dollhouses. And while Dean's mom was the one with grandma fever, even his dad had made a comment about building a beautiful dollhouse for Lily when she was a little older.

Dean had played it off by saying Lily might not like dolls. She might like race cars or horses instead. Of course, then his dad had simply pivoted and said he could make those too if that's what she preferred.

He tried not to think about how his marriage dissolving and the twins moving states away was going to break his parents' hearts. They'd already been fond of them, but his marriage had really upped their attachment to those little cuties. His too, if he was being honest.

As he stared out across the ranch that had been such a huge part of his entire life, he realized that the deal he'd made with Sunny had little to do with his desire to make his professional dreams come true. She'd needed help, and he'd agreed to it without fully thinking through the consequences. People were going to get hurt, and there was no way to prevent it.

Unless…

He shook his head at the idea of trying to convince Sunny to stay in Jade Valley, to make a real life together. But that wasn't fair to her. He'd gone into this relationship knowing she didn't feel the same way about him as he felt about her, so trying to change the terms of their agreement midstream wasn't right.

Even knowing all that, he couldn't stop his thoughts from racing down that path. But every time he thought about trying to woo his wife for real, the other half of his brain would scold him for trying to take away the life she'd worked hard to build for herself. While she might love Jade Valley, her friends and the ranch, she wasn't in love with him. She'd lost enough. He wasn't going to attempt to be the reason she lost a job she loved too.

"I KNOW IT'S not Josh Carlson, but at least it'll give you more opportunities to bring in people than a single appearance." Sunny pointed at the printouts of her plan she'd brought to show Trudy.

"I feel like kissing you," Trudy said.

Sunny laughed. "Thanks for the sentiment, but that's not necessary."

She'd been in the middle of writing her second travel piece for Maya, this one on Thailand, after Dean left for work that morning, when she'd started craving *tom kha gai*. That was when a memory of the first time she'd had the authentic chicken coconut soup caused the proverbial light bulb to click on above her head. For the next couple of hours she'd abandoned the article in favor of mapping out a schedule of articles that Trudy could then pair with themed nights at the café. Maya was probably going to be thrilled with the idea too. Being able to link an article about Portugal to a tasty night of *caldo verde* and *bifanas* with *pastel de nata* for dessert and a drawing to win a bottle of Portuguese wine was a win-win for two of the most important women in Sunny's life.

And she had gotten a thrill out of the planning for the effort—picking the countries, selecting the menu items, researching the best giveaway prizes from each country. She loved being able to bring so many beautiful parts of her travel back home to Jade Valley. She just hoped the whole effort didn't bomb spectacularly. In her articles, she was deliberately highlighting the similarities between those faraway places and Wyoming to help locals feel not only a kinship with but also an interest in learning more about the various countries. Hopefully it also would bring them and their taste buds to Trudy's for a little something different.

"No wonder that company of yours sends you all around the world to help people with their businesses," Trudy said as she stacked the papers in front of her. "It's a shame the same thing isn't available to the small business owners who can't afford expensive consultants."

Sunny kept thinking about Trudy's observation as she went to Eileen's for her first meeting as the new chair of the Fall Festival committee. It really was a shame that small communities didn't have access to the same type of opportunities as cities, but that was how the world worked. Professionals migrated to cities because it was where they could actually make a living doing what they wanted. Not only were none of the Jade Valley business owners appearing on any billionaires lists anytime soon, but many of them were probably also barely getting by.

By the time the festival committee meeting was over, not only did the festival have a new, flashier name—the Jade Valley Autumn Extravaganza—it also had a whole list of new activities, several additional volunteers, assignments made and deadlines set. Once Sunny got on a roll with ideas, she'd had to forcibly rein herself in before they had more activities than residents to coordinate them.

When she reached her dad's house and collapsed onto the couch, he chuckled at her.

"I see the stories I'm hearing are true, that you're working harder here than when you're in LA."

"It does feel that way." And yet, she was enjoying herself. It was one thing to bring an effective business plan to a multimillion-dollar company, but there was a different type of rush when helping those for whom her insights and hard work could mean exponentially more.

Nothing was standing in her way of helping out the people she knew in Jade Valley whenever she had the time after going back to LA. The problem was she'd rarely have any spare time with work, helping her dad take care of the twins and looking for a home that was more suitable for all of them.

Why did LA seem so far away in that moment? Like it was a place other people lived? That didn't make sense when she'd paid her next month's rent that morning.

"What have you been up to today?" she asked, wanting to get her mind off her own confusing life.

"The usual. Spoiling my grandkids, letting the TV rot my brain. And I made your mother's corn bread to go with that stew you put in the Crock-Pot this morning. I'll have you know my stomach has been rumbling for hours."

"Wait, you cooked?"

He gave her a look that said she was being a smarty-pants, which of course she was.

"How do you think I feed myself when you're not here?"

"Uber Eats?" She grinned at the very idea of Jade Valley having meal delivery of any sort other than pizzas from Little Italy, which had to be the smallest pizzeria in the country. There was room for exactly two people to stand in the little lobby of the takeout-and-delivery-only eatery. And even delivery didn't extend beyond two miles outside the city limits.

Her dad snorted, not even bothering with an answer.

"The corn bread sounds good. I haven't had it in a long time."

"Did you bring anything sweet home?"

"I think we've all had about enough sweets since I've been back. I'm calling a moratorium on sugar."

"Now you're just adding to my sad existence." He tapped his cast.

"The self-pity act really doesn't suit you."

"It doesn't, does it?"

She shook her head.

"I was so bored today that I also did the books," he said.

"Whew, that is bored." Though keeping up with the financial bookkeeping for the ranch was not her dad's favorite thing to do, it was a necessary evil.

"You could ask Dean if he'd like to take that over." She needed to start taking steps toward the ranch passing into Dean's hands, because she kept expecting a call from Mike telling her that if she wasn't in LA the next day she was going to be fired. And Dean might meet someone he liked and not want to be tied to a fake wife.

No, she didn't want to think about that possibility, or the reason she didn't want to think about it.

"Didn't you have to tutor him in high school?"

"In English, not math." She was surprised by how much his question irritated her. "You should have more confidence in your foreman. If you let him, Dean could do a lot more."

When she caught the way her dad was grinning, for some reason she felt as if she'd walked into a trap. What a strange thought to have.

"I suppose I should involve my son-in-law

more in the decision-making since he's family now."

"It shouldn't have taken a wedding in the front yard and a marriage license for you to do that. He's lived on this ranch longer than I have. I've looked at his ideas for diversifying, and I think they have a lot of merit. I added some of my own."

"That right?"

She shared a couple of the smaller ideas, oddly not wanting to share all of the plans she and Dean had come up with together. She didn't want to hear her dad possibly shoot them down or give him any reason to not want the ranch in Dean's hands.

"Sounds like you and Dean are a good team. That makes me happy. Your mom would be overjoyed. She used to tell me how nice it would be if the two of you grew up and fell in love."

Sunny sat up at this unexpected revelation. "She did? I never knew that."

"Of course she didn't say anything to you. After all, you were still pretty young, too young to date. Not to mention kids are known to do the opposite of what their parents want."

A familiar sadness settled in the place in her heart left empty by the loss of her mom.

That hole had company now, areas once filled with her brother's laughter and her sister-in-law's sweetness. She wondered if somehow her marriage to Dean had helped fill up similar holes in her dad's heart.

Not for the first time, she almost confessed everything to him. He would no doubt be angry and hurt, but wouldn't it be even worse the longer she waited?

"What did you think about what she said?"

He shrugged. "Probably that she was getting ahead of herself."

Sunny watched as a familiar cloud of sorrow came over her dad's face.

"As you got older, she didn't say anything because she knew you were probably going to leave and find your life somewhere else." A sigh filled a few moments of pause. "I wish she could have seen how beautiful and happy you looked on your wedding day."

"I'm sure she did," she said before she could think that saying so was a bad idea, in a way adding to the mountain of lies. But in a way not. After all, she hadn't been unhappy on her wedding day, but any outward happiness simply hadn't been for the reason her dad assumed.

And yet when Dean joined them later for

dinner, she found herself laughing and smiling and feeling as if they were a real family. She realized everything about Dean made it easy to slip into that mindset, and if she didn't guard against it she might end up getting hurt by her own plan.

CHAPTER FIFTEEN

DESPITE TELLING HERSELF she needed to make more moves toward convincing her dad to sign over the ranch to her and Dean, perhaps as a wedding gift and solid acknowledgment of Dean as a part of the family, more than just the ranch foreman, she kept avoiding it. Every time she said she'd start the next day, she ran into a mental wall of how to do so without it being painfully obvious what she was doing. And without guilt gnawing at her.

Instead, she focused on work—for her job, taking care of the twins, helping out her dad and the various local irons she had in the fire. To her and her dad's surprise, the first travel piece and associated special menu night at Trudy's had gone over amazingly well, so much so that Eileen had asked her to do a series of talks at the art center with photos of the same locales. Sunny didn't know if people were really interested in Thailand, the article topic that Maya had chosen to run first, or there weren't many other local entertainment options. Whatever the reason, her first presentation at the art center was packed, as well.

On top of all that work, she also found herself repeatedly going back to the master document she'd made of marketing and business strategy ideas for the ranch. She'd be in the middle of driving down the road or feeding the twins and another idea would pop into her head. She'd get so excited about it that by the time she had her laptop in front of her again, she couldn't type up everything fast enough. Dean was going to have to have help implementing even a fraction of what they'd mapped out.

She tried not to give too much thought to how every time she pictured someone else, perhaps a female someone, helping him make those ideas become reality, her mood soured.

There were times when she thought perhaps Dean was having similar thoughts, but she always ended up attributing it to her imagination giving more meaning to simple kindnesses than was there. No doubt the forced proximity of living in the small house together wasn't helping in keeping imagination and reality separate.

She should be thankful for nights like tonight when she had space to herself while Dean was at her dad's house for a poker night with Billy, Carlos, AJ, Dean's dad and Tom Rifkin. It had started out as an effort to alleviate some of her dad's boredom but had turned into a battle for bragging rights that was likely to go late into the night.

She'd decided to decline the half-hearted invitation from her dad in favor of quality time with her niece and nephew and then some quiet for knocking out a chunk of quality work for her actual job. Hopefully it would prevent unwanted questions from Mike about when she was going to ever make an appearance in her LA office again.

But she kept getting drowsy. Granted, lying stretched out on the couch with the laptop propped against her upturned legs didn't help. Neither did the sound of rain on the roof that had started a few minutes before. She kept shaking her head and blinking, determined to stay awake long enough to get through a proposal for a potential client in Norway.

Norway, land of long, cold nights perfect for curling up next to a fire with a good… book…and…

She jerked awake, grabbing for her falling laptop. Only it wasn't falling. Dean had his hands on it, lifting it from her lap to the coffee table. When his gaze met hers, she realized how close he was. Too close, so close she could feel his breath. And he didn't look away or put more distance between them. Instead, he slowly lifted his hand and pushed some strands of her hair off her forehead.

His fingers barely touched her skin, but she was nevertheless vividly reminded of that kiss they'd shared on their wedding day. Had that kiss opened up something within her that now saw Dean as a man, an attractive man, instead of only a friend she'd known all her life?

"How did poker night go?" she asked, her voice barely above a whisper. This moment seemed to demand quiet, as if speaking normally would break some sort of magic spell.

"Your dad cleaned us out." Dean also spoke softly, and she looked at his lips before she could think to stop herself.

When she lifted her gaze to his, her breath caught. And as he started to lean closer, she could not find a single word to stop him.

She didn't want to stop him.

It was a light kiss, soft, tender, what she had expected at the wedding instead of the very real kiss she'd received instead. For the space of a heartbeat she thought she sensed him about to deepen the kiss, but instead he broke contact and offered a little smile.

"I think it's time you go to bed and get some sleep."

You, not *we*.

"Oh yeah." After he stood to his full height and stepped back, she quickly swung her feet to the floor and grabbed her computer to her chest like armor. "Sorry I fell asleep in your space."

"It's okay. I shouldn't have come back so late."

Instead of telling him that he did not have to coordinate his schedule with hers, she simply stood, said good night and barely kept herself from running to the bedroom, then barricading herself inside. Not to keep him out but to put up barriers that would at least force her to think while removing them if she was tempted to go out and kiss him some more.

DEAN STOOD STARING at the door, halfway wanting Sunny to come back out and halfway wanting her to stay safely on the other side. He'd only had one beer at Jonathon's, wanting to have a clear head for poker—not that it had done him a lot of good—so he couldn't even blame alcohol for that impulsive kiss.

No, it had been entirely his attraction to her combined with how much he had to constantly hold himself back from revealing it. To be honest, he was surprised she'd never scolded him for the kiss at their wedding. Maybe she'd thought it better to pretend it hadn't happened at all.

When he'd come home tonight to find her lying along the couch where he normally slept, illuminated only by a single light spilling out from the kitchen, his ability to keep his distance had cracked. But judging how quickly she'd retreated to the bedroom, he'd be lucky if she didn't wake up in the morning and start divorce proceedings. Considering he didn't think they were any closer to his gaining the ranch and her convincing her dad to move with her to California, this whole fake-marriage thing might have been for nothing. Well, nothing other than making him want her even more than he had before.

Buzzing drew his attention but he quickly realized it wasn't his phone since it was in his pocket and not vibrating. He spotted a lit-up screen on the couch. He picked up Sunny's phone and saw the message was from her boss.

Why was the man texting her after eleven at night? Well, he could just wait until the morning for a response. He placed the phone on the coffee table and sank onto the couch, then ran his hand over his face.

His lips still tingled from where they'd touched Sunny's. He wondered if she'd once again pretend that the kiss hadn't happened. Or would she wake up in the morning upset with him for acting outside the boundaries of their agreement?

A part of him wondered if he should just spill the truth about how he felt. What's the worst that could happen? She was planning to leave Jade Valley for good anyway.

You might not ever get to talk to her again.

Maybe that would be the healthier outcome. If there was no true future for them, then cutting all ties would make it easier to move on. All those hours in the saddle riding the ranch's acreage had given him a lot of opportunities for self-reflection. He hadn't had to fork over hundreds or thousands of dollars to a therapist to figure out that the reason he'd never had a lasting relationship with any other woman was because he was still attached to Sunny. When she drove away the final time, that attachment needed to have been severed.

That or he had to muster all his courage and confess his feelings in the tiny hope that some of them might be reciprocated.

THE MORNING AFTER Dean kissed her, Sunny went into full avoidance mode because she still didn't have a clue how to act around him. Had he been caught up in another moment as a result of them living together, the same as she had? Or did he harbor actual feelings for her? When she thought about asking him outright, the thought of either answer made her nerves spasm all throughout her body.

So she did what she always did when she didn't want to face difficult-to-navigate situations—she threw herself into work, even more so than she had before.

It seemed every day she was being asked for advice from someone new. Even a former classmate, Matt Lyons, had insisted on buying her lunch at Trudy's and had agreed to help out with the building of some decorations for the festival in exchange for her advice on how he could best market his wooden carvings. She'd ended up spending a good three hours at Trudy's, well beyond the lunch rush, helping him map out a plan because she was so impressed with his work. He'd been so thankful he'd offered her one of his pieces. She'd chosen not to examine too closely that a box containing a carving of a cowboy astride a horse, a birthday present for Dean, now sat beside her suitcase in Dean's bedroom.

Dean seemed to be on the avoidance train, as well. He always left early in the morning, but he was coming home later each evening too. He evidently was catching up on miscellaneous upkeep in the barn or so she'd heard from her dad, who'd given her a curious look that seemed to ask why a newly married man was avoiding going home. She could have used the opportunity to tell her dad things weren't going to work out with Dean and she wanted her remaining family to move to California with her, but it was too soon. She was beginning to think that her dad's passing comment about Dean only gaining access to the ranch through marriage to her had only meant sometime in the distant future when her dad passed away.

Her impulsive actions really were making her feel like an idiot now. Still, she had to salvage the original plan. She and Dean needed to talk about what steps they should take when, how she might get her dad on board with the transfer of the ranch, but she kept putting it off whenever Dean came home and looked so tired each night.

But she couldn't put it off any longer. She didn't like the new, distant wariness between them since that soft kiss had sent her emotions and any semblance of coherent thought reeling. Had caused her to miss him at the same time she was actively trying to avoid too much time together. She was not someone who was often confused, but that was exactly what she felt when she thought about Dean.

When it started to rain yet again, she decided to make a big pot of chili and thick grilled-cheese sandwiches. And she texted Dean to let him know so that he wouldn't spend extra time finding things to do that kept him away from his own home. Their avoiding each other was making that kiss into more than it had been.

Even though he'd acknowledged her text with a simple okay, it was still after dark when she heard his truck pull up outside. She stirred the pot of chili then glanced over her shoulder as the front door opened. In the same moment, Dean sneezed three times in quick succession.

Sunny dropped the lid back onto the pot and walked toward him.

"Are you sick?"

He looked up as if he was surprised to see her there then shook his head.

"I'm fine. Just a little chilled from the rain. The wind shifted and it's cooler than normal."

She pointed down the short hallway to the bathroom. "Go take a hot shower then come eat."

He grinned. "Yes, ma'am."

While he was in the bathroom, she fed the twins and played with them, dutifully laughing every time they stacked then knocked over a few of their soft fabric blocks decorated with letters and animals. When she heard the shower shut off, she caressed Lily and Liam atop their heads then left them to amuse each other within the safety of their playpen.

After Dean was dressed in dry clothes and emerged from the bathroom, she heard him sneeze again. She needed to get some hot food into him to finish driving out the chill.

As soon as he sat down at the table and she placed his food in front of him, her phone rang. She started to ignore it but then saw it was her boss. Considering he typically texted, she figured she should pick up.

"Sorry. Duty calls." She took the phone and retreated to the bedroom.

"Hey, Mike. What's up?"

"You, on an airplane soon."

She resisted sighing at Mike's no-filter way of speaking. He only managed to filter himself when speaking with clients.

"I've been doing my work satisfactorily from here, right? And by me taking a break from traveling, it's giving others more experience in the field."

"While all true, you're going to want to come back soon. A position is opening up that will allow you to build a new division and pick the type of clients you want."

A surge of excitement shot through Sunny. "Really?"

"But you're going to have to work for it. It's company-wide, so you will be competing with the top people from other branches. Each of you will be presenting a proposal for the new division, and the executives will choose the one they like the best and let the new division head launch their proposal."

"How long do I have to prepare?" Being in charge of an entire division built by her was more than she'd dreamed of for the immediate future.

"That's still being discussed. I'll let you know as soon as I hear, but I wanted to give you a heads-up so you could start working up a killer plan."

Her excitement dimmed a fraction. She was already so busy, but this was a huge opportunity.

One that would take her away from Jade Valley sooner than she'd expected.

When one of the twins let out a wail, she thanked Mike again then ended the call. But by the time she took the few steps required to return to the living room, Dean already had Lily up in his arms, bouncing her gently as he talked in a soothing voice.

"Your aunt's on an important call," he said as if Lily would understand what he was saying. "We need to be quiet so she can talk."

Sunny stopped and stared at the picture they made together. If she didn't know Lily was her brother's child, she could easily assume Dean was her father. He seemed so at ease with the twins, as if he knew exactly how to speak to them in order to bring calm to their little world.

He spotted Sunny but didn't stop his movements meant to soothe his tiny companion.

"Sorry, I should have shut the door before I came to pick her up."

Sunny shook her head. "No, I was at the end of the conversation when she started crying. I should check her diaper."

"I checked. She's not wet. I think she just missed being able to see my handsome face."

The comment was so unexpected, especially after how she and he had been keeping their distance since the kiss, that she didn't immediately react. But when she saw his teasing grin, she laughed. Then she directed her attention to her niece.

"Lily, never date a man who is full of himself. Nothing but trouble."

Dean made an exaggerated expression of shock, which alleviated more of the tense feeling Sunny had been walking around with lately. She stepped forward and took Lily from him then pointed at the table.

"Finish your dinner."

Lily continued to border on being fussy, so Sunny held her in her lap as she ate her own food and listened as Dean talked about how the mountain lion that had given everyone a scare on their wedding day had been trapped farther up the valley and relocated to a more remote area to protect not only residents and cattle but the lion itself.

"That's a relief."

"Now if Mother Nature would cooperate. I don't want a drought, but I'd like to not have to swim through my days either."

But as the next few days progressed, the unusual rain seemed to have settled in for a good long stay. Sunny felt bad that her job allowed her to stay dry and warm indoors while Dean got wet on a regular basis despite his inclement-weather gear. Despite trying to keep her focus on taking care of the twins and the various projects she had going, her thoughts strayed to him often. Strayed to the kiss that hadn't been given for the benefit of a crowd they needed to convince of their relationship.

After a long session at her computer communicating with festival committee members, writing her next travel piece for Maya and working on her proposal she planned to present to the company in hopes of earning the promotion, she quickly loaded Lily and Liam in the car and headed to her dad's house. She and Dean had started having family dinner with her dad a couple of times a week, and each time she had to try to ignore how domestic and easy it felt.

"First day it isn't raining, I'm going to grill so much meat I'll be able to feed the county," her dad said as she set about fixing dinner. He stood staring out the window at the gray day outside.

"Sounds good to me."

When Dean arrived and left his wet coat, hat and boots on the front porch, she asked if he wanted to go home to shower and change before eating.

He shook his head. "I'm okay. I'll dry off in a few minutes."

They'd barely taken their seats at the table when there was a knock at the door. When her dad called out for the person to enter, Carlos quickly stepped inside, concern on his face.

"What is it?" Dean asked, already getting to his feet.

"Billy just rode in, said there's a break in the fence and the cattle are filing through."

Sunny knew not only the logistical problems with getting all the cattle back into the pasture so they could fix the fence, but also the danger if the herd got too close to the swollen river. All the rain had the river higher than she'd ever seen it, even during spring runoff, and it was flowing fast.

As Dean headed for the door, she followed.

She didn't even need to tell her dad to take care of the twins.

"You don't have to go," Dean said when he noticed her intention.

"One more set of experienced hands will make this go faster. I might not have done it in a while, but I still know how to herd cattle."

Thankfully her slicker, hat and boots were still in her room, so she prepped quickly. By the time she reached the barn, Dean had both his and her horses ready to go. Even wearing protective gear, the slanting rain made its way down her collar and she shivered as she rode alongside Dean. When they met up with Carlos, AJ and Billy, who had gone ahead with a utility vehicle loaded with fence-mending supplies, she realized that the incessant rain had probably loosened the soil so that some of the poles had toppled when brushed against by cattle.

Though it had been a while since she'd done this type of ranch work, it was still second nature. As AJ prepped the mending materials and Carlos and Dean rode farther out, down toward where the river was out of its banks, she and Billy herded closer to the break in the fence. When they had the cattle where they were supposed to be, they made sure the cattle didn't stray back over.

A yell drew her attention toward the river, where Dean had lassoed a calf that had managed to get too close to the rushing water. She couldn't look away as he struggled against the panicking calf. And then his horse stumbled, dumping Dean into the river.

"Dean!" She spurred her horse, racing toward where he'd disappeared below the churning brown water.

No, no, no! She couldn't lose anyone else. She wouldn't.

His head and an arm appeared above the water, and Carlos headed in that direction. Sunny followed in his tracks. She could barely keep her eyes open against the rain, but she was determined not to lose sight of Dean. Carlos quickly threw out a lasso, but it fell behind Dean and out of his reach.

Sunny spurred harder, hoping her own horse didn't slip and fall. She had to get out ahead of Dean so that the timing of her own lasso would be right. Her heart beat faster than the horse's hooves as she prayed her aim was true. When she let the rope fly, it honestly felt as if it moved in slow motion through the air.

Please, please, please!

At first Dean's reach for the rope failed, but then the water swirled in the right direction and he latched on. Sunny didn't even have time to sigh in relief before she quickly wrapped her end of the rope around the pommel of her saddle and started backing her horse up, not willing to take her eyes off Dean while he was still in danger. Though he was no doubt exhausted, he wrapped the rope tightly around his arm and kicked himself in the direction of the shore as she pulled.

She made the horse take a couple more steps back even after Dean was free of the water, irrationally worried that the rushing river would reach out and pull him back in. When he weakly held up a hand, she leaped to the ground and rushed toward him as Carlos, AJ and Billy joined them.

Dean was coughing up the water he'd swallowed during his brush with death, and she immediately helped him sit up when she dropped to her knees beside him. She didn't ask if he was okay because that was a stupid question. Instead, she placed one hand against his back and wrapped the other around his upper arm. It felt like a decade passed before he finally stopped coughing.

Sunny fought tears even though they'd probably be indistinguishable from the rain rolling down her cheeks since she'd managed to lose her hat somewhere.

"Are you injured anywhere?" Carlos asked while Sunny wondered if the fear she'd just experienced had eradicated her ability to speak.

Dean shook his head, but his fatigue was obvious.

"How's the horse?"

"Fine, calf too. Spooked but no injuries."

"Stop worrying about the horse," Sunny said, but her words were so quiet they were swallowed by the weather.

Dean started to push to his feet. "We need to get these cattle rounded up and the fence mended."

"We'll handle that," Billy said.

Again, Dean shook his head. "Faster with all of us working."

"Are you an idiot?" This time her words were heard loud and clear by everyone. All four men looked at her, but her focus remained on Dean, who coughed again. "You almost died just now and you want to go back to rounding up cows as if nothing more happened than a sneeze?"

Dean looked confused, as if he couldn't understand why she was so angry.

"You're going home, taking a hot shower, eating some hot soup and going to bed with every quilt in the house piled on top of you."

"I'll do all that once the work is done."

She tried to get him to listen to reason but finally gave up, deciding that helping get the work done would get him home, dry and warm faster. By the time all the cattle were accounted for, the fence repaired and they'd ridden back to the barn, Dean was coughing and sneezing. Sunny would bet every penny she had he was shivering too.

"You get him home," Carlos said when they reached the barn. "We'll take care of the horses and let your dad know what's going on."

She looked toward her dad's house, hoping he was coping with the twins okay.

"Don't worry. The kiddos will be fine. I'll help him out if he needs it."

"Thank you."

It was a testament to how bad Dean was feeling that he didn't argue to take care of his own horse, instead letting her drive him home and get him into the house. All potential embarrassment fled as she escorted him straight to the bathroom after he discarded his slicker and toed off his sodden boots outside the front door.

"I can manage," he said in a not very convincing tone.

"Hush." She pushed his hands out of the way and proceeded to unbutton his shirt. Her heart rate kicked up again when his bare chest was right in front of her. She'd of course seen it when they were younger and they'd swum in the river, but it was the chest of a full-grown man now and nicely made. The chest of her lawfully wedded husband.

She shook her head.

"What's wrong?" Dean asked, his voice tired but also holding a hint of teasing.

"You scared me nearly all the way to death." She said those words to distract herself and him from any physical attraction on her part, but they were also painfully true.

Dean placed his hands on her shoulders.

"I'm fine." But then he coughed, and she didn't like how deep in his chest it was.

"Yeah, that doesn't sound fine." She spun out of his grasp and turned on the hot water in the shower. Before she could face him again, he hugged her from behind. Sunny froze and not because of how chilled his skin felt.

"Thank you for saving me," he said close

to her ear, then pulled away and pushed her out of the bathroom. "I'll manage the rest myself."

She turned around in time to see the door close in her face, which was probably for the best since the only thing he'd still been wearing that wouldn't have been really embarrassing to remove were his socks.

A knock at the front door startled her from her thoughts.

Please don't let something else have happened.

When she opened it, Maya stood there with two plates covered in aluminum foil.

"Your dad told me to bring you these," Maya said. "He called me when you rode out, and Carlos just told us what happened. Is Dean okay?"

"He's taking a hot shower. After he gets some food in him, I'm sending him to bed. He's already coughing and sneezing, so I don't want it to get worse."

Maya gave her a look that Sunny was too tired to identify. Instead, she accepted the plates and stepped back so Maya could come in out of the damp air. But Maya shook her head.

"I'm just making the delivery. I'm going to

go back and help your dad with the babies. I doubt Dean wants company right now anyway."

"Thank you."

"You know you don't have to thank me for stuff like this. I love every opportunity I get to give your dad a hard time."

Sunny smiled, knowing that both her dad and Maya loved their routine of good-natured teasing.

After Maya left, Sunny realized that Dean didn't have any clean clothes in the bathroom. She deposited the food on the table then hurried into his bedroom to pull out something comfortable to sleep in. Right as she reached the bathroom door, the water shut off. She knocked lightly.

"I'm going to open the door to leave some clothes for you."

"Okay." Even that single word sounded as if it took a lot of effort.

She opened the door only wide enough to slip the clothes through and place them on the vanity. Her gaze lifted to the mirror, but thankfully it was fogged over.

If Dean didn't need to eat, she would have sent him directly to bed as soon as he walked into the kitchen. Instead, she pulled out his chair then went to grab one of the quilts off the couch. She wrapped it around his shoulders but left his arms free so he could feed himself.

She didn't initiate conversation, partly because he didn't need to expend the energy but mainly because she didn't think she could talk about what happened without crying. To be honest, she felt very close to the edge simply sitting across from him.

"I'm okay," he said, unprompted, repeating what he'd said in the bathroom as if she either hadn't heard him or hadn't believed him the first time.

Against all her efforts, two tears broke free and rolled down her cheeks.

"I can't survive losing anyone else," she said, not looking up at him and trying not to think about how much he'd come to mean to her, more than he had even during their long friendship.

"You didn't. I'm right here." He reached across the table and placed his hand atop hers. When she tried to pull away, he didn't let her. "Look at me."

She hesitated, not quite sure why since she'd already lost the battle with her tears.

When she finally met his gaze, he squeezed her hand.

"You're not going to lose me."

That's where he was wrong. Whether she convinced her dad to come to California with her or not, she was eventually going back. Sooner rather than later because of the promotion presentation. And when she went, Dean wouldn't be with her. It would be the beginning of the end for them.

CHAPTER SIXTEEN

DESPITE REASSURING SUNNY that he was fine, words she needed to hear, Dean felt like death. He'd come closer to actual death in that flooded river than he ever had in his life, and he had zero energy left. It was all he could do to lift his fork to his mouth to fill his empty stomach. He couldn't even clean his plate though.

"Come on, you're going to bed," Sunny said, rounding the table and putting her arm around his back as he stood. When he tried to head toward the couch, she steered him instead toward his room. "You are sleeping in your own bed tonight. You need room and comfort and every quilt and blanket I can pile on top of you."

He offered her a weak smile. "Just try not to smother me. I don't want to expire that way after surviving a flood."

"If you didn't feel so sick I would punch

you right now," she said without any real heat in her voice.

He'd given her a powerful scare, so he allowed her to fuss over him. To be honest, it was nice having her obviously care so much about his well-being. But that was the only thing that felt good now. His body ached, his head throbbed, his throat was raw and his chest felt tight. Not to mention he managed to feel both hot and cold at the same time.

As Sunny tucked him under half a dozen covers, he was happy to have them because the shivers were beginning to take hold of him and he didn't want her to see. Didn't want her to worry when he'd done his best to reassure her that he was fine.

When she placed a glass of water on the nightstand, he managed to dredge up a tired smile.

"If this whole business-consulting thing doesn't work out, I think you could have a future in caretaking."

"I only do this for people related to me."

While he might technically fit that description now, someday he wouldn't and he'd be on his own. Sunny would still be taking care of family members, but he would no longer be one of them.

"I'll leave the door partially open in case you need something."

His eyelids already heavy, all he could offer in response was a single nod. At least sleep would release him from thoughts about how at some point he was going to lose the woman he loved and how he wished he was selfish enough to tell her the truth and ask her not to go.

SUNNY JERKED AWAKE on the couch. Thankfully this time she wasn't holding her computer. She'd given up trying to concentrate on any of her work and curled up under the one quilt she'd left for herself. Had a dream woken her? She listened but heard nothing other than the gentle hum of the refrigerator. Even the rain seemed to have stopped or was only falling so lightly that it couldn't be heard inside.

Since she was awake, she decided to check on Dean. She hadn't liked how he looked as he'd been falling asleep, and she feared him developing pneumonia or some sort of infection after his near drowning.

A chill ran down her spine and she sat up rubbing her arms. She had to stop thinking about what might have happened because it hadn't. Dean might be sick now, but he was alive. That was the most important thing. If she'd lost him…she would have become convinced this ranch was cursed and would have stopped at nothing to get her dad and the twins away from this land before it claimed someone else she loved.

That thought startled her. Did she love Dean? Well, of course she did. She loved Maya too. No matter how much she traveled and how many people she met, Dean and Maya were still her two best friends in the world. She hadn't really thought of Dean that way until she'd come back this time, until they'd spent more time together and he'd agreed to help her with a plan that anyone else would have walked away from in a heartbeat.

She eased into the bedroom and noticed that Dean had tossed off at least half the coverings she'd layered atop him. Maybe she had gone a bit overboard, it not being the dead of winter and all. But when she moved closer, Dean groaned in his sleep and her instincts immediately told her something was wrong. She felt the heat radiating off him before she even touched his forehead.

Her heart shuddered. He was burning up with fever.

She rushed to the kitchen and filled a metal mixing bowl with cool water then grabbed a couple of clean washcloths from the bathroom. After placing one wet cloth on his forehead, she pulled down the covers with the aim of using the other washcloth to cool his arms and hands. She startled when she saw he'd pulled off the T-shirt he'd been wearing and was bare chested.

Stop staring and take care of him.

Dean woke as she was wiping down the feverish flesh on his chest.

"What are you doing?"

He sounded hoarse, so she helped him lift himself enough to take a couple of fever reducers and wash them down with plenty of water.

"Go back to sleep." Without thinking, she reached up and smoothed the furrows that had appeared on his forehead before she replaced the freshly cooled washcloth.

He did exactly that within moments. Throughout the night, she kept up her vigil. It was a balance between helping him through the fever and not letting him become chilled. As the time crept closer to dawn, fatigue started weighing heavy on her eyelids. But she wasn't willing to leave Dean alone. She harbored what she knew was an irrational fear that if she left him for more than a few moments, he'd take a turn for the worse.

Sunny eyed the empty half of the queen-size bed. Maybe she'd stretch out and catch a few winks. It was nothing romantic, simply her being there in case he needed her. But if she kept sitting in the chair she'd brought in from the kitchen, she was in danger of falling over into the floor. The last thing she needed to do was knock herself out on the nightstand.

Still, as she lay down beside Dean, lying on her side to face him, it felt like a step she'd never thought to take. Okay, that wasn't entirely true. After that second kiss they'd shared, she'd imagined it more than once. But despite being married, that kind of intimacy was not part of their deal.

The deal. It felt as if they'd made that stupid deal a lifetime ago. Did she really think it would work? Not to mention the longer she was back in Wyoming, back on this ranch, the more difficult it was to imagine her dad in California. Would things really be okay once her dad's leg healed and she'd gone back to hopefully her new position at the company? She could plan to visit more often, even if the visits were shorter. Her dad could hire another caretaker for the twins while he worked. Dean obviously liked Lily and Liam, so he'd keep an eye out for them too.

Still, she couldn't dispel the knot in her stomach at the idea of being separated from her family again. From Dean.

No, she couldn't have those kinds of thoughts. Or could she?

No. The kiss hadn't meant anything. It would be incredibly stupid to let their relationship progress further knowing that she'd be leaving soon. It wouldn't be fair—to either of them. She closed her eyes, wanting to escape her confusing thoughts in the blissful oblivion of sleep.

DEAN WOKE SLOWLY, his body still achy but no longer feverish. He'd realized before falling asleep the night before that he had a fever, and he had vague memories of waking a couple of times feeling like his skin was on fire. But Sunny had been there, taking care of him. How long had she stayed at his side?

Movement next to him gave him the surprising answer. Not only was Sunny still next to him, she was actually in the bed with him, though she lay atop the covers. The way she was curled up, however, told him that her body had cooled in the night. He covered her with the comforter that wasn't trapped beneath her.

He watched as she instinctually snuggled into the warmth. He eased onto his side facing her. Even asleep with mussed hair and dark circles under her eyes she was beautiful. He resisted the need to wake her, tell her what she meant to him and ask her to stay, to make their marriage real. Despite her care for him the night before, his confession would likely send her running.

But as he thought about how each day brought her closer to leaving, he couldn't help but wonder if he should take a chance. What was the worst that could happen? She'd leave, which she planned to do anyway. He'd lose his job and any opportunity to own the ranch? It wasn't as if he hadn't thought about what he'd do if those things happened. Starting over from scratch wasn't high on his list of wants, but he'd been moving closer and closer to the conclusion that seeing if there was a real chance with Sunny would be worth it.

As if she could sense that he was thinking about her, Sunny's eyelids fluttered open. She blinked a few times before her eyes widened and she placed her hand against his forehead.

"Your fever's gone." She looked so relieved that he fell more in love with her, something he didn't think was possible.

When she lifted her hand from his forehead, he grabbed it to keep her from leaving. Her gaze met his and she didn't avert her eyes.

Expecting her to realize what was happening and make a speedy exit from the room at any moment, Dean released her hand and lifted his own to Sunny's cheek. He let his fingers slide through her hair to the nape of her neck. As he ran his thumb softly along the edge of her jaw, she perhaps unconsciously leaned her head back against his hand. It felt like an invitation and he took it.

This wasn't going to be a light feather of a kiss like the one they'd shared that night in his living room. No, this time he kissed her deeply, with all the feeling he'd held in check for years.

SOMEWHERE AT THE back of her mind, a little voice was trying to remind Sunny that she shouldn't be kissing Dean like this, that she should pull away instead of letting him wrap his arm around her back and pull her closer.

But that voice was an increasingly faint echo at the far end of a canyon.

She'd been so worried about him, afraid that despite her having saved him from the raging river, the cruel hands of death would still claim him. To have him emerge on the other side of the fever with more strength than he'd had the night before felt like a miraculous gift, and she couldn't hold back how relieved and happy she was to receive it.

Neither of them spoke. If they had, she probably would have come to her senses and pulled away. Instead, she let herself enjoy the feel of kissing her husband.

When she started to worry that things would go too far, past the point of no return, and that she would let them, Dean seemed to sense her concern. Instead of pressing for more, he lifted his mouth from hers, tucked her against him and dropped a soft kiss on her forehead. Without words, he was telling her to rest, that she was safe from going further than she was comfortable.

She thought she'd be too excited, too nervous, too…everything to sleep, but the accumulation of worry and late-night hours spent trying to reduce Dean's fever joined forces with the normal warmth of his body to lull her toward the rest she needed.

Her last thought before succumbing was that she'd never felt more comfortable, more right in her life.

DEAN RESISTED THE urge to whistle while he cooked breakfast. Though he ached from his unfortunate fight with the river the day before and fatigue still tugged at him, he simultaneously felt fantastic. He'd imagined sleeping with Sunny in his arms but had never thought it would really happen. He'd swear he could still feel her lips on his as she'd kissed him back with every bit of passion he'd felt. He'd barely stopped himself from going further, but he suspected that he should take things with Sunny in careful steps. But the fact that she was obviously attracted to him, had stayed beside him even after his fever had broken instead of running to the relative safety of the couch, gave him hope.

As he waited for the biscuits to bake awhile before starting on eggs and bacon, he started moving Sunny's work materials that were scattered across the kitchen table. She'd obviously put in some time at her computer and sketching out notes on one of her projects after he'd gone to bed but before she'd discovered he had a fever.

Her pretty handwriting in an open notebook caught his attention, and he found himself skimming the words she'd written. As he moved through one bullet point after another, however, his happy mood started to evaporate.

It wasn't more ideas for the ranch or directions for the festival or even things for Trudy to add to her themed dinners. Staring up at him was the end of his marriage.

Suddenly realizing he was snooping where he didn't belong, he closed the notebook and moved it along with everything else to the coffee table. He hurried through the rest of the breakfast preparations, made himself an egg-and-cheese biscuit. Then he left the house before he had to face Sunny and the knowledge that no matter how nice things had been between them early that morning, she was still going to leave. She was always going to leave.

SUNNY STRETCHED LIKE a cat in the sun streaming through the window. It took a few ticks of her internal clock to remember where she was, which then caused her to freeze for a moment before turning her head to her right. But Dean was no longer beside her, and she wasn't sure if she was thankful or sad. Maybe a confusing mixture of both.

She lifted her hand to her lips, remembering what it had felt like to really give in to the attraction she now fully admitted was there. And who could blame her? Dean was a very handsome man, a grown-up version of the cute kid and good-looking teenager she'd always known.

How was last night going to change things between them? Would it? It certainly shook the foundation of the plan they'd agreed to.

Knowing she couldn't avoid him or the conversation they obviously needed to have, she got up and left the bedroom. She expected him to be in the bathroom or perhaps drinking a cup of coffee, but she quickly realized she was the only one in the house. She discovered her computer and various work detritus had been removed from the kitchen table. In its place was a note.

I let you sleep in, but I made breakfast. Enjoy your day.

She stared at the note, which had none of the warmth he'd shared with her earlier despite the kindness of the words and his making breakfast for her.

A glance out the window revealed his truck was gone. Had he gone back to work less than twenty-four hours after nearly drowning?

As she turned back to face the kitchen, she wondered if it was possible their kissing had been no more than an incredibly vivid dream. No, it had been real. But he hadn't stuck around. Either he didn't think they had anything to talk about or he'd assumed she'd be upset when she woke. Maybe that's why he'd made breakfast, as an apology for going too far.

She wasn't prepared for the rush of anger that surged up within her, nor did she understand it. And it didn't wane as she ate breakfast, showered, dressed and got to work. When Maya showed up at her door with the twins midafternoon, the anger had only simmered down to annoyance. But she pushed it away and smiled at her niece and nephew, hugging and kissing them as if she hadn't seen them in months.

"I saw Dean out working this morning," Maya said when they sat across from each other at the kitchen table a few minutes later, each with a fresh cup of coffee. "That man does not know how to take a break, does he?"

"Evidently not."

"Is that annoyance I hear?"

Sometimes it didn't pay to have a best friend who could peg you so perfectly.

"Of course I'm annoyed. I save the fool from drowning, make sure he doesn't die of a fever in the aftermath, and what does he do? Just up and goes back to work the next morning as if nothing at all out of the ordinary happened."

"At least the sun has made a reappearance."

"Well, I guess that's something."

When Maya laughed, Sunny looked up from her coffee, confused. "I fail to see the humor in this situation."

"Of course not. You're too busy being mad at the man you love."

Sunny stared at Maya as if she'd lost her mind. "What in the name of heaven are you talking about?"

You know what she's saying. You just don't want to admit it, not even to yourself.

Shut up!

Maya leaned forward and pointed straight at Sunny. "You, my dear friend, are totally in love with your husband."

"Maya Pine, if I had pulled you from the river yesterday and nursed you through the night only to have you—" she made a fluttering motion with her hand toward the front door "—not even take a day to recover, I'd be ticked at you too."

Maya propped her chin in her upturned palm. "So you nursed him all night, huh?"

Sunny rolled her eyes, sat back and took a big gulp of her coffee while she tried not to think about how she was even wondering if Maya's accusation could be true.

"What was I supposed to do? Let him fend for himself while he burned up with fever?"

"Why are you resisting the truth so much?"

"Because it's not true." It couldn't be. "We're just friends."

That felt like a lie because it was. One did not kiss their "just a friend" like she'd kissed Dean only a few hours ago. She had the craziest thought that Maya might be able to tell Sunny's lips had been kissed well and recently, so she brought the cup to her mouth again and drained it.

"I think you're fighting the truth because you're afraid to admit it. You're afraid of caring about anyone else, afraid of losing them."

"Wouldn't you be in my position?"

"Yes, I would," Maya said with surprising honesty. "But I also wouldn't refuse to grab happiness wherever I could because you, of all people, know that life can be short. And what's the use of living life avoiding being happy?"

"I'm not. That's why I'm in this crazy position." She gestured at the home in which they sat, Dean's home. "I'll be happy when Dad and the twins are with me in California, and I have a new position that gives me greater freedom to do what I want."

Maya's brows moved slightly toward each other, picking up on the new piece of information.

"I'm up for a promotion that will let me choose my clients. I fly to LA on Thursday to give the presentation to the panel making the decision about who to promote."

Maya stared at her for a long moment before she lowered her gaze to her cup, which she fiddled with while seeming to try to figure out how to respond.

"I think you're going to regret it if you get what you think you want."

Sunny couldn't believe what she was hearing. While Maya missed her, she'd always been supportive of Sunny's ambitions.

"I can't believe you said that."

"I mean, I wish you all the happiness in the world. You know that. But I think you're letting stubbornness, fear and blind allegiance to goals prevent you from seeing what's right in front of you."

Sunny didn't know what to say. Like she literally didn't know because her feelings were a jumbled-up mess and she didn't even know where to start untangling them. She was saved from having to respond by Maya's phone ringing.

After Maya answered and engaged in a short conversation, she ended the call and stood.

"I have to go." When she reached the door, however, she turned back to look at Sunny, who hadn't moved from her chair. "Only you can make decisions about your life, but really think about what I said. Your mom, your brother, Amanda—none of them would want you to use their deaths as an excuse to not allow yourself to love someone."

Long after Maya drove away, Sunny sat at the table not knowing how to feel. Confused? Hopeful? Excited? Scared out of her mind? All of the above?

After what felt like hours, she shook her

head. She couldn't let other people project their ideas onto her. She was the type of person who made plans and stuck with them. Dean and she had made a deal, and she wasn't going to back out of it.

But what if he wanted to?

"No," she said out loud.

She could literally explain away each one of the kisses she and Dean had shared. Kiss one, performing for an audience that needed to believe their marriage was real. Kiss two, caught up in a soft, late-night moment. Kiss three? Wait, how many kisses had they shared that morning anyway?

She lifted her fingertips to her lips, remembering the press of Dean's. The memory of how it had felt to be pulled close to him by his powerful arms, how safe and comfortable it had been sleeping next to him, made her blush.

Going back to LA for the presentation was a good thing. While the situation with her family and the ranch was still unresolved, she needed the time away from Dean and their continued forced proximity to clear her head and remember who she was, what her goals were, what kind of life she led.

She needed to remember that Dean Wheeler was her friend and nothing more.

CHAPTER SEVENTEEN

SUNNY HADN'T BEEN this nervous at work in a long time. During the years she'd worked at PTG Consulting, she'd grown more and more confident in her ideas, her approaches to projects, her presentations to clients. But this was different. If she nailed this presentation and was given the promotion, she could go back to Wyoming knowing she was in an even better position to care for her dad and the twins. Surely her dad would see how much having them all together meant to her and agree to the change.

But you are already all together, and you have Dean too.

She shook her head. No, she couldn't think about Dean or what it had felt like to be kissed by him, held in his arms, right before she had to walk into the conference room and give the presentation of her life.

She also couldn't think about how distant

Dean had seemed before she'd left while obviously trying not to appear that way.

With a deep breath, Sunny put all her effort into shoving confusing thoughts of her... of Dean away and going over her notes one more time. She focused on how excited she was about the idea that had sprung to life as she'd sat listening to it rain a thousand miles away from LA, one that Trudy had unknowingly planted.

The door to the conference room opened and one of her competitors, Jalene Lerman from the Miami office, walked out. Jalene offered Sunny one of those smiles that said, *Good luck but not too much good luck.* She was spared any awkward, insincere chitchat when Mike motioned her into the conference room.

After a round of reintroductions to the vaguely familiar faces seated at the table along with those she knew far better, Sunny launched into her presentation. Excitement filled her as she proposed that she head up the new division by creating a network of smaller satellite offices that would tackle working with businesses with growth potential but without the big budgets PTG's clients normally had.

"These strategically placed satellite offices could operate with only one to two people in certain situations, only a handful in others. Many could be home based, thereby not acquiring larger expenses such as office space, utilities and all the typical affiliated costs. But there are a lot of great small businesses across America that could grow into even larger businesses, creating more jobs in areas that need them, if only they were able to access some top-tier consulting such as what PTG provides."

Sunny had to pace herself because when she became this excited about possibilities, she had a tendency to talk fast. Working with Trudy on ideas for her café, brainstorming and launching ideas for the reimagined festival and all the other bits of advice she'd given to the residents of Jade Valley had shown her that her proposal was a good one. And it would make her stand out among what she suspected would be the usual types of ideas presented by her competitors.

So when she clicked off the screen at the front of the room and turned to look at her audience, she was surprised to not see equal excitement. Instead, the faces that were not looking at her seemed to reflect disappointment and a profound lack of interest.

Still, she kept on the bright expression for which she was known and asked, "Does anyone have any questions?"

"Is this a joke?"

Sunny actually startled at the question from Penelope Fields, the manager of the New York office, a woman who always looked as if she'd just stepped out of the most expensive salon in Manhattan. Even though Sunny had encountered Penelope's cool demeanor before, the tone of her question felt like the crack of a whip.

"Pardon?"

Penelope gestured toward the blank screen behind Sunny.

"You're one of the company's top consultants, so imagine my shock when that was the best you could come up with."

"I think what Penelope means," Mike said, looking uncomfortable, "is that this was really unexpected, and not at all what the company is striving toward with this new division."

"I thought you wanted innovative thinking." Sunny heard the hint of snappishness in her voice but couldn't seem to prevent it.

"We are, but you're very familiar with the type of clients PTG handles."

"Which is why I purposefully crafted a proposal that would go beyond what the company already has covered." It was truly out-of-the-box thinking, though she hated that overused phrase.

Bill Edmonds, head of PTG's overseas operations, leaned forward.

"While the thought and effort that have gone into your proposal are admirable, I believe the concern is that expanding in such a way would dilute the company's image."

At least he had the decency to be kind as well as honest.

Though Sunny had a wealth of experience in getting resistant people to come around to her way of thinking, she went silent. It actually hurt that the people facing her were not as excited about her proposal as she was, which of course was silly. They were looking for someone to make the company even more money, boatloads of it. She felt beyond stupid for never realizing before that she might very well be the only PTG employee who actually cared about her clients and their businesses, not only the money they brought into PTG's coffers.

Instead of further arguing her position, which she knew without a single doubt would be futile, she simply gathered her materials, thanked the assembled management for their time and strode out of the room without sparing them another glance.

She stopped by her desk only long enough to grab her purse, not making eye contact with any of her coworkers, before heading out to an early lunch alone. Though after she picked up a California roll, she sat on a park bench not eating it. Instead, she watched a couple of little kids squealing with delight as they played with their puppy. She'd been back in California for less than a day and she already missed Liam and Lily. Her dad. Maya and Trudy.

She sighed.

And Dean.

Maya's words echoed in her head. Then the memory of Dean's lips capturing hers, the way he'd gently, tentatively deepened their kisses. How she'd responded without thinking and how right it had felt.

That rightness had been what scared her, even though she hadn't fully acknowledged it. She'd left Jade Valley, the ranch and Dean behind, made a good life for herself. Did she really want to give up everything she'd worked for only to go back to the place she'd left almost as soon as she'd been handed her high school diploma?

Yes.

The answer was as clear as the water in Lake Tahoe.

As she sat with the Southern California warmth soaking into her despite sitting in the shade, she also had to acknowledge another truth. Maya had been right. Somewhere in among all the faking of their relationship, she'd fallen for Dean for real. Even knowing that it was true, she still couldn't quite wrap her mind around it. She'd known him forever, had never thought of him in a romantic way before.

But she did now. She caught herself smiling and her heart rate kicking up when she thought about him, as she looked down at the copper ring he'd chosen for her and placed on her left hand when he proposed.

What if loving him made her too vulnerable? What if she lost him? She almost had even before admitting the truth of her feelings to herself.

But she hadn't lost him.

The question was how did he feel about

her? Did he care as deeply as she did? Had their past as friends and their agreement stood in his way of admitting it too? Or was he just a guy who'd stolen a few kisses?

She had to find out, but she wasn't about to do it on the phone.

When she returned to the office, she found Mike had left her instructions to plan for a trip to London. As she stared at the message, she couldn't muster the excitement she normally did for a trip. It wasn't that she didn't love London. It was rich with history, and she always made sure to visit some interesting new historic site or museum each time she went there on business. But no place was calling to her at the moment in the same way as Jade Valley.

Sunny lifted her gaze from her computer and scanned her surroundings, then made her decision. Even though it was the right one, her hands shook as she began to type.

AFTER CARLOS AND Billy went home for the night, Dean headed to the barn to clean his horse's tack. He draped his saddlecloth over the door to an empty stall, planning to take it home to wash it, before he set to work cleaning the saddle, girth and finally the bridle.

He took his time despite being tired because walking into his empty house didn't hold the appeal it once had.

Before he'd shared it with Sunny.

He shook his head. He'd known what he was getting into when he'd agreed to Sunny's crazy plan, but he'd walked right into additional heartache and frustration with himself anyway. He had no one to blame but himself. He'd instigated all their kisses, so it was no surprise that he'd finally sent Sunny running back to California.

He supposed he should prepare to start divorce proceedings soon. And then to figure out what he was going to do next because there was no way he could stay on this ranch even if Jonathon didn't fire him. He couldn't even sleep worth a dime in his bed or on his couch because memories of kissing the woman he loved were attached to both.

Damn, he was a fool and a half.

He was running water over the bit to clean it of saliva and pieces of hay when Jonathon surprised him by coming into the barn on his crutches.

"Hey, is something wrong?" He glanced beyond his boss toward the house. "Need help with the twins?"

Jonathon shook his head. "No, they're asleep. Not that they didn't protest that loudly."

Dean shook the water off the bit then wiped it down before setting it aside to air-dry.

"Have you heard from Sunny?"

Dean's moment of hoping Sunny didn't come up in conversation obviously didn't help. He shook his head.

"I'm sure she's busy since she hasn't been in the office in a while."

"I can't believe she went."

Dean glanced over at Jonathon. "It's a big opportunity for her."

"What if she gets it?"

"I'm sure she will. She has more creativity and talent in her pinkie than I have in my whole body."

"And you'd let her go?"

Dean realized he had to tread carefully until he discussed their next steps with Sunny. He plastered on a smile and gave a little laugh that had no true amusement behind it.

"Has anyone ever been able to stop Sunny from doing something once she put her mind to it?"

Jonathon sighed as he leaned back against the feed storage box.

"You're every bit as stubborn as she is."

"Me? What did I do?"

Jonathon settled his gaze on Dean. "When are you going to tell her you love her?"

Remember your role.

"Don't you think I've done that already since we're married?"

"You mean that fake marriage she cooked up to try to get me to move to California?"

Dean was certain that shock showed on his face, but he couldn't help it. And he couldn't lie anymore.

"How long have you known?"

"About your current relationship or how long you've been in love with my daughter?"

Dean stared at Jonathon until the older man laughed a little.

"I've known how you feel about Sunny since you were in high school, and about the dating and marriage since the beginning."

Dean gripped the top of the stall he was standing next to.

"Why didn't you say anything, about any of it?"

"Honestly? I was selfish and wanted my baby girl to come home for good, but I promised her mother I'd never stand in her way of doing what she wanted with her life."

"Wait, that doesn't make sense if you knew

she was doing this to get you to sell the ranch and move to California."

"Sure it does because I thought you'd finally tell her how you feel."

"How would that change anything?"

"Because I thought given enough time and living together, she'd fall for you too and realize that this is where she wants to be, with her family. With you."

"Well, that's where you're wrong." He motioned toward the open barn doors in the general direction of California.

"Are you sure about that?"

"The fact that she's in LA right now seems to support my statement."

"But would she be there if she knew how you feel?"

Dean turned to fully face his temporary father-in-law.

"This is unlike you, talking about feelings and stuff."

Jonathon nodded once.

"You're right about that, but I've learned the hard way that you have to say things when you have the chance. When someone is gone and you can't tell them how you feel anymore, it makes you realize how stupid it is to be embarrassed to tell someone you love them."

The idea of losing Sunny in the same way Jonathon had lost his wife hit Dean in the gut like a boulder the size of Grand Teton. Was it possible Sunny could really come to care about him the way he did her? Love him? Or would confessing to her only make her feel guilty and awkward around him? Would it lead to her making sure they never crossed paths again?

"It's because I care about her that I don't want to stand in her way. She's made her choice, and that's okay." Despite the kisses they'd shared. "She lights up when she talks about all the places she's been around the world. I'm happy she gets to experience that."

"Being a martyr isn't as admirable as you might think."

"I'm not trying to be a martyr. Sunny has lost enough in her life. She deserves all the happiness and success she sets out to achieve for herself."

"So that's it? You're just going to what, divorce? Go on with your life alone while she does the same?"

"That's what we agreed upon, and I'm a man of my word."

"Well, I'm more convinced than ever you're

perfect for each other, both as stubborn as can be."

Dean grinned. "Pot, meet kettle."

Jonathon fixed him with a stare then sighed. "Fair. That being said, really think about if you're willing to take this route. I don't think it's a right decision, for either of you."

Dean didn't respond because they weren't going to agree on this. And he didn't apologize for the lie he had told along with Sunny because Jonathon had gone along with it despite knowing the truth. He'd wanted the situation to yield desired results, the same as Sunny and Dean had. He almost said that maybe Jonathon should take his own advice by being honest with Sunny, but that would put the same kind of pressure on her that Dean being honest about loving her would.

Jonathon must have figured that he wasn't going to make any inroads with Dean, so he pulled himself up to stand on his crutches.

"Best get back and make sure the kiddos are still sleeping."

"Call me if you need anything."

And just like that, they were back to employer and employee as if the conversation about love and loss hadn't happened.

After making sure Jonathon got back into the house safely without his boss knowing he was being watched, Dean finished cleaning and putting away the tack. Then he grabbed the saddle blanket in need of laundering and made his way to his truck to head for home.

But when he stepped into the home where he'd lived his entire life, it felt profoundly wrong and empty. Though Sunny's time living with him had been relatively short, he'd become accustomed to seeing her at the end of each day. Now he wouldn't be surprised that if he said something it would echo endlessly within the walls, continually slapping him with the reality of his loneliness.

Was he ever going to be able to step into his home again without thinking of her? The only room she hadn't been in was his old bedroom, which was little more than storage now. It didn't even have a bed he could use to escape the memories.

Needing to get away from everything that reminded him of Sunny and how he wasn't willing to be selfish when it came to her, he turned and walked right back out the front door. With no destination in mind, he got into his truck and took off. Maybe if he drove long and far enough, he could finally break free of the love he held for a woman he couldn't have.

CHAPTER EIGHTEEN

SUNNY'S NERVOUSNESS THAT had accompanied her on her flight back to Wyoming didn't wane any as she drove from Casper toward Jade Valley. In fact, it was increasing to the point where she felt as if she was vibrating. She'd always had a plan before she did anything, so winging it based on nothing more than the hope that Dean wouldn't be averse to making their relationship real felt more foreign than any country she'd visited.

What if he didn't feel the same despite the kisses? What if they'd been nothing more than the hormones of a man who lived alone suddenly having a woman under the same roof with him?

She shook her head. That didn't feel like the Dean she knew at all. And yet, how could she know what was real when their entire marriage started as a lie? He'd done it because he wanted to take the ranch to the next level and to help out a friend. But was there any possibility it was more than that?

Did the answer to that question lie in those last kisses they'd shared? She had to believe those came from genuine feelings.

The inky blackness of the Wyoming night stretched out in all directions outside the illumination of her rental car's headlights. She could have stayed at her apartment and flown out in the morning, or gotten a room in Casper and driven to Jade Valley in the daylight, but she wasn't going to be able to sleep until she had some answers. She hadn't given Dean a heads-up that she was returning tonight, and she knew if he was asleep she was going to have to wake him up.

But when she arrived at Dean's house, she found it empty. Surely he wasn't working this late, but who knew with Dean? The man had gone back to work the day after almost drowning. Maybe he'd gone to visit his parents.

She drew the line at hauling him out of his parents' house to have an honest conversation about their relationship. She'd waited all the way from LA, so she could wait awhile longer.

But as the minutes ticked by and she alternated between pacing, fixing then trying to eat a sandwich and flipping channels, only to start pacing again, she thought she might go crazy with the waiting. It was as if once she finally admitted the truth to herself, a burning need to see Dean had burst to life inside her. See him, hope he felt the same and kiss him again—this time with all the feelings she'd been confused about or outright denying before.

She stared at the front door as if doing so might make Dean materialize.

Where was he?

All her travel and lack of sleep finally caught up to her, and even her nervousness couldn't fight fatigue off any longer. She stretched out on the couch and let her eyes drift closed. What felt like only a few moments later, the sound of a truck engine outside jolted her awake. She sat up and rubbed her face, then smacked her cheeks to wake up more fully. The next few minutes were important, perhaps the most important of her life, and she had to be fully alert.

Unable to sit still, she stood and barely resisted the urge to jerk open the front door and run out to meet Dean. Only remembering that she wasn't sure how he felt about her kept her from doing so. The moments stretched until she wondered if Dean had fallen asleep out there. Or was he avoiding her?

When she finally heard his truck door shut, she took a deep breath to try to get her nerves under control. Her husband was going to step through that doorway in a few seconds, and she still didn't know how she was going to start the conversation. She only knew that she wanted him to be her husband for real, to stay together, and hoped he'd at least be open to the idea of giving it a try.

It was quite possible she looked like either a fool or an eager puppy when Dean finally entered the house because he appeared startled to see her despite her rental car sitting outside in plain view.

"You're back late," she said.

"I thought you were still in LA."

Her stomach tightened because she was not imagining the new distance in his eyes, in his expression and posture. Even more than had been there before she'd flown to California.

"Is something wrong?"

He shook his head. "No. Why?"

"I don't know. You seem different."

"Just tired. You probably are too. We should go to sleep."

As he took a step, presumably toward the bathroom, she took a couple of her own.

"Wait. I...I was hoping we could talk."

He was quiet as he visibly inhaled then exhaled a deep breath.

"I guess we should."

Sunny couldn't help the flicker of worry when Dean didn't move to sit, instead leaning against the back of the living room chair and crossing his arms.

"So, how do you want to handle things? I suppose we don't actually have to be in the same state to do all the paperwork. And you don't have to worry about me. I've decided to withdraw my interest in the ranch, get my own place. Start small and build up gradually. That makes more sense anyway." He looked as if he wanted to say something else but stopped himself.

That tightness in Sunny's stomach moved to her chest. Had she been wrong about what she'd thought she'd seen in his eyes each time he kissed her?

No. In that moment, as she stared at the way he was holding himself, at the invisible wall he appeared to have erected, she became certain she wasn't the only one with deeper feelings.

"Is that really what you want?"

A momentary flicker of confusion on his face was quickly replaced by a head nod.

"Yeah. I've thought about it a lot, and this ranch is too big. With only me at the beginning, it makes more sense to start small and only expand if the initial venture does well. If not, then I'll just run a small herd of cattle since I know how to do that."

He was trying so hard to convince her, but it wasn't working.

"I don't believe you."

"What?" This time he couldn't hide his surprise.

"I don't think that's what you want at all."

Please, please let me be right about this and not about to make a complete and utter fool of myself.

He sighed. "The charade isn't going to work. Your dad told me today that he's known from the beginning that we were faking the relationship."

"What!"

"I know. I was surprised too."

"Why would he do that?"

"You'll have to ask him to answer that. What I'm saying is that nothing I do now will help you get what you want, and I'm sorry about that. I'll stay on until your dad hires a new foreman. Hopefully he'll choose Carlos since he has experience here. I'll also make sure that he hires someone to help him with the twins."

"That won't be necessary."

"I don't mind—"

"I'm not going back to California."

"Are they going to let you continue to work remotely?"

Was that a hint of hope she heard in his voice?

"No, I didn't get the position."

"How is that possible?"

She smiled at his indignation on her behalf.

"You don't even know what I proposed. It could have been total garbage."

"I don't believe that for a minute."

"Well, the powers-that-be didn't agree with you. So I quit."

Dean uncrossed his arms and placed his palms against the back of the chair.

"You did what? You love working there, traveling the world."

"There are things I love more, some of which I didn't realize until I was back in LA."

"You missed your family even more than before?"

She nodded. "I did. I missed the twins' grins and giggles, even Dad's complaining about his cast and running commentary on those hunting and fishing shows. I missed how beautiful the valley is at sunrise, how peaceful and quiet." She paused right at the edge of the cliff she was about to jump off. "And most of all I missed my husband."

Dean stared at her without moving, almost without blinking. What was going on in that head of his?

"What do you mean by that?" he finally asked.

With her heart thumping hard, she took a step toward him. "What do you want it to mean?"

For a long moment, he seemed to not breathe.

"I don't want you to leave," he said, his voice quieter than normal, almost as if saying the words out loud would make her do the opposite.

A smile tugged at the corners of her mouth. She'd been right.

"Good. Because I'm staying."

"With your dad?"

She shook her head slowly. "Here, with you, if you're not opposed to that."

"Sunny…"

She could almost see the gears working in his head as he tried to figure out what to say next.

"I want our marriage to be real because I've fallen in love with you. Don't feel you have—"

Dean pushed away from the chair and closed the space between them before she could finish whatever it was she'd been about to say. The moment he wrapped her in his arms, pulled her close and brought his mouth to hers, she forgot everything but the feel and taste of him.

When they finally stopped kissing long enough to breathe, Sunny chuckled.

"I take it that means you're okay with making the temporary situation permanent?"

"It means that I love you. I've loved you since we were in high school."

Sunny leaned back so she could see his face more fully.

"Are you serious?"

"Completely."

"Why didn't you ever say anything?"

"Because I knew you had big plans for your life, ones that would take you far away from Jade Valley and this ranch."

"So...all this time you kept your feelings to yourself?"

He nodded once.

"Oh, Dean. You were going to let me go a second time." Her heart broke at his selflessness. And how oblivious she'd been.

"You've lost a lot in your life. You deserve to accomplish every goal you set for yourself, go to all the places you want to visit. As the saying goes, live your best life. Be happy."

"You make me happy."

"What about your career? Your world travels?"

"I'm going to take the idea I pitched to the company that they belittled, and I'm going to do it myself. I'm going to make it so successful that they're going to have a *Pretty Woman* store clerk 'big mistake' moment."

Dean smiled. "I have no doubt you will."

"I'll also have plenty to do helping you implement all these awesome ideas on the ranch."

"Your dad will have to agree first, though I have a feeling he might be more willing now that he's getting what he wanted."

"What's that?"

"You to come back home for good."

"He never said that."

"He did to me. It's why he went along with our marriage even though he knew we were trying to maneuver him."

"So you're saying he maneuvered me instead?"

"Yep. And you're not alone. He's known how I felt about you all along, since high school."

"When did my dad get so smart and crafty?"

"No idea." Dean ran a thumb across her cheek, making her skin tingle. "Won't you miss the world travel?"

"Who said I'm giving up traveling? After all, we haven't had a honeymoon."

Dean chuckled. "I guess I better apply for a passport."

"Yes, sir. But first, how about you kiss me again?"

"I think I can handle that."

And he did, so well that Sunny felt as if she was flying.

EPILOGUE

AFTER WHAT FELT like half an hour of trying to attract their attention, Sunny was finally successful in getting both of the twins to look her way at the same time with grins on their faces.

"Quick, take the picture!" She swatted Dean's back, perhaps a bit harder than necessary, for emphasis.

Instead of being annoyed, however, he chuckled as he snapped several pictures of Lily and Liam sitting atop the hay bale, surrounded by pumpkins, various other types of gourds, cornstalks and more hay bales. They wore matching jeans, little tan work boots and sweatshirts sporting cartoon pumpkins and ghosts. Thankfully, festival day had turned out pleasant and sunny, and the various photo spots her committee had set up around town had proven popular with families with young children, groups of teens and couples of all ages.

"You two go over and hold them and I'll take some family photos," a lady she didn't recognize said.

She must be one of the many out-of-towners who'd flocked to Jade Valley, helping to make the rejuvenated festival even more successful than she'd hoped. Trudy had informed her when they'd stopped by that she'd even had to hurry up and bake more pies because at the pace they were going they were going to sell out halfway through the afternoon.

"If you don't mind, that would be wonderful," Sunny said, handing over her phone to the smiling woman.

Sunny picked up Liam, and Lily went to her favorite person in the whole world. Each with a toddler on their lap, they scooted close to each other. Dean reached over and took her hand, threading his fingers with hers. Now that he'd finally admitted his long-held feelings, he had no problem expressing them often. She wondered if her heart would ever get used to his open affection and not beat a little faster when he held her hand, smiled at her, when he held her close and kissed her until her entire body tingled.

She'd honestly never thought a whole lot about being in love, but she'd come to the conclusion that Maya had been right. Without even realizing it, she'd kept herself from feeling too much for anyone for fear of losing them. She still sometimes struggled with worry about Dean's health and safety, same as she did for the twins, her dad, Maya, Trudy and everyone else in town she was getting to know again. But she supposed that was true of anyone, and she did her best to not let those concerns get the better of her.

She was the happiest she'd ever been, and she firmly believed her mom, brother and sister-in-law were happy for her. Happy that she had taken the role of mother that Amanda could no longer fill, that Dean had stepped into the role of fatherhood as if he'd been born to be a dad.

She squeezed Dean's hand in return, gave him a smile she hoped reflected how very much she loved him and then turned that smile toward the camera.

"You have a lovely family," the woman said when she handed the phone back to Sunny.

"Thank you."

After putting Lily and Liam back in their double stroller, Sunny walked hand in hand with Dean around the business district of Jade Valley. They chatted with neighbors;

she checked in with the various merchants to see how business and the mystery game were going and stopped at the booth selling chocolate-covered pretzels.

"No, you're too little for this," she told Liam when he reached for a pretzel.

He did not like her answer but his attention was quickly diverted by the start of the pet parade.

"We should get them a puppy," Dean said.

"They already have cats to play with."

"Okay, maybe I want a pup and I'm using the kids as an excuse."

"Well, you are awfully cute, so I guess you deserve a puppy."

"Yes!"

Sunny laughed then planted a peck on his cheek, not caring who saw.

Ever since she'd decided that she really, truly wanted to make Jade Valley her permanent home, a surprising inner peace had blossomed within her. Though she was starting small, her business was off to a good start. She already had clients as far away as Cheyenne and West Yellowstone, Montana, and only two days before she'd begun discussions with a former coworker who had also left the company about her coming on board to cover the small towns in Southern California.

"What are you thinking about?" Dean asked as they headed to the main stage where the winners of various contests would be announced soon, including the mystery game.

Even Sunny didn't know the identity of the "killer," though she was intensely curious.

"About how happy I am," she said in answer to Dean's question.

"To have the festival almost behind you?"

She shook her head. "No, that ended up being fun to work on, even if it was a lot to do in a short amount of time." She stopped and turned to face him. "I knew when I came back from LA and told you how I felt that I was doing the right thing, but I underestimated how incredibly happy I would be back here. My job feels right—my family feels right." She ran her thumb across the back of his tanned hand. "Being with you feels so right that I often feel stupid for not realizing sooner that this is how it should be."

"You're not. Maybe it had to be the right time for everything to fall into place for us."

"Maybe. I'm really glad that it did."

"Me too." He dropped a light kiss on her forehead.

"How many times are you two going to kiss right out here for God and everyone to see?" Trudy teased from her perch on the end of the bleachers set up facing the stage.

"I think we still have a few in us," Dean said, suddenly taking Sunny in his arms, dipping her backward and giving her a quick peck on the lips.

Sunny wasn't easily embarrassed, but blood ran to her cheeks. Dean winked at her before righting her on both her feet.

"Whew, I think I need a fan," Trudy said, drawing a few chuckles from the people seated near her.

Sunny spotted her dad sitting with friends in lawn chairs across the park, a huge grin on his face. He was probably telling his friends for the eight hundredth time that her and Dean being together was all his doing, that he thought he might have a second career as a matchmaker.

"Ladies and gentlemen," announced Brent Foley, the radio DJ they'd brought in to emcee the festivities, "it's time to reveal the winners of both the pet parade and the Jade Valley Murder Mystery."

An adorable golden retriever named Bella

won the pet parade, much to her elementary-age owner's squealing delight.

"We don't even have to do a drawing among all the right answers in the mystery game because only one person guessed the identity of the culprit correctly. And that nefarious merchant is…Alma Graves."

"Ha! I knew it!" Trudy said so loudly that the twins startled and several locals who were familiar with the ladies' feud started laughing.

As the afternoon waned into evening, musicians filled the stage and couples gathered in front to dance the night away.

"So, Mrs. Wheeler, care to take a spin around the dance floor with this cowboy?"

"I think we can make that happen, Mr. Wheeler."

They left the twins with all three of their doting grandparents and joined all the other locals and visitors enjoying the cool fall evening filled with lively tunes. Dean pulled her close, and that familiar little thrill went through her again. She hoped that never changed.

"I'm proud of you," he said as they began to dance. "The festival is a rousing success, and I've seen a lot of happiness and hope on people's faces today."

"I'm glad it's gone well. And speaking of pride, that goes for you too."

After they'd gotten back from their belated honeymoon in Ireland, construction had started on the first cabin along the river with plans to add a second and a greenhouse the following spring. With her connections, both cabins were already booked solid until next Thanksgiving.

"We make a pretty good team."

"That we do."

Whether it was business, parenthood or being in love, she doubted they could be any better suited.

"I love you," she said.

He smiled. "That came out of nowhere."

"You make me want to say it all the time."

"I'm not averse to that." He pulled her closer. "Because I love you too, more every day even though that shouldn't be possible."

"Imagine how much we'll love each other when we're old, gray and wrinkled like a Shar-Pei."

"You'll be the most beautiful grandma the state of Wyoming has ever seen."

"And I'll have to beat the other grannies away from you with a big stick."

Dean laughed and guided her head to rest against his chest. As they danced, she listened to his heartbeat and couldn't stop smiling. Loving someone with your entire heart and having that love returned really was the best thing ever.

* * * * *

Get 4 FREE REWARDS!

We'll send you 2 FREE Books plus 2 FREE Mystery Gifts.

Love Inspired books feature uplifting stories where faith helps guide you through life's challenges and discover the promise of a new beginning.

FREE Value Over $20

YES! Please send me 2 FREE Love Inspired Romance novels and my 2 FREE mystery gifts (gifts are worth about $10 retail). After receiving them, if I don't wish to receive any more books, I can return the shipping statement marked "cancel." If I don't cancel, I will receive 6 brand-new novels every month and be billed just $5.24 each for the regular-print edition or $5.99 each for the larger-print edition in the U.S., or $5.74 each for the regular-print edition or $6.24 each for the larger-print edition in Canada. That's a savings of at least 13% off the cover price. It's quite a bargain! Shipping and handling is just 50¢ per book in the U.S. and $1.25 per book in Canada.* I understand that accepting the 2 free books and gifts places me under no obligation to buy anything. I can always return a shipment and cancel at any time. The free books and gifts are mine to keep no matter what I decide.

Choose one: ☐ **Love Inspired Romance Regular-Print**
(105/305 IDN GNWC)

☐ **Love Inspired Romance Larger-Print**
(122/322 IDN GNWC)

Name (please print)

Address   Apt. #

City   State/Province   Zip/Postal Code

Email: Please check this box ☐ if you would like to receive newsletters and promotional emails from Harlequin Enterprises ULC and its affiliates. You can unsubscribe anytime.

> **Mail to the Harlequin Reader Service:**
> **IN U.S.A.:** P.O. Box 1341, Buffalo, NY 14240-8531
> **IN CANADA:** P.O. Box 603, Fort Erie, Ontario L2A 5X3

Want to try 2 free books from another series! Call 1-800-873-8635 or visit www.ReaderService.com.

Get 4 FREE REWARDS!

We'll send you 2 FREE Books plus 2 FREE Mystery Gifts.

Love Inspired Suspense books showcase how courage and optimism unite in stories of faith and love in the face of danger.

FREE Value Over **$20**

YES! Please send me 2 FREE Love Inspired Suspense novels and my 2 FREE mystery gifts (gifts are worth about $10 retail). After receiving them, if I don't wish to receive any more books, I can return the shipping statement marked "cancel." If I don't cancel, I will receive 6 brand-new novels every month and be billed just $5.24 each for the regular-print edition or $5.99 each for the larger-print edition in the U.S., or $5.74 each for the regular-print edition or $6.24 each for the larger-print edition in Canada. That's a savings of at least 13% off the cover price. It's quite a bargain! Shipping and handling is just 50¢ per book in the U.S. and $1.25 per book in Canada.* I understand that accepting the 2 free books and gifts places me under no obligation to buy anything. I can always return a shipment and cancel at any time. The free books and gifts are mine to keep no matter what I decide.

Choose one: ☐ **Love Inspired Suspense Regular-Print** (153/353 IDN GNWN)   ☐ **Love Inspired Suspense Larger-Print** (107/307 IDN GNWN)

Name (please print)

Address   Apt. #

City   State/Province   Zip/Postal Code

Email: Please check this box ☐ if you would like to receive newsletters and promotional emails from Harlequin Enterprises ULC and its affiliates. You can unsubscribe anytime.

Mail to the Harlequin Reader Service:

IN U.S.A.: P.O. Box 1341, Buffalo, NY 14240-8531
IN CANADA: P.O. Box 603, Fort Erie, Ontario L2A 5X3

Want to try 2 free books from another series! Call 1-800-873-8635 or visit www.ReaderService.com.

HARLEQUIN SELECTS COLLECTION

19 FREE BOOKS IN ALL!

From Robyn Carr to RaeAnne Thayne to Linda Lael Miller and Sherryl Woods we promise (actually, GUARANTEE!) each author in the Harlequin Selects collection has seen their name on the *New York Times* or *USA TODAY* bestseller lists!

#391 A COWGIRL'S SECRET
The Mountain Monroes • by Melinda Curtis
Horse trainer Cassie Diaz is at a crossroads. Ranch life is her
first love...until Bentley Monroe passes through her Idaho town
and helps with the family business. Will this cowgirl turn in her
boots for him?

#392 THE SINGLE DAD'S HOLIDAY MATCH
Smoky Mountain First Responders
by Tanya Agler
Can a widowed cop and single father find love again? When
a case leads Jonathan Maxwell to single mom Brooke Novak,
sparks fly. But with their focus on kids and work, romance isn't
so easy...is it?

#393 A COWBOY'S HOPE
Eclipse Ridge Ranch • by Mary Anne Wilson
When lawyer Anna Watters agreed to help a local ranch, she
wasn't supposed to fall for handsome Ben Arias! He's only in
town temporarily—but soon she wants Ben and the peace she
finds at his ranch permanently.

#394 I'LL BE HOME FOR CHRISTMAS
Return to Christmas Island • by Amie Denman
Rebecca Browne will do anything for her finance career. Even
spend the summer on Christmas Island. But she didn't expect
to have to keep secrets...especially from the local ferryboat
captain she's starting to fall for.